The Piano Raft

Sara Alexi is the author of the Greek Village Series.

She divides her time between England and a small village in Greece.

http://facebook.com/authorsaraalexi

Sara Alexi

THE PIANO RAFT

oneiro

Published by Oneiro Press 2017

This edition 2017

ISBN: 9781520439778

Also by Sara Alexi

Chapter 1

Even with his eyes still shut, Neil knows he is not where he expects to be. The surface he is curled up on is hard, and the world seems to be rocking ever so gently.

He sucks in a deep breath in the hope that this will rouse him. The air is unusually clear and sharp, and there is a chill that urges him to hug his knees tightly to his chest for warmth. He keeps his eyes shut tight, reluctant, as yet, to leave the world of dreams. He was – perhaps still is – dreaming of Kimberly, who is at the piano. Her playing is confident in the dream, and more accomplished – not simple and soft, as is her normal style, and he doesn't recognise the tune. Sleep slips away as the minutes pass, until he is pretty sure he is awake. The sound of the piano, oddly, is still there. The notes are pure and floating, and there is no echo off the wall like there usually is in the flat.

Waking up to find himself in a strange place – someone else's house, a friend's sofa – is always perplexing, and, in that confusion, the moments it takes to remember where he is are either oddly delicious or deeply unsettling, depending on his mood, on how much his head is throbbing. Neil knows this well; how many tipsy evenings in the last two years have ended up with him staying the night with friends or acquaintances? There was even that one time when he and Sleet dozed, slumped against each other, for a few hours in the bus shelter, waking shivering to disapproving glances from commuters.

The music continues but he is not ready to open his eyes yet. The pulsing in his head is making the world spin, and it feels safer to keep them shut for the moment whilst he tries to recall where he might be. He was in the flat last night; he remembers that for sure, so it stands to reason that he must still be there. Maybe the back door is open, which would account for the chill, the fresh air. Slowly, painfully, and far too brightly, the world appears beyond the veil of his eyelashes. But as he peeps through one half-open eye, it seems as if the room has expanded to a thousand times its normal size, and the walls, usually a rather grubby magnolia paint over peeling embossed wallpaper, have been replaced with a majestic line of trees, delicate green and waving in the morning's spring breeze.

Cold adrenaline flows through his limbs. How have the walls of the house been removed? Have the flats finally been condemned? Is there a demolition ball aimed at his head right now? His eyelids snap open now, his senses on alert. All around are trees and bushes, grass and flowers. The flat is absent entirely and, stranger still, it seems that the floorboards he is sitting on are actually floating down what looks very much like the canal that flows past the bottom of the garden. If this were not surreal enough, this odd sight is accompanied by the sound of the piano, which is still playing, filling his ears, and it is definitely not Kimberly at the keys.

He lifts his head and looks in the direction of the music, and there, sure enough, is Kimberly's upright piano, silhouetted against a pale-blue sky, the watery first rays of the sun catching the shiny veneer. A slim girl in a long black dress is seated at the instrument, her fingers flashing with chunky silver rings as they travel across the keys, nails a dark red. Her face is pale, contrasting with her raven hair and heavy, dark make-up. Neil cannot be sure what is reality and what is not, but one thing he does know is that he has never seen this person before. He rubs his forehead, puts his thumbs into his eye sockets and massages, trying to ease the headache that is cutting slices from the back of his eyes.

The air smells of ozone and woodsmoke and something else very familiar. It is a musty smell that seems connected with a cold and clammy sensation down his left leg, from where large, soulful, eager eyes look up at him. A wiry tail thumps against the wooden deck, and the smell reveals itself as that unique aroma of wet dog.

'Bushy-Mush, get off!' Neil lifts his legs and sits up carefully, pushing his canine friend away and taking care not to jar his own head.

'Morning!' The young woman stops playing abruptly and flashes a cheerful smile.

Neil is not sure which bit of her to take in first: the black lipstick or the skull rings that dwarf her thin fingers. Perhaps she is on her way to a fancy dress party, or maybe he is still dreaming.

'Sleet says he had to go to work,' the girl informs him; her voice, though matter of fact, and despite its monosyllabic cadence, is warm and friendly. 'He says that if you don't pay the rent today the landlord will change the locks and chuck all your stuff out on the street.' She twists one of her big rings, which has slipped around the wrong way, and pulls it down her finger a little to anchor it against a finger joint.

Sleet! That might help explain this situation. Neil looks about for evidence, and his eyes light on a rocking chair, half hidden behind the piano. It's the Victorian chair with a torn canework seat that he and Kimberly bought in a tiny junk shop in Garfax last year – the first item they bought when they moved in together. A smile traces over his lips at the memory of carting it back to the flat on the train, people staring at them. He carried it upside down on his head from the station, and Kimberly called him a clown but with light in her eyes. That was back in the days when he could do no wrong.

It was cheap because the canework was torn in one corner, and by the time they got it home it was even worse. In the six months it sat in the flat, he never got round to fixing the hole, and stuffed through it this morning is what appears to be an empty whisky bottle – clear evidence of Sleet's involvement, if proof were required.

There is another bottle on the keys at the far end of the piano, and several beer bottles litter the floor, jammed in underneath the instrument. There are also one or two bottles floating in the brown water, the Cheerios effect causing them to cling to the side of the raft.

The raft. He is definitely on the raft.

'So solid it could survive the Atlantic,' he recalls boasting to Kimberly whilst they were building it, not much more than a week ago.

Taking him at his word, she jumped on board. The thing pitched so unnervingly that she wrapped her arms around him and they sank to their knees laughing, and when the rocking subsided they lay down and watched the sky, or rather she watched the sky, and he leaned on one elbow and gazed at her until she pulled him towards her and demanded a kiss.

Kissing was a frequent occurrence during the construction of the raft. Each stage was celebrated with a cuddle or a kiss. Typical Kim – how she could distract him and squander time by the bucketful. It took four days to build the thing, and it was launched without ceremony late one night, after the pub, and before it was really ready to take to the water. Large blue plastic drums provided flotation: six of them salvaged from the waste ground at the end of the terrace. They arranged the barrels on the tiny back lawn, two rows of three, with joists laid across to form a platform. On top of the wooden beams they nailed boards, all scavenged from various sources, and just because he knew it would delight Kim, Neil cut into one of the plastic drums, and made a flap that could be lifted up to reveal a secret storage space. As he expected, this prompted a squirm and a shriek, her face shining. Then she pulled him to her, forehead to forehead as she hung her arms around his neck and looked deep into his eyes in a way she knew would make him squirm in return. Beautiful Kimberly. They hadn't devised a way to steer the raft, so they attached a couple of mooring ropes to the corners, and with these he towed the raft a few feet up and down the canal, drinking in her delight as she floated under the trailing branches of the weeping willows that lined the bank, brushing through the reeds.

'Don't let go!' she shrieked, her feet planted wide for balance. There was no special reason to build the raft; it was just one of her whims, prompted by the discovery of the dumped barrels. Something to amuse them whilst they waited for answers to all her job applications, and whilst he continued to ponder if it was really possible for him to make a living as an artist. At least, that was what he told himself he was doing.

He secured the raft to the back fence and helped her off as the light faded and hunger drew them indoors. The following morning, he got up late to find Kim all red-cheeked, eyes shining.

'I've registered the raft with the canal authority,' she said, hanging up her coat. 'Because, guess what, there's a race to raise money for a local charity.'

He ruffled his hair, slid out of bed to pull on his jeans, rubbing his face. 'I don't suppose they'll let you enter without a canal licence and you can't get a licence without insurance, and we can't afford insurance,' he objected, stretching and yawning. They had lived long enough by the canal for him to know that boats needed licences.

'You can if the boat doesn't have power,' she replied.

'But if it's unpowered how on earth are we going to win this charity race?' he said, filling the kettle.

Kim rolled her eyes at this. 'We don't have to win! We just have to get sponsored to take part. It's about raising money and awareness, not winning.' And then she produced the entry form from her pocket and, together, over coffee, they filled it in.

But the next day the letter arrived from London with her job offer, and all thoughts of the raft and charity races were abandoned in favour of the serious business of work, and Neil sensed the beginning of a gap opening up between them. Their beautiful raft was left to float by itself, a cast-off plaything.

He watches a duck paddle past; it's curious and unafraid, pecking at a beer bottle. He is pretty sure he can recall Sleet turning up at the flat with beer last night. From there, it's not too great a mental leap to figure that they sat down by the canal at the end of the garden, drinking. But then? Did the mooring knots slip, did they work their way loose? That would explain being on the move now, but the rocking chair, the piano, and this stranger? How on earth?'

He shakes his head slowly and becomes aware of the girl in black staring at him.

'You want this?' The girl's pale face and black lipstick are half obscured by her curtain of hair as she bends to pick up a paper cup. 'It's still quite hot.'

For some reason, the weirdness of this strange vampire woman producing a coffee from the floor by her black-booted feet seems to fit the stark reality of waking up floating. Maybe he really is still asleep. What do they call it? – lucid dreaming.

'Thanks.' He takes the drink. The cardboard cup is very hot; he swaps hands and blows on his fingers. The first drop of coffee burns his tongue but he really needs to drink something so he blows across the top and takes little sips. Tail wagging, Bushy-Mush is now sniffing at the girl's long black skirt.

'You can thank Sleet, he bought them.' She sips from her own cup, and with her skull-encrusted finger she points to a cafe some way back along the towpath, a small building with picnic tables and benches outside, all of which is slowly drifting into the distance as the current carries them on.

Neil sips the coffee and tries hard to focus, to work out his priorities. His landlord needs dealing with. Yes, that should be dealt with first, otherwise he'll be homeless. In fact, as soon as he has drunk this coffee he will tie up and take the bus back to Greater Lotherton and sort that out. Or maybe he could phone. He checks all his pockets, finds his phone, only to discover the battery is flat, as usual.

The coffee is not settling well; his stomach feels fluttery, his head too fuzzy to think straight. If Kim was here she would already have organised things.

He rubs his chest with his free hand, but the sensation that feels like heartburn is not eased. The ache is for Kimberly. With no Kim, the flat is just a poky, rather grubby space. Why would he make an effort to go back to save that, when all it is going to do is remind him how empty the place is without her? In his temples, his heartbeat quickens; he takes another sip of coffee but it does not calm him. Some sort of decision needs to be made, but the details

11

elude him. Still, continuing to sit here is obviously not the answer.

He takes another sip of coffee and his gaze rests on the piano. Someone is going to have to sit here, though, because he cannot just leave the raft with Kim's piano on board; she will kill him if any harm comes to it.

'How do you know Sleet?' He tries to force himself to sound calm, to concentrate on something normal, like a conversation. Maybe if he could recall whether there was a plan that would explain why he and the piano are now on board the raft, floating downstream, the whole situation might not seem so surreal ...

They started at the flat, that's for sure. He has a vague memory of Sleet announcing that he had the cure for everything and presenting him with a whisky bottle and a six-pack of beer, but then?

'Oh, I don't know him,' says the girl. 'I just met him this morning as he was leaving. I was walking along the towpath. I asked if he played, you know, the piano, else why would he be on a raft with a piano on it, floating down a river ...'

'Canal,' Neil interrupts, but she carries on as if he hasn't spoken.

'He said he didn't and asked if I did, so I said yes, and so he said prove it, so I did and then he told me to tell you about your rent and said he had to go to work.' She stops to take another sip of her coffee. 'He seems nice. Well, he bought me a coffee, anyway.'

All Neil can manage by way of reply is a grunt. What was a dull sense of panic in his chest begins to bubble into anger. Is this whole thing Sleet's idea of a joke? A little joyride and then abandon ship and not even think to tie up to stop him floating further down the canal? Typical.

The hills behind the trees on the bank seem familiar, but how can he judge how far they have come? Have they passed Little Lotherton or haven't they gone that far yet? Certainly it's going to take hours, going against the current, to tow the raft back home, and by the sound of it, if he does not get back pronto he is not going to have a home. But what's the point of going back without Kim?

He groans inwardly; he is back there again. Surely there is a simple solution, if only he could see it, but the more he tries to think, the cloudier his mind seems to become. The logical thing to do is to moor up, get back there and see his landlord. But it is also logical not to leave the raft, because if someone helps themselves to the piano or the chair whilst he is gone, then what? Take it a step at a time. First, stop the raft. Get it to the bank and tie up. He'll do that. In a minute. Just as soon as the coffee takes effect …

Now, where was he? Oh yes – trying to figure out how last night morphed from whisky and beers with Sleet at the flat, to this … He can recall the evening breeze last night, through the back door, ruffling the notes on the corkboard, and he can remember staring at them for some time, thinking of Kim. It was her handwriting on the yellow squares, ideas she was forever jotting down and pinning up to develop into articles and storyboards later. Outside, he can remember, her rug lay abandoned on the grass, the form of her body impressed into the tartan folds where she had sat – alone – before the taxi arrived to take her, and her bags, to the train station. Beyond the tiny garden, he can recall the canal glinting in the dull, flat light: thick and oily, without a ripple. He can remember standing there, not quite believing life was real, after Kimberly slammed the door behind her. He could hear the raft knocking hollowly against the makeshift jetty. At some point, later, an empty bottle stood upright next to a rolling glass on the wooden deck – his bottle, his glass. That might have been the first bottle, or several bottles into the evening. It all feels a bit messed up, confusing, and depressingly familiar.

'Oi, hey!'

He is jolted back into the present by this new voice, coming from somewhere behind the piano – stressed, urgent. The girl in black looks over the top of the instrument and her eyes widen, and Bushy-Mush starts to bark in the irritating, high-pitched way he does when he is excited.

'Hey, oi!'

The voice is more urgent this time. The girl looks expectantly at Neil.

With a hand on the edge of the keyboard he levers himself up, but his knees don't seem to be able to support his weight and his stomach lurches and his mouth starts to produce saliva. Staying motionless for a moment helps the nausea recede. This section of the canal is quite narrow, with boats moored on either side, making the channel narrower still. He could step off the raft onto one of these boats and across the path to be discreetly sick in the bushes. They almost scrape along the hull of the next boat. The girl pushes them away from it with her foot and the raft drifts out into the middle of the waterway, moving with the current, and spinning ever so slowly. Bushy-Mush barks even more frantically, running around the perimeter of the raft. Some yards away, coming upstream towards them, is a narrowboat that must be at least sixty feet long, steered by a stout man with a very red face.

'Oi!' he shouts again. His boat is pristine, with shiny red and green paintwork. Tubs of geraniums are spaced at intervals along the roof. The brass edges of the windows gleam in the morning sun, framing carefully drawn chintz curtains.

'Watch out!' The man's voice is desperate now, and the girl with the black lipstick edges towards the back of the raft, away from him. Bushy-Mush is at the front, barking manically.

15

Neil braces himself for the inevitable impact, and with a splintering crunch the raft judders to a sudden halt.

'You bloody idiot!' The man is furious now. 'Look what you've done.'

He pulls down his stiff-brimmed green hat firmly, straightens his sleeveless jacket and leans over the side of his boat, poking at the raft with a boathook.

Bushy-Mush chooses this moment to make a leap onto the narrowboat, still barking. This invasion seems to infuriate the man even more than the collision.

'Get that yapping rat off my boat!' he howls, and his face takes on a crimson hue.

'Here, Bushy-Mush, get here.' Neil closes his eyes to shout, so painful is the noise inside his head, but at least the sick feeling has receded.

Quite remarkably, Bushy-Mush does as he is told and leaps across the widening gap from the polished craft, splashes into the canal and disappears from sight under the water. Silence ensues for a moment as Neil, the girl, and the man on the narrowboat all peer into the water, united by their horror. No one speaks, but the girl glances towards Neil, who looks back at her, eyes wide as he rips off his jumper, ready to jump in after his pup.

Then, suddenly, with a mad series of splashes, and yapping as wildly as before, Bushy-Mush breaks the surface and thrashes at the water, propelling himself towards the raft. Neil throws himself flat on the deck to reach out, grabbing the dog by the collar and pulling him to safety. Once on board, the dog shakes himself violently and water sprays over Neil, the raft, the piano and the rocking chair.

'You got a licence for this thing?' The man with the red face has found his voice again and he gives a final shove with his boathook.

'Yes!' Neil retorts smugly.

The girl with the black lipstick looks down at her skirt, brushing the water off. The narrowboat is slipping away, upstream now, but just before it disappears round a bend in the canal, the owner calls back at them, 'And you need to learn to control your dog!'

The push from the boathook has added to the raft's rotation, but Neil's attention is on Bushy-Mush. He towels him dry with his T-shirt and the little animal curls up on Neil's jumper, exhausted by the commotion.

Despite the encounter with the narrowboat, the raft has lost no momentum; it slips silently downstream again, and the stillness of the canal smooths away the memory of the incident in seconds.

The girl grins at Neil. It seems as if the encounter with the shiny narrowboat has united them, and he grins back.

'Phee, by the way ...' The girl points to herself.

'Neil.'

'Yes,' she says, as if she already knows his name. Perhaps Sleet told her.

'This is Bushy-Mush.' He points to the dog with his toe. It's not really his dog. Kimberly took him in, named him and fed him. He frowns. Why did she not take the little wiry thing with her down to London?

'Good name. So, where are you going?' Phee asks.

Chapter 2

Hasn't that been the question since he left college, the big question for two years now: where is he going? And the answer? Well, there isn't one – so far, at least. There's nowhere he is going, nothing he is doing. Isn't it this very fact that caused the rift between him and Kimberly?

The caffeine begins to take effect and memories of the day before bleed into Neil's consciousness. Yesterday was Kimberly's last day, and they did not speak from the moment they awoke on their cushion-separated halves of the bed. The gulf between them felt too great to bridge. If they had both been willing, they could still have reached out, grasped each other's hands and pulled themselves back to the safety and tenderness of their relationship. But he knew Kimberly was not willing; in her mind, the frustration he caused her had pushed her too far past that point. So he lay in bed pretending to still be asleep because he didn't know what to say and was worried that anything he did say would lead to another argument and make things worse. In retrospect that was crazy – she was leaving anyway, so how could it be worse?

She dressed hurriedly and stuffed her few belongings into her rucksack with force, dumping other things in the bin: a T-shirt he had bought her six months before, a bag with a zip that didn't work. With the same angry energy. she declared that she would stick yellow Post-It notes on the things she wanted to keep, or was coming back for, or something; it wasn't clear, and with Kim in this mood Neil was loathe to ask. She stomped around the room, yellow squares in hand, as if preparing to fight for what she wanted, but there wasn't much to claim. She ignored what she considered to be 'his' television and 'his' beanbag, which lost more of its little polystyrene balls every day, even though they had bought both with joint funds. He rolled out of bed and put the kettle on. Waiting for it to boil, he watched as the piano was claimed with its own little yellow flag, which seemed absurd as she had brought it from her family home and had been playing it since she was six. It annoyed him that she stuck a sticker on it, pressing it hard to make sure it would stay, as it suggested that he might challenge her for it, which of course she knew he would never do!

He could have made instant, but he took the time to brew real coffee, and not selfishly just for himself, as many people might say he would be justified in doing. After he'd made it, Kim didn't drink hers anyway. She kept looking around the room until, finally, she had stuck a yellow square on the rocking chair and the black-spotted, gold-framed mirror that had already been on the wall when they moved in. There was nothing else to claim, unless she wanted the thin mattress on the floor.

He desperately tried to think of something to say, to redeem himself, to make her understand he still loved her, that he had always loved her and that she had misunderstood, but the words never got any further than a twist in his tongue or an exhalation of his breath. She had her jeans on – her statement of practicality – but she also had on an impractical, floaty, white lace top with long, dripping sleeves that were stained at their pointed ends where they had trailed in life's dusty corners on previous occasions.

The coffee was far too weak, and as he drank the useless brew and watched Kimberly pack he had the feeling that by standing there doing nothing he was making the biggest mistake of his life. The fluttering in his stomach turned his insides over; the beat of his heart in his ears became deafening. His breath quickened until he was sucking in little pockets of air. But what was he to do? All the unspoken signals she was giving out assured him that he did not have a choice any more; that had been taken away the week before when they went to buy the tickets.

'For someone not going anywhere, you are very deep in thought.' Phee sits down on the piano stool again and plays a dramatic chord followed by a trill of light notes. It makes Neil think of a Tom and Jerry cartoon.

'I was just thinking,' he mutters, and peels the yellow square off the side of the piano. Phee plays a new chord, changes key and breaks into song:

'When your rooster squawks at the break of dawn,

La la la la la la, and I'll be gone.'

Neil wonders if she is changing the words to the song deliberately, or if she has previously misheard them. Her voice is clear and sweet, incongruous with her black hair and grungy appearance.

'You're the reason I'll be travelling on. But don't think twice ...'

She stops playing and, in one breath, as if it is a single word, she finishes the song with 'I-am-happy-enough-stuck-on-a-raft-going-nowhere-down-a-canal-with-no-specific-destination.'

And then she completes her song with a crashing chord that starts Bushy-Mush barking. Neil squats to pat his head and the dog quietens down.

'Okay, so where are *you* going, then?' Neil counters, and he sits in the rocking chair. Bushy-Mush jumps onto his knee and curls up, still damp.

'This morning my world changed,' she says brightly. 'I decided to do things differently, to do everything differently, so with each step I take I'm choosing the one that goes against the grain. Like jumping onto your raft. Totally the wrong thing to do. Waiting for a bus or walking would have been a more solid choice.'

'To get where?' Neil asks. He turns the now-empty coffee cup upside down and puts it over the neck of the whisky bottle and wonders what canal people do with their rubbish.

'Don't know.' She doesn't sound in the least concerned. 'But finding somewhere to stay in Greater Lotherton was the obvious thing to do. So, instead, I wandered to the canal edge and started walking.'

She swivels round to sit sideways on the piano stool so that she is facing him.

'So come on, what's your story?' she asks.

It's a typical icebreaking sort of question, one that people often ask, but it's too general and he hasn't the faintest idea how to answer it. Does she mean the story of the raft, the story of him and Kim, the story of his life? How can he know, how can he answer? He is aware that this uncertainty is part of what frustrated Kim. He dithers. Decisions elude him. To tell Phee his story, he would have to decide what she meant by 'his story' and then he would have to unpick events and decide what they meant, and he hasn't a clue about any of that.

'Um, well, yeah, I admit it looks a bit odd.' He eyes the piano and the raft and the passing water. 'But really, there isn't one.'

She tips her head to one side and frowns, and he gets the sense that she thinks he is withholding, which he isn't. He really isn't, it's just that …

'It's complicated,' he says in summary.

'No, it's a simple question,' she says. 'How did you end up on this raft with a piano?'

He feels his cheeks on fire under her gaze. At least her question is more specific now; he must try to fashion some sort of an answer.

'You see, Sleet's a bit of a pisshead, and – well, Kimberly, she walked out. Sleet brought round whisky, you know, to numb the pain. My head feels like – well, like you just wouldn't believe.'

He rubs his forehead with the flat of his hand; this isn't going well.

'Anyway, we drank too much, which is about standard, and I guess in our drunken stupor we must have pushed Kim's piano onto the raft. God knows how it didn't fall in, or how we didn't fall in. Maybe we did.' He looks at his clothes. 'Well I'm not wet, not now, anyway, so I presume we didn't fall in. I don't know, but what I do know is that it's a right royal mess.'

As he speaks, a memory of last night returns. Sleet also called him an idiot and confirmed to him that he had just made the biggest mistake of his life.

'I can't believe you let her go.' Sleet had taken over the beanbag at the flat, Bushy-Mush on his chest, a bottle of whisky in his hand. It was early evening but they hadn't put the lights on yet, and it was fairly dark outside.

'Whaddya mean?' Neil retorted, dropping his empty beer bottle onto the others and cracking open a new one. 'You're the man who's always saying don't get tied down, don't succumb to the status quo, live free and all that.'

And as he took his first slug of the new beer, he noticed that Kim had taken the poster of the black cat against a yellow background, yellow eyes staring, that used to be on the wall by the front door. Blobs of Blu Tack where each corner had been highlighted its absence. He liked that picture, and he had bought it, but he did not feel angry that she had taken it – he just sighed.

'Come on, man, why would you listen to me?' Sleet spluttered. 'I spend half my time drunk' – he swung the bottle by its neck as if to reinforce his point – 'and the other half working for my dad. For Christ's sake, I still listen to the same bands I did when I was fourteen, and wear the same T-shirts, and I've never really had a girlfriend. Not a proper one. You have to admit, you'd be pretty sad if you took advice from me …'

'Well, I still like the music we listened to at fourteen, too,' Neil protested. 'And it was you who said that she hadn't considered me in her plans and that I should stand up for myself.'

Neil kicked out at the beanbag Sleet was sitting on, and missed, sending his chair rocking violently. His beer bottle toppled over and rolled across the threadbare carpet, leaking a wet trail.

'Well, yeah!' Sleet's gaze followed the dark line spreading across the floor. 'But when I said stand up for yourself I didn't mean to this point! I meant, you know, just get a bit of a say. I mean, she was telling you how it was going to be, not asking. Like how quick she wanted to go, and stuff.'

'She got a bloody job offer, it's not like the start date was her choice.'

'Like I said, best not listen to me.' Sleet took a swig of whisky and they continued bickering back and forth for some time. The conversation became harder to follow with each new bottle of beer, and then Sleet said something funny and Neil laughed so hard he fell off his chair. Bushy-Mush started howling, and Sleet said something about the yellow stickers on the piano and on the rocking chair, and somehow it seemed so very clear to their intoxicated minds that they should load these items onto the raft! With unnerving certainty, the lunacy of what they did next rushes back to Neil, followed by an impression of the smug look on Sleet's face at the fulfilment of his plan.

'She'll have to talk to you if you turn up in London with this,' Sleet argued, laughing as they manhandled the piano out of the back door. In an odd way it felt good to be taking positive action.

His recollection of yesterday's events is brought to a sudden end as Phee asks, 'Okay, so Kimberly walked out and Sleet got you drunk ... Kim's your girlfriend, I presume?'

'Well, ex-girlfriend, I suppose.' Neil takes comfort in ruffling the dog's wiry coat.

'Ah. So, girlfriend left ... So, what, you were going to drown her piano in revenge?' Phee laughs.

'No, I was going to take it to her.'

'Oh, where is she?' Phee looks down the canal the way they are going, as if expecting to see Neil's ex-girlfriend standing on the towpath, waiting for them.

'London.'

'London! What, as in *London* London, the capital of Great Britain? That's – what, something like two hundred miles away?'

'Two hundred and fifty.' Neil studies an oak tree as they pass and then looks up at the sky. 'Give or take.'

The pale blue of first light has darkened and saturated with colour and one or two full, white fluffy clouds dot the tops of the distant green hills.

He is shocked out of his thoughts as Phee begins to shriek with laughter, or is it excitement? She does not seem to be able to control herself. Then, with a hand just below her throat, she steadies her breathing and composes herself. Neil is mystified.

'So, let me get this straight,' she says. 'You are floating a piano down to your ex-girlfriend who lives two hundred and fifty miles away in London?'

She waits for him to answer. He grimaces at how ridiculous he must look, but manages a curt nod.

'Oh my God! How romantic is that?' Phee screeches, and Neil wonders if they are talking about the same topic. 'That's one heck of a story.' He can feel her gaze on him and he tries to work out how serious she is being, or if she is just teasing him. It's a pretty cruel thing to do if she is.

'You know what,' he says, 'I don't need someone taking the piss.'

Her eyebrows rise in astonishment. 'What? Who, me? Why are you saying that? I'm serious. I would just die to have someone sail a piano down to me if I lived in London. It's like … Knights in shining armour, and white stallions …'

Phee is choking on her words, she is so excited, and almost bouncing up and down on the piano stool.

'It's a great heroic journey to show the hero's love. It's just awesomeness incarnate!'

Chapter 3

Neil blinks and stares back at Phee, who is looking at him, if he is not mistaken, with an expression of awe! It would be lovely to soak it up, drink it in and believe he was worthy of such a reaction, but if she had been at the train station last week when he and Kimberly went to buy the tickets she would not be half as impressed.

'So, I guess we should make sure we get there in the daylight.'

Kimberly was in her organised, grown-up state of mind, and he felt a little squeezed out, as if it was unimportant whether he was there or not.

'Once we're in London, we go three stops on the Tube, so we need to allow time for that. They said it was a fifteen-minute walk from the Tube to the house, so we should allow half an hour, in case we get lost. Better to arrive early and wait than be late, right? Right ...? Neil, are you even listening?' Kimberly joined the queue for tickets.

'Are there trees?' he asked. Once Kimberly had had the job offer, there was no stopping her. She had found a flat online, transferred the deposit and been sent the keys by post. To him, it felt like the whole thing had been accomplished in a whirlwind: Kim was in the still eye of the storm and he was catching some whipping gusts of momentum on the edge of the vortex. The whole process of her acquiring the flat in London left him stunned. He found such major transitions hard. When he had moved to college, only an hour away from Greater Lotherton, that had been tough enough, but when he imagined London, two hundred and fifty miles away, all he could see were concrete roads and concrete tower blocks. So, knowing whether there were trees would have helped.

'What?' Kimberly swivelled her head to look at him, her eyes wide, her mouth open.

'On the street where this flat is, are there trees?'

'How should I know? They only sent interior shots.'

Her skin puckered between her eyes, and she had that look she would get in the Chinese takeaway when he agonised over veg satay or sweet and sour veg with cashew nuts. He liked them both, and it wasn't the easiest of choices, but when they were ordering she always gave him that look.

'Why do you want to know if there are trees?' Her face was close to his, so clear, so beautiful, it was an effort to concentrate on anything else.

'Well, it's all concrete and tarmac, isn't it? London, I mean.'

He did not say this loudly; instead he sort of muttered it, sensing he was taking a bad route with this observation.

'It's London, Neil!' She emphasised his name as if talking to a child. 'It's a city. We are not moving to Watership Down.'

That was a dig, a reference to his favourite film. A classic, and ahead of its time in his opinion, for the artwork, the colours. He had always been attracted by animation, and he would be happy enough if he could spend his life drawing cartoons.

'I was just hoping there would be trees …'

'Oh, here we go.' She sighed heavily. 'I get it.'

Her brow dropped and the corners of her mouth twitched downwards.

'All this time you've been encouraging me, egging me on to apply for these jobs and saying, "Of course I'm going with you, Kim." But what was actually going on in your head was, you never thought I'd get an offer, did you? You thought you would earn brownie points by encouraging me, but you never really thought it would happen. Well it has!

I'm going to London, I've got a job with Channel Doc, and I'm taking it. I'll have a career in the media and you, *mate*' – she created distance with this word, stepped out of their intimate relationship – 'need to wake up.'

Then she stopped for breath. Her chest was lifting and falling as if she had been running, her eyes glassy as if she had been chopping onions. He, on the other hand, looked around him, embarrassed because she had not spoken quietly. This was clearly the wrong thing to have done because it started her off again.

'You care what they think –' she was shouting now, flinging her arms to indicate everyone else at the station – 'but not what I think?'

He tried not to look around him again, at the people who must be staring at them; he tried to stay focused on her face, her eyes, but he was sure he could feel the stares and, despite himself, he glanced to one side.

'Look at me!' she shrieked.

... Well, no, in truth – if he was really honest – she did not shriek. In fact, she had hissed the whole conversation through her teeth very close to his ear. But to him it had sounded like she was shouting and shrieking, and one or two people *had* looked at them.

'Look at me, not them! This is about us,' she continued. 'I thought we were a team, I thought we

33

had committed. I thought you were encouraging me like partners do, like partners should.'

'No – I mean, yes, I am, I do.'

He had no clue what the right thing to say was. Of course he had thought she would get one of the jobs, and he was very impressed that she had landed one with Channel Doc. She was great, he knew that. It was just that he had not, until that moment, really pictured what the reality of living in London was going to be like, for him. He had this sudden image of a narrow, urban road with not a tree in sight and all the solid terraced houses broken into flats, all the front gardens tarmacked or gravelled for parking, no one knowing each other, and the whole idea suddenly seemed just as drab and depressing to him as it was wonderful and uplifting to her.

'You haven't given this a thought, have you?' Her eyes were no longer glassy; now they were hard.

'Of course I have,' he lied, and he knew that she knew it was a lie.

She knew him so well; sometimes he felt that she knew him better than he knew himself. Having grown up together, the only time they had spent apart was when she went off to university, all the way up in Edinburgh, and didn't come back for three years. During that time, he studied at the local college. After that, his dad signed him up for what Neil thought was a proper job in the arts. That was how Dad made it sound, but he should have known better because the truth was his dad had never felt that art had much value, and he considered Neil's interest in the subject neither worthwhile nor a realistic basis for his future. As it turned out, it was temporary, underpaid work loading boxes in a factory that produced art books. The placement lasted three months and when it came to an end he swore he would never listen to his dad again. His blood had boiled with anger and he had moved out of home. Sleet, such a funny guy, had helped with the move, whilst making a joke out of the whole thing, especially after a drink or two.

But, seeing as he could say he had had some experience in a printer's, maybe he could find something similar in London – to start him off, at least.

'I have given it a lot of thought,' he lied. 'I thought I might get a job like the one I did before, you know, in a printer's,' and he looked Kimberly boldly in the eyes to show his sincerity and his commitment to living in London.

She made a derisive noise at that point, and the woman behind them in the queue pushed forward, urging them to fill up the space in front.

'You just thought of that now, didn't you?' Kimberly snorted.

'No, I've been thinking.'

'Two years you've been thinking what to do next while I've been applying for every job I could find. Didn't I say for you to apply for jobs too, so we would both be working? You know, like a proper couple.'

'What do you mean, a proper couple? My mum never worked.'

She rolled her eyes then and stepped up behind the person in front. They did not speak whilst the next three people were served. He thought he was off the hook, but then, just before it was their turn, she turned to him and said, 'You know what, just go.'

What did she mean go? Go as in leave? That didn't make sense, but if not that, what *did* she mean? As it seemed he kept doing the wrong thing, he decided the best thing to do was just stand there.

'Go, I said,' Kimberly continued. 'I don't want to spend any more time with someone who is A, not committed to me and B, not committed to making something out of his life. So I'll go to London on my own. You can stay in the poky little flat, which, I presume, having not seen this move to London as a reality, you've not given notice on as we agreed?'

His cheeks flamed at that.

'I see I'm right, so that's it. You can stay in your poky little flat, 'cause I'm off. If you manage to get yourself and your life together I would be overjoyed to see you in London because, believe it or not, I really love you, and I know you give me space to play, which is good, but I do not want a dead weight who is not committed.'

'Next!' the woman behind the glass called, and Kimberly stepped up and bought a one-way ticket to the capital. She returned the change to her drawstring purse, turned away from where she knew he was standing and walked off without even a half glance back.

'Next,' the woman on the other side of the glass called again, and the woman behind Neil in the queue gave him a push.

'Er, no, er, nothing, sorry – er, thank you,' Neil stammered, and ran after Kimberly, who had turned the corner, left the station and disappeared into the crowd in the street.

She didn't come back to the flat that night. The next day, when he returned from the shop with beers and a loaf of bread, she was there and so were two pillows down the middle of the bed. He had a week to try to think of something to say, some way to rectify the situation, but he couldn't think of anything, and she continued frostily ignoring him. He would go out and meet up with Sleet just for someone to talk to, but Sleet, trying to be the loyal friend, said unkind and untrue things about Kimberly – male clichés about being independent and not getting stitched up by some girl who wants a picket fence, and then he would drift off into platitudes about life being art and how you only get one canvas, and other stuff they had already said a hundred times at college.

He still didn't think Kimberly would really go. Either that or he hadn't properly visualised the day when she would actually leave. Or maybe he thought a miracle would happen and he would know what to say to change her mind. Whatever the case, he did think *something* was going to happen – other than her packing her rucksack and banging the door behind her and walking out to the taxi without even a goodbye.

No, he was no superhero. He was, and is, a bit of a ditherer, which, along with the happy bubble created by living with Kimberly, has amounted to him not doing much of anything with his life since college. Of course, he has spent countless hours filling countless sketchbooks with his observations of life around him and his life with Kim. Sleet, bless him, has always praised these and encouraged him, saying how, as an artist, everything he did was productive and creative. Everything was a part of the artistic process, he said. Even the raft, in Sleet's eyes, was a piece of art. However, in the real world, building rafts doesn't pay the bills, and the truth is Neil has done nothing for the last two years to make his life sustainable without government handouts. So, no, he is no hero.

He sighs loudly, but he shares none of these thoughts with Phee.

'Wow, you are quite a guy!' Phee whistles through her teeth. 'Pulling her piano all the way to London. Now that's commitment! That's true love. Wow. Lucky girl. Wow.' She whistles through her teeth again and shakes her head.

'Only because I was too dumb to go with her when she left,' Neil says, but only in his head. Outwardly, he manages a smile and sits up a little taller.

Chapter 4

The raft drifts onwards, slower than a man can walk, and Neil feels strangely lulled by the gentle pace. It is a natural speed, and he has a growing sense that he is one with the world, the trees, the plants, the soil. Ducks come swooping down onto the canal's smooth water, webbed feet splayed, skiing across the mirrored surface, to splash down and loiter around the raft for a while, hopeful for bread, and then float away. In the fields beyond the towpath, rabbits and hares nibble the grass, alert, twitching, and horses graze quietly.

It feels like they have been floating for hours, and judging by the sun it is already early afternoon, which brings with it a keen hunger, but he doesn't mention this to Phee. They are deep in the countryside now; there are no shops to be seen – or any kind of building. The next village could be just around the next tranquil corner, or it could be miles, hours – days, even, at this rate – before they draw in to anywhere inhabited. This timeless drifting might be very seductive, but he is beginning to realise that, considering the practicalities, there is no way he can make this heroic trip.

Neil feels in his pocket and pulls out a handful of change and a couple of notes. He checks his wallet.

At least he has his card, but there is not much more in his account than what he and Kimberly had saved for next month's rent. With a twist of his head, he looks back the way they have come. Even if he started walking now he would not get back before dark. It's quite likely that the landlord, who is a grumpy toad, will have been as good as his word and will have turned out all his belongings. What was there in the flat, anyway? A few clothes, a mattress, pots and pans. Just the paraphernalia one accumulates to stay afloat in the world. That lot would not make much of a pile if Mr Toad dumped it on the waste ground at the end of the road – the very place where they found the blue plastic barrels which now keep him afloat.

He snorts at the irony of the exchange.

Is there anything personal that he would wish to rescue from that potential bonfire? Anything he will actually miss? Is it not all just 'stuff'? Maybe his portfolio from college and the drawings he has done since, but even those have had their time, or most of them, and they are undeveloped ideas for the main, started but then abandoned. A strange sensation creeps up on him, as if someone has just poured cool water over his brain and filled his arms and legs with helium. To be suddenly free of material things produces such a feeling of lightness, and a bubble of joy ripples across his solar plexus and up into his throat.

There are memories, of course; it was his and Kimberly's home, but it was not a home they would have chosen. It was simply all they could afford: a poky, dark flat whose only redeeming feature was the tiny patch of grass at the back and the canal beyond that. Within their budget, the estate agent said, there was that and a two-roomed basement in town that smelt of damp. No choice at all, really.

He lets go of these thoughts and drifts, the sun on his face, the smell of the outdoors in his nostrils, bird calls all around.

Up ahead, a large weeping willow trails the ends of its branches in the water, the slight current strong enough to draw the ends downstream, curving the leafy tendrils. It would be fun to pass underneath it, be inside its canopy, in a house of green, but with no way of steering all he can do is watch as they pass by.

'I wonder what it would take to make something so you could steer a little?' Phee says, as if reading his thoughts. Bushy-Mush lifts his head at the sound of her voice, then stands eager for something to happen. Maybe he needs to be walked, taken for a pee.

'It would be good to steer so Bushy-Mush could jump onto the bank and take himself for a walk,' Neil says.

'He could probably do with some food, too. I know I could.'

Neil looks up at the clouds that are gathering. It could rain tonight, and that would be a problem.

Not only is there himself and Phee to keep dry, but the piano too.

A splashing from the far end of the raft stirs him from his cloud-gazing: Phee is on her knees, scooping water with her hands. Their gentle spin stops and they edge towards the towpath. Bushy-Mush starts to pace, also alert to this new sound. As they near the bank, Bushy-Mush leaps, back arched, legs outstretched, ears flying behind him. He lands on the bank with a thump, rolls over, jumps up, and runs full pelt down the towpath and round the bend they are approaching.

'Oh, do you think he has run off?' Phee says.

Neil looks after his little canine friend, his eyebrows rising.

Phee resumes her splashing. 'You paddle that side. I'll paddle this side and we'll round the corner more quickly, see where he's gone.'

Neil does as she bids him and so they scull, the banks now passing at twice the speed, almost at casual walking pace.

'Why do you keep looking at the bank?' Phee asks.

'This tremendous speed we are travelling at! I could walk faster.'

'Good idea, let's head for the bank.'

A little more splashing guides the raft gently into the muddy bank, and Phee's black skirt flaps around her legs as she jumps ashore, mooring rope in hand. She marches off down the towpath, and with a jolt the raft moves off again and Neil sees her plan.

'Hey, I'll do that,' he calls, but then he finds there is another job to do. Since the rope is pulling them towards the bank, the raft constantly collides with the edge and stops. They need to make a rudder that will steer them out towards the middle of the canal, but for now Neil kicks at the bank with his foot each time they approach, and this way they keep the raft moving in a snake-like fashion. The pulling and the kicking both fit into the lazy mood the day's drifting has instilled in them.

The corner is passed to reveal a bridge and a pub. Neil reads the sign: *The Bridge Inn*.

'Well, that's a bit unimaginative, but maybe they do food. I think we should tie up here and walk the rest.'

He does not welcome the inevitable comments and questions about the piano, the raft, his life, and this hair-brained scheme Phee is encouraging him to embark on. He looks up at the sky again, which is grey and moody. It might not rain, or maybe it will just drizzle. Perhaps by the time they come out of the pub it will have passed. The rocking chair will be okay but the piano might not fare very well. As far as he can see, though, there is nothing he can do.

'Use a bowline,' he suggests as he jumps ashore to check Phee's handiwork. The knot is a mess so he quickly reties it and then trots to catch up her up.

'Is Phee short for something?' he asks as they fall into step. The towpath is a line of compacted mud edged with grass, with water on one side, hawthorn bushes on the other and tree branches hanging over their heads.

'Ophelia. Mum lived in a fantasy world. Look, there's Bushy-Mush.' She points to where a man is sitting at a rough wooden table outside the pub, sharing his food with the wiry creature. Bushy-Mush, chewing on a discarded bone, ignores them as they are lured past him into the pub by the smell of food.

'Funny things, pubs. We think they are here to provide a drink, and now they all serve food too, but the truth is they supply a way to stop people feeling isolated,' Phee observes. 'I mean, it's not as if we can't buy the drink and the food from a shop for half the price and take it home.'

She scans the chalkboard over the bar. 'I think I'll have the soup and a roll. I'm on a budget.'

'I think they provide a sanctuary, a place to go to take time off from life,' Neil offers.

'Really? What are you having?'

'Dunno. I was brought up in one.'

'In a pub?'

'It felt really safe, they still do. Every pub feels like home. I'll have the soup too. Two soups, please. You want a beer?' he asks.

Phee nods.

'And two lagers, please.' Neil counts his change. It feels like the right thing to do to offer to pay for Phee's food too, but she has already put her share in the bartender's hand.

'You on a boat, then?' The barman smiles and passes the drinks over the bar.

'Not exactly a boat,' Phee starts, and Neil grimaces, but the barman is not really expecting a reply.

'Inside or out?' he asks, ringing the money into the till.

'In,' says Phee, choosing a table at the end of the bar that has a wooden top on ornate curved cast iron legs.

'I'll bring your food over when it's done,' the barman says.

'So why didn't you want the man to know about the raft?' Phee asks quietly. Then she drinks deeply before wiping away the thin froth moustache the cool amber has left behind.

Neil feels flattered that she picked up on his reluctance to answer the barman's question, but he wonders what else she has noticed about him.

'It's a few boards on six plastic barrels with a rocking chair and a piano on top, and you ask me that question?'

He snorts and takes a long drink himself. The lager is like nectar, mother's milk – a lifetime of familiarity.

'The raft's interesting,' Phee states.

'It's embarrassing.'

'It's romantic.'

'It's nuts.'

'It's art.'

'Is it?' he stops drinking and looks at her, a little adrenaline churning his stomach – excitement. Their gazes are locked.

'The raft is art, that's what Sleet said.'

The moment is broken by loud laughter, and two big men, sleeves rolled up, tattoos visible, enter the pub.

'Ha, Jeff,' one of the men addresses the barman, 'you seen that thing moored back along the way there? Someone's tied some sticks together, shoved a piano on top. You've never seen such a sight in your life!'

The men lean against the bar, still laughing. Jeff is already pulling a pint.

'Not that you need to worry about the eyesore,' the other says. 'I reckon it will have sunk by nightfall.' And he slaps his friend on the back, hard, and they both laugh again.

'Well, if it doesn't sink and it doesn't move it's nothing a match and a can of petrol won't sort out!' Then there is silence as they both drink deeply.

'Two soups?' A woman with a long apron on approaches Neil and Phee.

'Yeah, thanks.' Neil's face feels like it is on fire. 'Come on, we'll sit outside after all,' he says quietly, and he takes both the bowls and hurries to the door, leaving Phee to follow him with the drinks.

Chapter 5

The clouds hang heavy as night gathers. It has taken all day to travel only a couple of miles along the shallow valley that the waterway follows. Squares of orange light dot the surrounding hills, marking cosy farm kitchens. The canal is nothing more than a black mirror, and the thickets and trees by the towpath are dark shadows.

Warm light seeps out of the pub's windows and around the door, and the tiny car park has filled up. With bay windows either side of the porch, the building might be just another farmhouse if it were not for the tables and chairs on the grass beside the car park – that, and the hand-painted sign in the style of many of the canal boats in this area: the lettering is swirling and dotted, with simple brushstrokes, and there are flowers against the black background. Painting the canal boats was something Neil thought he might like to do after college, but it seemed there was not enough work for one man, let alone two in competition, and apparently an old codger called Bill has cornered that market around these parts.

The soup is thick and warming.

'Did you hear those men?' Neil says, tearing at his hunk of bread and dipping it into his soup.

'The two inside?' Phee tuts as if to dismiss them.

'Hmm,' Neil replies.

'I don't think I'll ever understand why men show off to each other in that way. You must have heard that sort of talk all your life in bars and pubs ...' Phee pauses, spoon halfway to her mouth, as a van draws in to the cobbled car park.

Even in the twilight, the vehicle is a riot of colour. *Balloonatics Children's Parties* is emblazoned down one side, and the back doors boldly declare *More Bounce to the Ounce*.

'Oh, here's trouble,' Neil says to Phee, who now watches the van expectantly. The man who climbs out of the driver's side is wearing oversized black-and-yellow-striped trousers and his face has a cloudy texture, as though he has recently wiped off a layer of white facepaint but without using a mirror. A reddish tinge surrounds his mouth and he is scowling.

'You all right?' Neil calls cheerily.

'Mate, you know what, I cannot do one more day of this!' says the driver. 'I can't, I just can't, I tell you. I feel like an idiot.' He pauses, expectant.

'You *are* an idiot.' Neil replies.

Sleet slides onto the picnic bench next to Phee. With his eyebrows raised, presumably surprised that Phee is still here, and with a big grin, presumably because he is pleased that she is, Sleet's face takes on an even more clown-like appearance.

'Anyone want a drink?' Sleet offers, making eye contact with Phee, but both she and Neil shake their heads. Sleet makes no move towards the pub for himself; instead, he rummages in the pockets of his oversized trousers and pulls out a small bottle of vodka.

Just as Sleet puts bottle to mouth he is interrupted. With a belch and a laugh, the two big men exit the pub and roll out to the car park. One of them gestures in Sleet's direction and makes a comment that his friend evidently finds hilarious. Neil drops his head closer to his soup. Sleet sits upright and flings one leg over the bench so that he is sitting sideways, ready to stand and face the men.

'Yeah, well I'm dressed like this for a reason,' he calls to the pair. 'I take it you two look like you do because you're a right pair of jokers!'

'Leave it,' Neil mutters without looking up from the table.

'No, sod them,' says Sleet. 'I've had a day to end all days, and I'm damned if I'll be laughed at by a pair of mugs like them!' He struggles to be free of the bench, fighting with his trousers, which have somehow wound themselves around the seat.

'They're just bullies,' Phee adds quietly, a hand on Sleet's forearm.

Neil doesn't rate her chances of calming him. When Sleet is in one of these moods he can create trouble out of anything. 'Brain-dead,' Kimberly would observe at moments such as this. She never quite understood Sleet, which made things difficult. She even referred to Sleet as 'that waste of human life', which was too harsh. Sleet, on the other hand, would dismiss his volatile behaviour as just his way of getting rid of some pent-up anger. Neil could see both sides.

Phee's touch, however, appears to have had the desired effect, as Sleet has made no further move.

'Er, sorry, mate,' the bigger of the two men says, car keys in hand. 'No offence meant.' His key fob reads *World's Best Dad*. Neil wonders about the accuracy of this statement.

'That was nice of them,' Phee says, and to Neil it sounds like a pacifying comment for Sleet's sake; she is obviously not convinced that he has completely calmed down yet.

'Yeah, well, I don't need it,' Sleet grumbles, and he slumps back onto the bench.

'How did you know we would be here?' Phee asks as Neil offers Sleet some of the bread that came with the soup. He declines.

'Well, I started back at Neil's old flat – I thought you might have pulled it back there.' Sleet looks up and down the canal until he spots the raft, the piano upright on top. 'Most of your clothes are in the van, by the way,' he tells Neil, 'and your mattress. The landlord was true to his word. Then I followed the canal from where I left you.' He chuckles these last words.

'Yeah, well, tying the raft up, or even just waking me this morning when you left, would have been a friendly thing to do.' Neil abandons his spoon in his bowl and sits back to contemplate the fact that his flat is gone. He is not sure how he feels about that now it has actually happened.

'Yeah, but not as funny.' Sleet is grinning now, his face alive, all tiredness and misery gone. 'Besides,' he continues, laughing, 'if I had done that, what would have happened?'

Neil shrugs, feeling a little overwhelmed by everything.

'I'll tell you what would have happened. You would have gone and paid your miserable landlord and you would have settled back into that dump for the next month and rotted in the swamp of your own festering mind.' Sleet presents this as a challenge.

'Oh right, so instead I'm without a place to call home, and with nothing to my name but a floating piano and a rocking chair?' Neil says.

'That has to be better than paralysis followed by rigor mortis,' Sleet goads, taking another nip from his bottle.

'I would have done something,' Neil mutters, but he knows Sleet is right.

'You would have wallowed in your misery without Kim, and I would have had to periodically deliver you from that hell with a course of whisky shots, which, by the way, would not be a solution.'

'If it's not a solution, why do you self-medicate so much?' Neil jibes, finishing his lager.

'Because, unlike you,' Sleet speaks grandly, an actor on a stage, 'I am tied by the unbreakable demands of duty and money. You can escape them one at a time but never the two together.' He wags his finger dramatically and lowers his voice as he speaks.

Phee's eyes shine, drawn in by the performance, and he smiles. 'Or, to put it more bluntly, my dear Orange Peel, and at the risk of boring you by repeating what I've told you a thousand times, my dad's got me. I will die the saddest, most pitifully paid clown in the history of children's parties …'

He grins at Phee as he delivers this statement, clearly very pleased with himself. Neil rolls his eyes.

'You know, I turned my life around this morning.'

Phee's interjection is sudden and both of them look at her. She stumbles now that the attention is focused on her.

'It's a bit of a long story, but anyway, the same things kept happening to me.' She focuses on Sleet as she talks. 'So this morning I decided to just do the opposite of what I would normally do.'

She looks at Neil, perhaps seeking a little reassurance, seeing as she told him all this earlier. Sleet is grinning, and, encouraged, she continues.

'Consequently, I have never had a day like today before in my life!' Most of the black lipstick has worn off her mouth with the passing of the day and because of the soup. She looks better for it, but it would be good to see her without all the eye make-up. Neil feels sure Sleet fancies her and he wonders if he could fancy her, too, but such a thought unearths all the love in his heart for Kimberly and he looks away over the hills.

'Nice idea,' Sleet replies to Phee, 'but if I do the opposite then that means no job, which means no use of the van, which means I'm stuck. And it also means no money, and no job means Mum whines at me. It's a trap! Talking of which, Mum says if you want to stay in the spare room tonight, you can, Neil, but only the night, mind, not like last time ...' His face takes on a serious expression.

'She never lets anything go, your mum, does she?' Neil says. 'That was two years ago, when I first moved out of home, before the flat, before Kimberly.'

The light is fading fast now, and the bulb over the pub door comes on, bright and harsh, the intimacy gone.

'You want a bed or not?' Sleet stands. 'I think it's going to rain. Come on, let's go.' He jangles the van keys in his pocket.'

'I can't just leave Kimberly's piano out in the elements.' Neil stands too. Phee goes inside, presumably to use the loo.

'I brought a tarp. We'll throw it over the top and tomorrow I should be finished by two. I'll get my motorbike and we can tow it back up to Greater Lotherton. Come on.'

'And what'll I do with it in Greater Lotherton?' Neil says glumly.

'I dunno. Worry about that then.' Sleet is at the van, unlocking the back door, taking out a paint-stained tarpaulin. Phee rejoins them, mouth freshly black.

'What are we doing?' she asks.

'Putting this over that.' Sleet nods towards the piano and marches off down the towpath, the tarpaulin over one shoulder. Neil and Phee follow him.

'I think we should push it down under the bridge, too,' Neil says. The piano and chair are silhouetted against the last of the light in the sky, where the sun slipped over the hills. Like a blow to the chest, the realisation hits him that his flat is gone and these are the last remaining pieces of the home he shared with Kimberly. How many times has she sat on that chair, writing and rocking herself, the toes of one foot on his shoulder to push herself backward and forward whilst he sprawled on the beanbag watching television? How many times has he sat on that chair with her in his lap, the hours passing, doing nothing in particular? The piano was solely hers, though, and he loved to listen to her play.

Actually, no, he is being a bit sentimental. Sometimes he loved to hear her play, especially 'My Funny Valentine', but once in a while they would argue because she would insist on playing very loudly, great crashing chords, when he was watching the news or something. But that was only because the news, or the 'state of the world', as she referred to it, made her sad and mad. She was so sensitive. In the first few weeks they lived together, it had quite shocked him how upset she could get just watching the news, until in the end he took to reading a newspaper if he wanted to know what was going on.

His chest feels heavy. Why, oh why, had she blown his reaction at the station into such a big deal?

For God's sake, she had already named their unborn children and he had agreed with her choices. How committed did she want him to be?

'Are you okay?' Phee says, shaking him out of his thoughts.

'Kimberly-struck!' Sleet diagnoses the cause of Neil's withdrawal as if it is a common condition. 'You know what, she hasn't even been gone twenty-four hours! Get a grip, man.'

The chuckle at the end tells Neil that Sleet is trying to be funny, but it doesn't feel funny. He wipes a hand across his eyes.

'Don't be unkind,' Phee says to Sleet, and Neil strides out, leaving them behind. He unties the raft and passes them again as he turns to pull it towards the bridge. Every now and again he shoves it away with his foot to stop it colliding with the muddy bank. Phee and Sleet don't seem to be in any hurry to help; they have stopped to talk about something, and he can hear her laughing. Sleet keeps using his sleeve to wipe at his face, to rid himself of the last traces of his clown make-up.

When they do catch up, she is still laughing and Sleet is telling one of his corny clown act jokes, suitable for a five-year-old. His words and her laughter echo under the bridge. Bushy-Mush reappears, barking joyfully. Phee makes a fuss of him whilst Neil and Sleet pull the tarpaulin over the piano and the chair, and the den it creates proves irresistible to Bushy-Mush, who leaps onto the raft and runs round in circles, then curls up, beating his tail on the boards.

'I'm not sure what Mum will say about Bushy-Mush staying,' Sleet says. 'I suppose he can stay in the garage.'

'Can you imagine how much he will howl?' Neil knows this from experience. The dog has to be on his or Kimberly's feet or no one gets any sleep.

'Well, I don't think she'll let him in the house.'

With a grin, Sleet turns to Phee.

'I've just remembered one I used to tell – there was a dog and a horse, have you heard it?'

Neil, who has heard it a thousand times, doesn't want to hear it again. Night is falling and this is the first time in two years that he will not go to sleep holding Kimberly. He wraps his arms across his chest and tries to hold his heart in. He wants to howl at the stars himself.

Chapter 6

'You coming, Neil?' Sleet walks off, Phee beside him. Neil hears him ask her, 'Where can I drop you?'

It's decision time. If he goes with Sleet, it's back to what he knows, and Kim is certainly not waiting for him there. Chances are, Sleet's dad will give him the odd bit of work here and there – again – and that will fill his days and his mind until he rents another flat, and then one day he'll be too hungover to get out of bed, Sleet's dad will sack him, and he'll go back on the dole – again. Sure, he'll keep drawing every opportunity he gets, but it's hardly a future.

As for Kimberly, she will have a magnificent career in London and he will keep packing the memory of her away in a box in his head marked 'history' until one day, hopefully, she will stay there and the thought of her will no longer hurt. Meanwhile, the government will stop giving him handouts and he will have to get a night job stacking shelves in a supermarket for minimum wage, as those are the only jobs around these days, it seems. Before he knows it, his bones will creak and his hair will be white and then everything will be too late.

'Come on, Neil!' Sleet is by his van now, leaning on an information plaque facing the canal. It seems they have them dotted everywhere these days; you can be in the most remote corner and suddenly there's a plaque with information and dates, taking all the romance out of being in the countryside.

'You know what, I think I might spend the night here.'

'Don't be daft, you'll freeze. Look, just don't worry. With the tarp over, no one's going to know it's a piano. No one will nick it. It'll be all right until we come back tomorrow for it.'

Neil looks at the odd floating shape.

'You know what ...' He speaks slowly. 'I'm going to do what we said, I'm going to float it down to Kim in London, woo her back.'

He can picture her waiting for him, a big smile, arms open, and for that it would be worth travelling twice the distance.

'A day in the fresh air has sent you soft in the head!' Sleet laughs. 'And "woo"? What kind of old-fashioned granddad word is that? Besides, it must be two hundred miles to London.'

'Two hundred and fifty,' Phee informs him. 'And I think it's a great idea.'

61

'Well, originally, it was my idea.' Sleet stresses the word 'my', and looks just a little disgruntled. Then he adds, 'But without a motor how are you going to do it?'

'I'll pull it.'

'That was my idea,' Phee says.

'How long will that take you?' Sleet asks, his eyebrows high, his tone incredulous.

'If you walk with it at about three miles an hour then it will take you less than one hundred hours in total,' Phee calculates. 'If you walk, say, ten hours a day … That's quite a lot, isn't it?' She looks at Sleet, who in turn looks blank. 'That's only ten days,' she calls to Neil, injecting hope into her voice.

'Yeah, but that's two hundred and fifty miles by road. This canal goes out towards the coast from here and then hits Wigan where you turn back inland to Manchester before you can find a canal that heads south.'

Both Neil and Phee turn to look at Sleet, amazed, only to find that he is reading from the plaque on the towpath. The pub's lights bounce off its plastic surface, and they gather round to study for themselves the short text, and the map with its thin blue line that meanders through villages and towns, marked with bridges and locks.

'It's very wiggly,' Phee says, looking over Neil's shoulder.

'It'll take you a year,' Sleet pronounces.

'The longer it takes, the more committed you'll look,' Phee says dreamily.

'Do you want all your clothes, then – your portfolio and your mattress?' Sleet asks, wrapping his arms around himself, obviously feeling the cold.

'The mattress won't fit, will it? The raft's too small for a double mattress and the other stuff.' Phee's practical voice has returned.

'Can you keep my portfolio at yours?' Neil asks.

'You know you're nuts?' Sleet says.

'It's a quest. Quests are meant to be nuts,' Neil replies, but already a seed of fear has lodged deep in his gut. But also, there is a glimmer of hope, an inkling of belief that such a journey will change him, make him more the sort of person he wants to be. Whatever happens, it must be better than staying and doing nothing.

'The old bouncy castle we use for repairs is in the van,' Sleet says. 'We could put that over, or under, the tarp, make it a bit warmer for you, if you like?'

'Could you fold the mattress over and tie it, so it only takes up the space of a single?' Phee suggests, picking at the knots in a length of rope in the back of the van.

The corresponding knot in Neil's stomach begins to tighten and twist. This preparation suggests his commitment to the journey, and the fear slowly spreads its wings, flutters up into his chest and morphs into what could possibly be excitement. A strange, floating feeling comes over him and he feels almost certain that Kimberly will be waiting for him at the other end. Not that she will openly admit liking such a big display of emotion; it is more likely that she will sidestep the question. But she will be there. How could she not be, after he has walked two hundred and fifty miles for her? Also, it is easier for him to deal with the journey if he views it as art. It is a concept he can grasp wholeheartedly and it returns him to the more solid rationale of his student days. It acts as an anchor and his world stabilises.

'Did you see Tracy Emin's *My Bed*?' he asks Phee.

'What a load of crap!' Sleet exclaims.

'I love her work,' says Phee.

'Yeah, well, when I say crap, I mean she intends it to be crap, right? That's the point … But it being crap doesn't make it any less art …'

Sleet stumbles over his words in his eagerness to redeem himself. Sleet's first project that first year only got him a grade C, but an additional note at the bottom of the report awarded an A for bullshit. He may not have much to do with art these days but he hasn't lost that skill.

Together, they drag the cannibalised bouncy castle out of the van, down the towpath and onto the raft. The bouncy castle is a riot of colour. Sleet throws it over the tarpaulin and pulls and tugs it about until it sits well. It appears to have a Disney theme, with the seven dwarfs painted down one side, under the words *Snow White's Fairy Castle*.

'Did you put those words at the front like that on purpose?' Neil asks.

Sleet sniggers.

'Typical.'

'Right. I'm knackered. I need to sleep.' Sleet yawns. 'You sure you'll be all right in your fairy castle?'

'Yeah. Fine.' Neil surveys the raft, with its new living space. Bushy-Mush has curled up inside the makeshift tent on one of his jumpers and is fast asleep. He will have to offer the mattress to Phee, obviously, but he can sleep on a pile of his own clothes.

'Right, I'll be off, then,' says Sleet. 'You coming, Phee? The guest room's all made up.'

Neil turns swiftly to look at the two of them. Did he miss something? Sleet has the key in the lock, and Phee's hand is on the passenger door. She smiles back at the raft and gives him the smallest of waves before her door is pushed open from the inside and she is absorbed into the Balloonatics van.

'Good luck, mate,' Neil whispers under his breath. It would do Sleet some good to have a girlfriend, give him a bit of self-worth. Despite this thought, a loneliness sweeps over him as he turns back to face the raft alone, and the knot in his stomach tightens. But no sooner does he feel his stomach churn than the sight of the bouncy castle – the dwarfs walking around the bottom, the wording framing the opening – brings a smile to his face.

'Sorry, Sleet, but no matter how warm your bouncy castle keeps me, it definitely has to go tomorrow.' He will turn the rubber material inside out first thing in the morning, but for now all he can think of is sleep.

An hour later, he is grateful that Phee and Sleet did not tie the folded mattress very tightly as he slithers off the top and wiggles his way between the ropes to become the jam in the mattress sandwich. It is instantly much warmer, and Bushy-Mush is quick to create a warm patch for his feet. With three jumpers on and one wrapped around his head, he can now say that he is almost warm. In fact, he would say his situation is pleasant. He can hear the rain, but there is a stillness in the tunnel and a sense that he is miles from anywhere.

Bushy-Mush stretches out alongside his legs. Neil reaches down and caresses his little friend's snout.

With no warning, the dog is suddenly alert, body tense, ears cocked. Neil's hand freezes as he listens. Voices, speaking quietly. Whispering. Oh God, is it the two men from the pub come to put a match to the raft? He should get out or he will burn to death.

The bile in his throat is matched by the adrenaline in his limbs as he squirms, trying to free himself of the mattress. He fumbles and struggles to find the opening to the tarp, sound rushing in his ears, and wriggles to get out from under the bouncy castle material; then, like a slug, a snake with no curl, he writhes and crawls onto the bank, Bushy-Mush by his side.

He slips as he scrambles to his feet. Hot blood courses through his veins and the question comes to him – will he run, or will he fight?

He looks around him. It is relatively light in the moonlight, and there is no sign of the two men. But there on the water behind him is a large dark mass that wasn't there before. He steps closer. A circle of light, a round window, provides the first clue. Then he distinctly hears a man say, 'Goodnight dear', followed by 'Sleep well', in a female voice; then the circle of light is snuffed out. A narrowboat has pulled in to moor behind him! He peers back into the tunnel, which is so dark he can hardly even see the outline of the raft.

'Rule one, then,' he tells Bushy-Mush. 'If we really are going on this mad venture then we mustn't park in tunnels. It's lucky they didn't hit us.' The thought of sinking, sandwiched in the mattress under the tarp and Snow White's thick rubber outer shell, is worse than the thought of the bullies and the match.

'Come on,' he says to his canine friend, and they make their way back into the fairy castle, find the warm spots they have just left and, reassured by each other's proximity, fall asleep.

'Good morning!'

A cheery voice greets Neil as he pokes his head out into the misty daylight. The water has a green sheen to it and above the surface floats a fog that grows thicker the higher he looks.

'We are in a bit of cloud this morning,' the voice continues, and out of the gloom steps a woman in white jeans and a zipped-up green hooded jacket, with a coffee mug in one hand. He eyes the latter, the steam curling and mixing with the mist, and she is quick to follow his gaze.

'Just made, you want some?' The woman smiles, and then calls over her shoulder, 'Trevor, another coffee. The raft is manned.' She turns back to Neil. 'We did wonder last night, it was hard to see you. Are you stationary or does it move?' She squints and peers under the bridge.

'Morning!' A new voice, annoyingly cheerful and brisk for such an early hour. This must be Trevor. Neil tries to control the curl of his upper lip. With concentrated force, he manages a smile to counteract his natural inclination.

Kim would often complain about his surliness in the morning. 'Everyone's tired in the mornings,' she told him soon after they moved in together. 'Some break through that and are cheerful, while others self-indulge.' And then she gave him that look before continuing, 'When you live with others who are not your mum, best to be cheerful.'

In his head, he called her a patronising cow, and he wondered if he had made a mistake cohabiting with her, but she looked so cute in his oversized T-shirt, and besides, he knew she had a point; so he slipped his arms around her and kissed her neck until she broke free to bang and clatter last night's dishes in the sink.

'So …' The new, cheerful, brisk voice comes out of the mist and a mug of coffee is thrust into Neil's hands.

Mr Cheerful, or Trevor, as the woman called him, casts a critical gaze over the raft. 'So, you're sailing Snow White's fairy Castle to where – Narnia?' and he chortles at his own joke.

After a sip of the hot brew, Neil finds his voice. 'No – London,' he says quietly, but he doesn't look up from his steaming mug.

The couple laugh so hard at this that he feels he should laugh with them, make out it is all a joke, tell them something else. But he doesn't. He just stands there as the mist slowly lifts, and Trevor and his first mate quickly control themselves as they realise he is serious.

'London. That's a fair way,' Trevor says in a deep voice. 'So, you're off to Wigan … And then the Bridgewater Canal to Manchester, or …'

Before he has time to offer an alternative, Neil cuts in. 'Yup, giving myself twenty-five years to get there.'

'Twenty-five years!' Mrs Trevor's carefully painted-on eyebrows rise.

'I doubt you'll need twenty-five years. Have you any power?' Trevor moves towards the raft again, walks past it to look at it from the other side.

'No, eh? Well, you still won't need twenty-five years if you get a move on.' He laughs again and comes back smiling. 'Curious craft. Why Snow White, is it a statement?'

'No, it's a bouncy castle,' is what Neil would like to say, but instead he explains the course of events and the need to keep the piano dry and himself warm.

'Oh, it's so romantic,' the woman says, and her eyes moisten as she looks at him anew.

'So you'll be adding to the craft as you go, then? You'll need something a bit more solid if you are taking your time over the journey. Do you know Bill and Cyril down the way here?' Trevor asks. 'They'd help. Just their sort of thing, isn't it, Joyce?' The woman smiles.

'I'll get breakfast on,' she says, and she makes her way carefully back to the narrowboat, avoiding the muddy patches. The fog has all but gone now and smoke curls from the narrowboat's shiny chimney in the still morning air.

'Ah, breakfast. Good idea, Joyce. Will you join us?' says Trevor. 'Then we'll give you a tow to Bill's. Nice bloke – does the old-style painting on the side of canal boats around here, and Cyril's a good sort too, but a bit shy, likes animals. I think it's Cyril who gets Bill all his stuff, and Bill is the artisan, creating all sorts out of other people's rubbish, painting it up, selling it on. Come in, have a look at our table. It was a door Cyril found, and Bill made it up for us.'

The brass frames of the boat's circular windows shine in the morning light. Along the roof of the barge, plants in pots add colour; a pile of firewood is neatly stacked and two bicycles are chained at the far end. In curling writing adorned with stylised flowers is the boat's name – *Bramble*.

Bushy-Mush gives a bark of delight from the towpath and hares off down the side of the canal, chasing the coots, which swim madly away on the still water as he approaches. Neil steps over the neatly painted side into the canal boat's bow area. Two deckchairs are folded and carefully stored, secured with bungee ropes, and a mat bids him *Welcome*. Inside, the craft is very narrow, little more than a corridor. It smells of fried food and air fresheners. Joyce is in the kitchen area; there is a worktop on narrow units down one side, with a stove on which she is frying eggs. There is just room for them to pass through to the sitting area, where the door that has become a table takes up much of the space. The old paint has been rubbed back here and there to show the layers of time, and the edge is decorated with painted flowers, and Neil has to admit it does look nice.

'Even the glass top is from an old shop cabinet. He doesn't buy anything, not even nails, doesn't old Bill. He pulls them out of whatever he finds and puts them in tins to use again. Well, he buys his paint, of course.'

'Here you are, boys.' Two plates are laid before them on the table, and Trevor motions to Neil to sit.

'Go ahead, I'll just get mine on the go,' Joyce says.

Neil cannot remember the last time he had a cooked breakfast – last time he was at Mum and Dad's, probably. Ha! Sleet and Phee will be chewing on Sleet's mum's burnt toast and sloppy marmalade, imagining him shivering in the cold. He chuckles to himself as he eats, and he studies the interior of the craft. Beyond the dining area where they are sitting is a sofa built in against one wall, and beyond that is a partition of polished wood with a door to whatever is beyond. Portholes down each side have curtains, secured top and bottom. On the walls are pictures of children and grandchildren, judging by Trevor's and Joyce's ages, and of a black cocker spaniel. One faded image displays a much younger Trevor and Joyce in old-fashioned technicoloured clothing. She has a scarf around her head and is holding a flower, and he is wearing a long top with tassels around the hem. They are both laughing, and seem free and full of life. Trevor must be about Neil's age in the picture.

'That you?' Neil asks, and he points with his fork.

'Our first Glastonbury,' Trevor says, cutting away at his breakfast. 'We go every year, but it's changed a lot since then, and not entirely for the better.'

With a jolt, Neil realises that Trevor, despite his early morning cheerfulness and pristine boat, might be quite an okay guy. Not exactly cool, perhaps, but he's seen some things, done some things. Neil stops chewing. One day this will be him, old enough to be someone's granddad, and maybe he will find himself with someone of his present age and they in turn will not be able to imagine what he was like at their age. Will they treat him with hidden disdain, as if he is a bit of a fool, just as he has been judging Trevor? Which begs the question – did Trevor think this when he was Neil's age, and does Trevor, sitting there now, see through his politeness to his real feelings of disdain? His cheeks feel a little warm at this thought.

So engrossed is he in his own thoughts, the food is finished almost before he feels he has started. He wipes his plate clean with a hunk of bread and sits back.

'So are you on holiday?' he asks.

'We're nomads,' Joyce answers from the kitchen area. 'We have one daughter in Greater Lotherton and one in Liverpool. Each with two children.'

'We couldn't decide which child to buy a house near' – Trevor takes up the narrative – 'so we tried to think "out of the box", and this seemed like a great solution. Sold our house, which means we have cash in the bank for six weeks abroad each year, and when we are in England we just potter up to one daughter and down to the other. Canal folk are very friendly.'

'Oh,' is all Neil can think to say. He looks again at the picture of young Trevor and Joyce. Boat nomads – that's pretty cool. It's impossible to think of his parents doing the same but it is quite exciting to think that he might do something like this one day – something 'out of the box', imaginative, unusual.

Whilst he is musing over these thoughts, a volley of barking heralds the return of Bushy-Mush.

'Oh, that's my dog!' Neil exclaims. I'd better go and see what the trouble is.' And with this as his excuse, he leaves hurriedly.

'Oh,' he calls back over his shoulder, 'and thanks for the breakfast …'

Chapter 7

Bushy-Mush is sitting on the towpath, barking at nothing in particular. He stops as soon as he sees Neil, who is glad of the fresh air now he is out of the narrowboat. It seems like as good a time as any to take down the fairy castle. The tarpaulin will be enough to protect the piano.

'Oh, don't take it down.' Joyce has followed him outside, plate in hand, a piece of toast paused near her lips. 'Bill and Cyril will love that! Leave it up till you get to their yard. Maybe they will do a swap with you.'

'I'll just fold it back a little to give myself somewhere to sit.' He ducks inside the tent and begins to fold his clothes, which are screwed up and dumped in a corner.

'We'll be off in half an hour if you'd like a tow along to Bill and Cyril's,' Joyce calls.

'Oh, yes, thanks.' His response is automatic but inside he feels a wave of uncertainty that tells him the decision to make this journey doesn't feel real yet. Even now he could catch a local bus back to Greater Lotherton and forget the whole idea. Accepting this tow will add miles on to his journey that he might find he ends up retracing. On the other hand, if he is indeed taking on this adventure, then a tow will be an amazing head start and will feel like real progress.

With the fog gone, his voice now echoes in the tunnel again. 'Thanks a lot. It's really kind of you – cheers!' he says, and he's rewarded with a smile.

He checks all the knots fastening the blue barrels to the boards as best he can and stores his clothes in the barrel with the opening. He puts his mobile phone in the barrel, too, and feels lighter without it. He has never liked the things. Packing away his phone makes him feel he is casting off the world and all its demands, and he sighs his relief.

By the time he has stowed everything neatly and feels ready for the next leg of the journey, the day has brightened and the sun is sliding from behind a cloud, illuminating all the dust particles and small insects that float on the surface. It is as though the canal has been dusted with a sprinkling of icing sugar. Neil lies flat on the raft and hums the tune of 'My Funny Valentine' to himself as he looks down into the water. In the depths, weeds trail, bending with the current, but whereas yesterday afternoon the water was flowing at a reasonable rate, this morning the surface barely creeps along. The twigs and leaves on the surface are almost stationary. He wonders if it's the wind that is responsible. Maybe it is the locks. Each time a boat passes through a lock, water drains away downstream, drawing more from higher up, and heavy traffic, with the locks opening and closing more frequently, will presumably mean a faster current, which will be great, so long as the direction of flow is in his favour. And if there is no traffic, the water will settle, become stationary. If this is true, then this should mean that he will float all the more quickly in busy areas – where the canal passes through towns, for example. For now at least the current is carrying him in the direction he needs to go.

Two swans sail towards them, slowing to inspect the raft, their graceful movements mesmerising Neil. As they draw alongside, the larger bird fluffs its wings out and pecks at a multicoloured floating object. Bushy-Mush naturally starts to bark, and Neil tries to wave the swan away. The larger of the regal birds hisses and curls its neck back; its chest rises from the water and it spreads its wings. There is no doubting its aggression as it hurls itself towards Neil's face, and he is at a disadvantage, lying on his belly so near to the water.

'Hey!' he shouts, hoping the sound of his voice is enough to put the beast off, but he scrambles to his feet just in case. The swan, unafraid, hurls itself at him again.

'Oh heck,' he gasps. Can he outrun the bird if he goes ashore, or will it fly after him?

'Territorial animals,' he hears Trevor observe from the bank.

Neil makes it onto the path next to him, and is relieved when the bird backs down and swims off a little way to where it can keep an eye on them.

'We'll push off now, as we pass,' Trevor continues. 'Throw your line to Joyce. Do you want to jump over to our boat once we're on the move, or do you think you need to steer a little?'

'Thanks – er, I'm not sure …' Neil can feel himself dithering, and he can imagine Kim becoming impatient with him if she were here.

'Perhaps I'd better stay on the raft,' he concludes, 'just to be on the safe side.' He is not sure what might happen, or what he would do if anything did happen, but it seems more responsible, somehow. Maybe, if this works, and more people are kind enough to offer lifts, he can go all the way to London relying on tows?

Bushy-Mush hasn't stopped barking.

'He's a jolly little chap, isn't he?' Trevor looks over his glasses at the dog. Neil picks him up and the silence is soothing.

'Little dog in a big world,' Neil says. Trevor smiles at him, and Neil can see him as the man in the picture, his own age, full of energy. Their eye contact lasts just a fraction longer than necessary and Neil feels he has bridged a divide, or Trevor did. Something has happened, anyway. The youthful granddad walks back to his boat, a slight skip to his step.

'You're just scared, aren't you?' Neil whispers in the animal's ear. 'The world seems a fair size to me too, but there are nice people in it, if you take your time to get to know them.'

He smiles to himself, straightens his back and lifts his chin. 'Just call me Neil the Wise,' he mutters to the dog before putting him down.

The narrowboat begins to chug, the swan moves out of the way and the raft lurches and bobs as the boat begins to pass.

'Here you go,' Neil says, handing the line to Joyce, who is waiting at the stern. The craft is moving at walking speed, and he wonders how fast they can go.

'All righty-roo, then.' She makes fast with a neat figure of eight over a cleat, and the rope uncurls from the raft's deck. Fearing that the sudden tension will jerk the raft and upset the piano, he picks up the rope and takes the strain himself. Better if he is pulled off and into the water than the piano. But the pull is gentle, so he slowly lets the rope out until the strain is taken by the raft.

Compared to yesterday, when the raft was just floating with the current, the speed of the narrowboat is impressive. But they are not travelling at more than a brisk walking pace. The stench of diesel from the boat's exhaust hangs in the air, but the rope is long enough to afford him some distance. He can watch Trevor's back as he steers his craft with its long tiller, but the engine noise is too loud for them to be able to hold a conversation. Trevor smiles and waves.

Neil settles back to enjoy the ride. The sun is now fully out; all signs of the mist have vanished and the sky is a beautiful blue, dotted with big fluffy clouds, like yesterday. As he starts to drift off, a flash of metallic green over his head is followed by another, and he sits up to trace the flight of a pair of kingfishers, which disappear into the bushes on the opposite bank. Trevor is pointing at them and nodding his head enthusiastically. They both watch and wait but the birds do not reappear.

As they follow the canal round a gentle bend, Neil tries to work out where they are. So far, the journey has been very slow and meandering. He reckons he must be somewhere near the outskirts of Little Lotherton, perhaps, or maybe not even that far yet, and if indeed he is not there yet he has come no distance at all. The bus would have taken twenty minutes to travel the distance it has taken him a day and a night to cover. His joke about twenty-five years might not be so ridiculous at this rate.

The waterway twists around clumps of trees and winds in between the hills, meandering like a river rather than a man-made course. In the distance he can see a tall grey stone building. It will be a mill, no doubt, and the canal will have been cut to go right past it, to pick up its produce. Wool, most likely, and he bets there is a river there that would have driven the water-powered looms. Not that any of the machinery will be left now. It is probably unused, abandoned, this far from civilisation. If it were nearer a town, someone would have converted it into flats, no doubt. He prefers them left abandoned – there is something romantic about nature reclaiming man-made structures. He checks the plastic bag of stuff Sleet left by the piano. He knows what will be in it, he knows Sleet so well, but he wants to check, just to be certain. Sure enough, there is a sketchbook, and his pencils in the pencil case Kim made for him out of a piece of bright patterned fabric. As they get closer, he will take the time to sketch the mill.

The raft is heading towards a weeping willow that hangs out over the bank, on a bend up ahead. The narrowboat steers around the tree, but without a rudder Neil is helpless. He ducks under the branches, but long wet tentacles slither across his legs, dragging trails over the plastic of the bouncy castle. Worried that a branch might push or even pull the piano from its place, he stands and wraps his arms around the instrument to keep it steady. It does not take long to see how ridiculous this is: if the piano goes, he will go too – there would be no stopping it.

There are thick weeds under the tree, and driftwood and plastic bags have become caught, as has a short plank. He grabs the plank, and once he is out in the open water again he experiments with using this to steer. It is quite efficient and he only needs to adjust his course every few minutes, or if he wants to steer around an obstacle. Trevor looks back and gives him the thumbs up.

Bushy-Mush, it seems, likes to be a prow dog, and he sits up front near where the tow rope is secured. The speed is very pleasant, but the sound of Trevor's and Joyce's motor is not; when the revs suddenly cut out and Trevor points to a waterway that veers off to one side, before waving back at him, Neil reasons that this is his departure point, and it is a relief to be free of the noise. Trevor throws the rope in the water and turns his back with a last salute.

'Have fun,' Trevor shouts, and Joyce appears from below deck to smile and wave madly at him.

'You're a hero!' she calls, and she waves again, and then she and Trevor turn in the direction they are going. Neil watches them for a moment, and although he's glad it's quieter now, he feels a sense of abandonment as the narrowboat slips away down the canal.

Without the tow rope pulling it, the raft turns in the current. Neil is adrift midstream but not going in the right direction. The raft still has some momentum and he turns his improvised rudder to steer into the side stream. As the momentum drops off, he uses the steering plank to paddle. The way narrows, with trees thick on either side. It cannot be right; did he miss where Trevor pointed?

Now he is pushing past overhanging shrubs and willows, and just as he thinks he should retrace his route the waterway opens up, and soon afterwards it comes to an end at what looks like a clearing in a tropical forest. It is all leaves and ivy, but as he looks more closely he can make out furniture in the undergrowth, as if it is a decaying reclamation yard, the whole of which is canopied in leaves. At the far end, where the bushes and trees present a solid wall, there is a small hut about the size of a garden shed.

The raft drifts right up to where the the yard begins and grounds itself. The rocking chair rocks, but everything else remains as it was except for Bushy-Mush, who jumps off at once to explore this exciting new terrain.

The yard is an overwhelming jumble of wooden furniture, old windows and doors, and more, all piled up or leaning with no obvious method. On one side is a stack of railway sleepers, six feet high, with an old desk balanced precariously on top. A collection of wardrobes, in various stages of decomposition, huddle next to this, and beyond these a contingent of old cast-iron radiators guard a delicate Victorian slipper bath, complete with brass taps. The perimeter is marked with impenetrable hawthorn bushes in front of a row of trees, and beyond, through the tangle of tree branches, the dark stone of the mill can be seen.

Neil would like to go and explore, find the passageways that would have diverted the water from the river to power the mill. Maybe parts of the waterwheel will still be there – more likely not.

'Hello,' Neil calls out tentatively, and he walks towards the hut, treading carefully between the piles of junk.

He can hear Bushy-Mush snuffling and rooting about to the side of him, and then a scampering and the same noise to his left. But there are so many ferns and so much ivy and grass and half-buried stuff he cannot actually see his dog.

'Hello?' he calls again, nearer to the hut. There is an attractive collection of fountain statues by the hut, and several stone gateway posts with urns on top jostling for room. The ivy is taking these over and it gives the appearance of a Gothic Victorian graveyard. Phee would love it!

'Hel–' he begins again.

'Hello.'

He leaps back at the unexpected closeness of the voice. Standing so still, he had taken the man in front of him, dressed in a shapeless, grey woollen suit and a grey hat, holding a grey mug of tea, for one of the statues.

'Oh, sorry, hello. I thought that you … No, never mind.'

'You wanting something?' says the man, but not unkindly. 'Or are you lost? Most people are lost if they're here. If they're here for a reason, like as not

86

they're still lost. But then most people are lost, don't you find?'

His face is lined and pitted with age and yet there is a youthfulness about the man, especially around the eyes. He is clean-shaven and his hair is short, and yet his sagging clothes give off the appearance of being unkempt.

Neil closes his mouth to consider this. 'Yes, I suppose you are right,' he agrees hesitantly.

'So are you lost, then?' the man demands.

'Well, that depends,' says Neil. 'Are you Cyril?'

'No, I'm Bill.'

'I'm Neil,' says Neil. 'Trevor and Joyce dropped me here and yes, I am probably lost.'

'Ah, now, that's a different sort of lost. First of all, because you know you're lost, and second, you don't seem to mind being lost. That's got to be the best sort of lost. What can I do for you?'

The question is tacked on so seamlessly to the monologue that it catches Neil unawares.

'Er … Not sure. I think I might be going to London.'

'Er, hmm,' Bill says, by way of acknowledgement, but he clearly wants more. 'Well, 'appen I've just put t'kettle on, so I'll tell thee what, find thisen a seat' – he indicates a fountain base beside him – 'and I'll mek us both a brew, and you can tell me all about it. You can't say fairer than that, can you now, young man?'

And at this invitation, Neil sits on his stone pew.

Once the tea is made, he feels obliged to explain his situation. It occurs to him that he can cast himself as the hero, explain his quest as Phee and Joyce might, which would make him feel good, but it also strikes him as being a little dishonest. Instead, he could explain how his friend played a prank on him after a night of drinking, but he risks coming across as a bit of a mug if he does that. He is also aware that he is dithering, and that Kim would have lost her patience again by now.

'I need to take this piano to a friend, my girlfriend, in London, so I thought I would make a bit of a journey out of it,' he says succinctly, and in his mind he conjures Kim on the banks of the waterway in the city, and it gives him the sense that it is he who is in control of their relationship and that she is passively waiting for him to arrive. It's an image that fosters hope.

Chapter 8

Bill sits silently, nodding his head whilst Neil relates the details of his journey so far and explains his quest to travel to London.

'I reckon that'll be quite a journey.' Bill speaks slowly. 'Summat worth doing, I expect. And you'll impress your lass in the process. Two birds with one stone.'

Above their heads, hidden in the tangle of branches, a bird twitters and another answers.

'When I were in Burma, the natives would build a raft at the drop of a hat. Not to win the heart of a lass, mind, but just because they needed a raft, like. Clever people, and lovely food. Of course, they used the raw materials around them. So much abundance, forest all around them, you see, but here we're only abundant in what we throw away. That's Cyril's thing. He can't stand it. He'll walk five mile with a wardrobe on his back rather than let it go to landfill. I keep telling him it'd be more efficient if he carried an axe, to chop what he finds into firewood. Folks'd be quick enough to tek it home then. Ah well. Anyway, I keep what he brings me an' when I need a bit to burn I've plenty and the rest goes back to the ground eventually. And people know I'm here now, and they know what I've got and they come if they want owt. Now, what were you wanting?'

'I didn't really say ... Trevor reckoned I needed a bigger raft if I'm to go to London, but, you know what, I'm not so sure. I mean, I don't want to bother you. I might just push off again. The tarpaulin and the rubber bouncy castle material kept me warm and dry enough last night.'

'Ah, so that's what it is, part of a bouncy castle. Colourful enough, isn't it?' Bill puts his mug of tea down on a derelict fountain and steps through his jungle of ivy and discarded furniture. As he nears the water's edge he begins to laugh. 'Did you put it over like that? Snow White's Fairy Castle? Aye, Cyril'll love that.'

Bill continues his inspection of the raft, his hands jammed in his front pockets.

'Right then, so what is it I can do for you? Do you want to buy some stuff, then?' He looks Neil up and down critically and does not pause for an answer. 'You'll not have any brass on you, to look at you. No one ever does these days. Never mind, I make enough to get by painting roses on t'boats ...'

'Oh yes, you're the man, eh? The boat painter? Now that's a job I would love,' Neil interrupts him.

'Can you paint?'

'Three years of art school.' Neil stands tall.

'Aye, but can you paint?'

Neil smiles, but quickly realises Bill's question is serious.

'I can paint,' he says solemnly.

'Well, you seem a likeable enough young man, so when I'm too old you can come and do an apprenticeship, how's that?'

When he's too old? He must be eighty if he is a day. Neil does his best not to smirk.

'That would be great,' he manages, and it would be – he would love it. Bill is back to concentrating on the raft.

'So, no brass right now, then. Ah well, 'appen we can arrange a swap of some sort. Cyril will love the fairy castle, any road. Oh aye, just his sort of thing. He'll be after that little dog of yours, too, mark my words – animal mad, he is.'

He pauses to scratch at Bushy-Mush's ears. 'That's his.' He points to the mill, the top of which can just be seen through the trees. 'He's turned it into an animal sanctuary. That's how we met – my land backing onto his. He'll be right interested in your raft too, I reckon. He likes to see folk reusing stuff. As for making it bigger, we could fix summat up, I suppose. Some sort of superstructure, as they call it, to keep you dry and that. There's all sorts of doors and windows we can use, and I've got bucketloads of nails. Can you do woodwork? No, probably not. They don't teach nowt any more. I'll teach you, though. You'll have to be learning if you're going to build this raft of yours any bigger. Did you see the table Joyce got from here? Didn't make it, didn't even touch it, apart from painting flowers round the edge and fitting it into their boat. Cyril found it like that, the paint rubbed back, all those layers of colour. The glass happened to fit. More money than sense, some people. Mind you, it keeps the wolf from the door. Have you been to India? No, probably not, no sense of adventure these days. Lots of wolves there. Was it India? Maybe. No money there. No sense either. Don't just stand there, roll your sleeves up, we've work to do. Let's get a good look at this craft of yours.'

Neil has fallen into a kind of trance, his eyes fixed on Bill's moving mouth, watching this torrent of words pour forth until the final call to action snaps him back into the moment.

With his mouth now closed in a tight, thin line, Bill takes his time to examine the raft, casting a critical eye over the knots that secure the wooden crosspieces to the barrels. Neil can remember tying each one of them, but the memory seems to be from a time so long ago.

'Well, there's nowt wrong with the basic structure but, like you said, you're a bit cramped. Perhaps we can tie on a few more barrels, elongate you a bit … It'll keep you from spinning in the current, too.'

Bill leaves the raft and starts to rummage around in his leaf-strewn furniture empire. 'Now, a wardrobe on its side won't be tall enough. If we put it upright, the square footage'll be too small for you to lie down. You see those there?' He points to a stack of wooden beams peeping out of a thick bramble bush. 'They could be the beams for on top o' the extra barrels. Good bit o' timber, those, from a barn up yonder, after the roof fell in one stormy night. Ah yes, what a stormy night! Mind you, nowt like the storms we knew in the tropics! Now *they* were storms, when the rain came at you horizontally, pierced your skin like needles.'

He continues his tour until they come to a hoard of blue barrels like the ones that started this whole raft idea back at the flat, over on the far side of Greater Lotherton.

'Grab a couple of these, here you go' – and between them they roll four of the barrels to the water's edge. 'Cyril will be very happy with you using these. Plastic, you see, don't rot, definite landfill.' He goes back for two more. 'Six enough, you think? Or shall we do eight?'

Neil shrugs. Bill, however old he is, has all the vitality of a much younger man. Was he in one of the forces, Neil wonders, and is that why he has been to all these places he names?

'We'll do six. It might take two of us to pull those beams out.' He nods back to the posts under the tangle of bramble.

'Were you in the army?' Neil asks.

'I don't think we have any pieces of wood big enough to create a wall for a cabin, though.' Bill scratches his chin, looking about. 'We'll have to cobble it.'

Maybe the old man is deaf. Neil is just about to repeat his question when Bushy-Mush appears through a hole in the backdrop of elder bushes, barking frantically at a man in a knitted tank top who is surrounded by a dozen dogs of various shapes and sizes.

'Hey, Cyril, come and meet …' Bill stops and turns to ask, without a hint of embarrassment, 'What did you say your name was again?'

'Neil.'

'Neil, Cyril.' Then he shouts to the approaching man as if in warning: 'This is Neil!'

Cyril's hesitation is obvious even from this distance, and Neil wonders if he is going to turn around and head back into the thickets.

'Neil's going to use your blue barrels,' explains Bill. 'He's going to swap them for that colourful plastic stuff over his raft.'

Neil was not aware that this was the agreement, and he looks across at his raft, but it takes no more than a glance for him to realise he has the better side of the deal. Cyril seems encouraged by this news and his hesitant step becomes more sure.

'Hello,' Neil says.

'That your dog?' Cyril asks. He has a soft face, kind, and a pair of thick, round glasses balances on his nose. He doesn't look Neil in the eye, and nor does he accept his outstretched hand. 'Shy,' Trevor had said, and Neil feels it is more than that.

'That's Bushy-Mush. These yours?' Neil is surrounded by the man's dogs, all sniffing at his trousers.

'That's Coco, Sabi, Zaza, Blackie Boo, Gorilla Head, Mr Perfect … and he's new, doesn't have a name yet.' Cyril pats each dog as he names them.

'So, Neil's going to London on this 'ere raft,' Bill explains. Cyril steps closer to inspect his swap.

'I reckon that stuff'll make a great cover for the rabbit runs,' Bill says.

'Aye, I reckon,' Cyril agrees. He traces the lettering with his finger and then pokes the image of Dopey on his big nose.

'The idea with this is to extend the raft and build a room. Same as we do with the animal hutches, but bigger. I thought we might get creative.' Bill has moved off with Cyril, the two of them in step, looking through their collection of wooden junk. Neil feels superfluous and he hangs back to let them talk.

'Here's what'd be fun – those chests of drawers over there, the backs have been in the bushes all winter and they've rotted, but the fronts are good. Look at the handles.'

They walk over to inspect them together. Neil stays just close enough to hear what is being said.

'Let's take the fronts of the drawers and piece them together to make a wall. Ha ha! That'll confuse people. They'll try to open 'em. Then, for the other side of the cabin, we can use these window frames, yes, and then at the end that door there. We can mek use of so much of this stuff all in one go!' He sounds triumphant. 'You just need a space to sleep, right, to keep dry?'

He turns to Neil to ask this, and Neil nods his head.

'Actually, Cyril, we could get rid of that old stove too,' Bill continues. 'Where did we put it? You'll need to keep warm, like.' He addresses this last comment to Neil.

The dogs have broken away and are running around chasing each other. Bushy-Mush is joining in, barking as furiously as he can. Cyril's dogs run back and forth, out through the gap in the elder bush towards the mill, but Bushy-Mush does not follow them that far. He is the only one barking, and as the pack circle back past Bill and Cyril again, Cyril crouches and picks up the little dog from among them. Bushy-Mush is initially shocked by this sudden intervention, but Cyril caresses him and appears to whisper in his ear, and he quietens down.

Cyril holds on to him for a while, whilst he and Bill choose pieces for the construction, and then with another word in the dog's ear he puts Bushy-Mush down and the dog runs away with the pack, no longer barking.

Bill appears to conclude his talk with Cyril, who starts to walk away. He talks to his dogs as he goes and wishes no one goodbye.

'What did he do to my dog to stop him barking?' Neil is curious. It is a trick he would like to learn.

'Who knows? Cyril's a law unto himself, him and his animals. He says why don't you go to London by train? It would be a lot quicker.'

The question catches Neil off guard, but he only hesitates for a moment.

'Er, yes, I realise that would be quicker, but the idea is to take a long time. It's a sort of quest-type thing.'

He can hear himself stumbling, dithering over his thoughts, and he makes a conscious effort to sound sure.

'The journey down on the raft, to deliver the piano, it's a sign of commitment to my girlfriend, the girl whose piano it is,' he explains. The idea seems so ridiculously fanciful when he describes it like this, to someone as down to earth as Bill.

'Women,' Bill remarks. He seems to think this word is funny. 'Altogether too complicated. Give your lass a call and be done with it.' Bill chortles as he pulls at the top of one of the posts in the brambles and rocks it back and forth to free it, then he lifts it out vertically.

Neil had almost forgotten his phone. He pats himself down, wondering where he put it and whether there is any life in the battery. Kimberly was always nagging him to keep it charged. Did he put it in the barrel with the opening? He goes to check and is delighted to find it.

Pressing the button does not light the blank screen, though. 'No battery,' he calls.

'Use mine.' The thought of Bill with a mobile phone seems odd, but Neil's surprise falls away as the old man points to his shed. He means a landline, but then, even that seems strange, here in this semi-wilderness.

I'll make a start, you make a call,' Bill says, and Neil walks towards the hut.

Chapter 9

Beyond the disassembled fountains, the door of the hut is ajar. Neil imagines the tiny cabin will be full of more junk: things forgotten, bric-a-brac stored. Maybe the ivy has even broken its way in and nature herself is beginning her repossession. In amongst the rot, Bill, no doubt, has a chair here, and maybe a small table too.

But as the door swings open, Neil's eyes open wide in shock at the bright metallic-orange walls that glint in the light of a strong lamp. Dotted over the surface are Polaroid photographs of happy, smiling people, each holding something that appears to be giving them joy. A young couple with a three-legged stool in front of the very hut he is standing in; a man with a carved cupboard door leaning against a moss-covered tree; a woman grinning broadly with her hand on the edge of what looks like an old wooden milk churn, which is surrounded by ivy in front of the broken fountains … And there are Joyce and Trevor with their table, on the quay in front of their boat, which floats on the spot that the raft now occupies. Cyril is in one of the photos, with an Indian woman in a purple top and mustard trousers, who is holding up a wooden spoon as if it is her most prized possession. Cyril is in the next photo, too, beside a woman in a grey cardigan who is laughing, mouth open, holding a huge rabbit. So many photographs of smiling people.

'Extraordinary,' Neil mouths as he examines one picture after another. So much happiness. One Polaroid catches his eye and he looks a little closer. Hasn't he seen that man on the television? Not looking like this, though – here he appears normal, in casual clothes instead of his customary sharp suit, and again looking so happy with the rustic wooden chair he is holding. Neil's eye is drawn from one face to another, to the flamboyance of the colours of the photographs, and to the metallic-orange paper stuck to the walls that is so at odds with the natural surroundings outside. He shuffles, looking from one delighted countenance to another until he knocks his hip against a vice on a workbench set along the back wall. The surface is covered with tools: smooth-handled rasps and worn hammers, small chisels with shiny sharpened ends, a brass hand drill lined up ready for use, and a selection of polished wooden planes, the likes of which he has only seen in television shows in which dubiously suited men ask meek and dowdy professionals to offer their valuations of old artefacts.

In amongst all this jumble sits the telephone, moulded plastic around a chrome rotary dial, all smooth lines and bright yellow, looking like it has just come off a nineteen-sixties film set. He doubts it works, and he picks up the receiver tentatively. The purring tone assures him that it does. Kimberly's mobile number comes to his mind effortlessly, and he watches the old-fashioned dial spin back after he has dialled in each digit. Wood shavings crunch underfoot as he paces nervously. What should he say? Will she still be angry with him? Maybe he should leave it a few more days ... If she isn't going to be pleased to hear from him, then what is the point of this journey he has started? And if, against the odds, she *is* pleased to hear from him, then he might as well take the train, be with her as soon as he can, so again there will be no point in the journey by raft.

The phone diverts to voicemail and Neil is quick to put down the receiver. It is probably best not to call her. Give her a little time. Her thoughts will be taken up with her move, no doubt, and she will not have had time to even think about him yet. Maybe he should try in a few days, in a week or so, when she has settled in and starts to miss him.

He grunts and takes a last look around the orange hut before stepping back outside into the green-leaf canopy, then he wanders down to where Bill is hammering away at something by the raft.

'What'd she say, then? Everything sorted now?' Bill stops hammering and begins to lash the barrels to a crosspiece he has fashioned.

'No answer.'

'Ah.' Bill nods. 'But you tried, so that's the main thing.'

'You've a lot of photos in your hut. Smiley people.' Neil holds steady the piece that Bill is lashing.

'Guinea – the people always smiled in Guinea. And the Gambia. That's all there is at the end of the day. Happy people, smiles. It's all you can do. It's like compound interest. It grows and grows.'

'Not sure I understand you?' Neil says as they move on to lash the last of the six plastic barrels.

'Avalanches. They're the same. Got caught in one in Austria once. Cold as the devil. But "happy people avalanches", they're the best.'

Neil doesn't know how to reply to this, and Bill goes quiet, grunting with the exertion. Neil has begun to think he has forgotten what he was saying when suddenly he continues.

'Make one person happy, they go away and make someone else happy. Maybe two more people, and so on, like compound interest. Compound happiness, you might say – an avalanche, making everyone it touches along the way happy. Shall we bring the raft up here so we can tie the two together?'

'It's a bit heavy with the piano on top … So you've taken a photograph of everyone you've made happy?'

'We can slide it off on these.' Bill offers two planks up to straddle the watery gap from raft to shore. 'It's easy to think you've done nowt with your life.'

Neil is about to object, to point out all the places Bill has said he has been to, but the old man has started to pull the piano off the raft and he hurries to help.

'Make someone happy and you've changed the world. So I keep a reminder. Like banknotes, they are. Printed money. Happiness banknotes. I aim to be the richest man in the world.'

The piano is safely ashore now, and the raft is quick to follow, and Bill gets to work.

Neil tries to find ways to be useful but the old man seems to like to work alone. He says little and asks nothing. After half an hour, Bill leaves the raft to go over to the line of rotting bureaus, where he begins to lever the fronts away from the drawers. Neil sees his chance to help and does the same. With a tap from his hammer, Bill indicates which chest of drawers Neil should disassemble next.

The work is strangely satisfying, and the pile of drawer fronts grows; the runners are in another pile, and the backs and sides, already warped and tempered with time and moisture, are stacked on their ends. Neil becomes so engrossed that when he straightens his back and wipes his brow he is surprised to see that Cyril has joined them and that he and Bill are working away in quiet harmony. The cabin is taking shape with unexpected speed.

Once the drawers are all done, Neil carries them by the handles to the raft, where Bill is busy setting in a frame for a door. The tarp is neatly folded and the thick plastic of the bouncy castle is nowhere to be seen. As Neil approaches, Cyril sets off wandering around the perimeter of the yard, looking for something. Neil's stomach grumbles. It must be mid-afternoon, and he's eaten nothing since his breakfast on the narrowboat.

Bill leaves the door frame and starts putting the drawers together. He arranges them face down on the floor and attaches the runners across their backs to hold them together. Neil catches on quickly and takes over this task, and Bill returns, without a word, to the door frame. They continue building in this way until Bill slams the door shut to prove it works and comes over to inspect Neil's handiwork.

'Aye, that'll do,' he says. 'Let's get summat to eat.' And with this, he drops his hammer and wanders over to the hut. Neil follows.

'He found it, then.' Bill pats a pot-bellied stove that has appeared by the door of the hut. Cyril is nowhere to be seen, but there is an amazing aroma leaking from the hut. Inside, the table has been cleared of tools and a line of small covered metal dishes have been arranged down the middle, and a smell of spices fills the air.

Bill takes a metal waste bin from the corner and turns it upside down. 'That'll do you,' he says as he takes the chair for himself and picks up a fork and one of the dishes.

'You can get a takeaway delivered here?' Neil says as he takes the top off the nearest curry dish, but then he wonders if Cyril might be the cook.

'Not likely,' Bill snorts. 'A friend of Cyril's does this. Does it every day for all them that works at the animal sanctuary.' Bill fills his mouth and talking is over. After a few minutes he taps on one of the pictures with the handle of his fork. Neil waits for him to say something about the people in it, but he just goes on eating until a few more minutes have passed, and then he taps another and nods his head. A conversation is being had, apparently, but not out loud: it is inside Bill's head. Neil wonders if he should feel sorry for the old man, but he has created a comfortable corner of the world for himself and seems happy enough.

With his hunger satisfied, Neil has energy to spare, and the remainder of the afternoon proves very productive. As the light begins to fade, Bill drags the mattress back on board and Bushy-Mush turns up. Neil can tell by his waddle that he has been fed to the point of bursting. Neil fusses over the dog, and when he stops he finds Bill has gone.

The place is eerie now that he is alone but he is not yet quite ready to sleep. He paces the quay and looks up at the sky, where an abundance of stars and the bright moon are clearly visible.

'Kim, are you looking up at the stars too?' he asks the night, and he closes his mouth tightly, in case emotion escapes by that exit.

'Oh Kim, my lo-o-o-o-ve, how I miss you after these forty-eight hours we've been apart …' The sarcastic voice that is the source of these words comes from behind him, and he turns sharply. With a rustling and snapping of twigs, a tall figure emerges from the bushes.

'How the hell did you find me?' Neil asks, all loneliness gone in a moment.

'I saw the enigmatic Trevor and the demure Joyce at the next lock. They're a right pair! I asked if they had seen you and they informed me that you were having some "general repairs and improvements" done here. Cripes! What have you done to it?'

Sleet stands and stares at the raft. 'And where's Snow White gone?'

'No idea. I think all this was a swap, and I quite liked Trevor and Joyce.' Neil is not sure now if he is pleased to see Sleet or not.

'Here, got you some beers.' Sleet hands over a six-pack as he steps across onto the raft and into the new cabin. Of the four walls that have been erected, one side is made of the drawer fronts and the one opposite of reclaimed windows; at the rear is a door, and at the front of the craft a louvre window sits on its end, looking out to where the piano rests, firmly strapped under the tarpaulin. With so much glass, there will be loads of light in the cabin in the day, and no privacy. It's a bit like a floating goldfish bowl, but Neil loves it. He takes hold of the pack of beers, rips one free, opens it against a metal post and decides he is very glad to see Sleet after all.

'Good in there, isn't it?' Sleet says, poking his head out. I mean, it's a bit too dark to see properly at the moment, but I can actually imagine this thing making it to London. Whereas the raft, well ….' He takes a beer. 'You kicking off again tomorrow?'

'I suppose.'

'I probably won't see you again for a while then. This was far enough to drive after work. Anyway, I've got something for you.' He reaches into his pocket and takes out a postcard.

'Went past your old flat. The front door was open, new people moving in. I felt a bit nosy so I was just wandering about as they moved stuff in, you know, to see who they were … Not that it matters, it's just – well, we had some good times there.'

'You should move out of your parents', you know. Do you good.'

'Yeah, well, I saw this and I thought it would do you more good than it would that woman upstairs. Besides, it gave me a bit of a kick to steal it.' Sleet hands the postcard over and Neil angles it so that the moon shines on the picture of Big Ben. His stomach tightens. It's from London, and the only person he knows there is Kim. He turns it over; sure enough, the handwriting on the back is Kim's. Why on earth would she be writing to the woman upstairs? They hardly ever spoke. His mouth becomes dry and he swallows hard.

'I reckon she sent it to you but didn't, if you know what I mean? She knew you would see it. I mean, it's always you who sorts through the mail.'

'Maybe,' Neil says, and he reads the message.

Hi, Jenny.

I hope you are OK. Sorry not to see you the day I left but things were rather hectic. The new place in London's amazing, with huge windows that let in this fantastic light. It's a perfect spot for my piano and opposite there is a park to walk Bushy-Mush. Please tell Neil to take care of them both. I will come to pick both up soon, as soon as I feel settled. (Please remind him to feed Bushy-Mush proper dog food, not just pizza.) I hope he is not turning the sound up on the TV too loud. Anyway, very busy with work, which is just as amazing as I anticipated. Got to dash, very busy. Kimberly.

He stops reading; his chest feels tight. Maybe it is indigestion from the curry, or maybe it's the beer.

'Does nothing but talk about you, eh?' Sleet comments and makes himself as comfortable as he can on an empty paint tin. He has finished his first beer already and has started another. Neil follows suit.

They sit in silence as they drink. Sleet looks down the canal, Neil up at the stars and the full moon. Kim always liked the moonlight. Is the postcard a sign that she is missing him and just wants to feel that she is making contact? He allows himself to nurture a little hope and again envisages her waiting for him in London.

The mattress, piano, chair, paint stool and bits of clothing that were on the raft are now on the quay next to Neil. He takes up his sketchbook and the pencil case Kimberly made and starts to draw, outlining the raft in the moonlight, making it look as romantic as possible in the hope that one day soon he will show her the sketch.

'You know what?' Sleet breaks the silence. 'I envy you.'

Sleet never reflects, or talks sentimental twaddle; nor is Neil sure exactly what he is referring to. Is he talking about Kim, the raft, him sketching or something else?

'I would love to have such an adventure before me,' Sleet adds after a long pause, and he drains his second beer, takes a third, stands abruptly and puts out his free hand.

'Good luck, mate, with everything.' And with a handshake and these parting words, he abruptly strides away, leaving Neil – sketchbook in one hand, pencil between his teeth, his extended hand left hanging – speechless. The night is young, Neil thinks, and there are more beers – Sleet leaving so soon just isn't like him.

Neil takes the pencil from his mouth so he can call after him but then closes it again. He nods, he gets it. This is the point where their lives go in different directions: Sleet back to the same old life and him off into the unknown. Best to make a clean break, avoid all the mushy stuff.

He takes a swig of beer to stop his chin wobbling and sits back down and continues to sketch.

Tomorrow he'll be in unfamiliar countryside, and by saying goodbye Sleet has cut for him the umbilical cord connecting him to all he has ever known. He stares at the gap in the undergrowth that Sleet disappeared through until long after he is gone.

Chapter 10

'Morning!' a muffled voice calls and Neil sits up, looks around in a daze.

'Now where am I?' he mutters, yawning. The roof of the space in which he finds himself is of rough planking, one wall all windows, mismatched, cobbled together, and through them he can see the canal sparkling and ducks floating, pecking at weeds.

'Oh yes!' The memory of yesterday comes flooding back, and he rolls over onto his knees and makes the effort to stand. Bushy-Mush complains then stretches, shoulders down, haunches and squirrel tail up, his sour breath too close.

Whoever called out is now clattering about, grinding metal on stone, shattering the morning's peace. With a rub of his eyes, Neil opens his new door to find Bill is on the quay, the pot-bellied stove in his grip, walking it from one cast-iron foot to another, inching his way towards the raft. The hotplate rubs against Bill's rough wool suit. He has on a very dark grey one today, three-piece, watch chain dangling, black flat cap pulled down, collarless shirt an off-white.

'Were you cold last night?' he asks.

Neil shivers with the memory. He finished Sleet's beers last night and passed out where he sat, waking hours later, shivering, with Bushy-Mush curled up on his lap. He wonders if he has lost the ability to sleep without a couple of drinks inside him, something that was never a problem when he was with Kimberly. The thought of Kim brings the now-familiar instant heaviness, and a gaping, empty sensation, as if someone has torn out his stomach, and he can see his bleak future stretching out in front of him. He focuses; Bill is waiting for an answer.

'A bit,' he manages.

Bill grunts his understanding. 'We'll get this set in and then you can be on yer way, eh?' Bushy-Mush pushes past Neil's legs and runs through the opening in the hedge towards the mill beyond. Presently, there is a distant sound of barking.

'Coffee up in the shed if you want it, and a bit to eat.' Bill is arranging the flue pipes that will draw the smoke from the stove up through the roof of the new cabin.

The undergrowth either side of the path to the hut is wet with dew and licks at Neil's ankles. Coffee will help – that's another thing he relies on. Alcohol to help him sleep, caffeine to wake up. With all this nature around him, living in such a way seems wrong, all of a sudden. But until this moment he has never given it a thought. It's just how life is – the pub serves coffee in the morning, beer at night. His parents live like that, and Sleet lives like that; it's normal. But it's not! It's far from normal, and what he is doing is far from normal too. Maybe he can change some of the rules?

He pushes open the door to the orange shrine of happiness. The interior glows, a tempting pot of coffee sits next to a tin mug, and someone has made a huge stack of pancakes, has filled them with all sorts of fillings and folded them into quarters. He's so hungry that he polishes off the lot before he has realised it.

When the coffee pot is drained he returns to the raft, rather slowly thanks to the weight in his belly. Bill is inside, sealing around a hole in the roof through which the chimney now protrudes.

'That should do it,' he says. 'I reckon you're set' – and as if on cue Bushy-Mush appears and jumps aboard. 'You'll find more wood than you need in the hedgerows for burning as you go. Ah, here's Cyril.'

Cyril carries a sack on his back, and he swings it over his shoulder and puts it by Neil's feet before holding up a Polaroid camera.

'Now, this sack should do you,' he says, without making eye contact. 'Newspapers for starting a fire, a bit of food, a couple of blankets. That sort of thing.'

'I don't know how to thank you,' Neil begins, and he feels at a bit of a loss, but then he recalls the sketch he did the night before, and after a leap and a rummage he returns, opens his sketchbook and tears out the picture he drew of the yard. It shows the ivy everywhere, the half-buried eclectic assortment of wooden furniture, the hut at the back, haloed in dark undergrowth so that it stands out. It's quite good, even if he says so himself. He hands it over without hesitation.

'I can't pay you, but I'd like to give you this,' he says.

'Well, that's right grand,' says Bill. 'Hey Cyril, look at this.' Cyril stands by his side and they examine the drawing together. 'Eh, you've caught it just right, got the atmosphere and everything. If you can paint as well as you can draw I'll be pressing you to take that apprenticeship when I gets older.'

Bill's face wrinkles into a rare smile, his eyes mere slits as his cheeks are pushed so far up by his grin. Cyril is grinning too, and his eyes are moist, if Neil is not mistaken. Knowing he has created that smile fills Neil with such a surge of energy, of life.

'I'd like one other thing, though,' Bill says. 'Just give us a good smile,' and he throws an arm around Neil's shoulders. Neil cannot help but feel lucky to have met him, and he grins as Cyril says 'cheese' and they are momentarily blinded by one flash and then another.

'Well, on your way, then,' Bill says, and Neil feels it is all a bit rushed, but he reasons that the two men must have other things to do.

He puts one foot on the raft. 'Here you go,' Bill says, and Cyril passes over the sack and one of the Polaroid pictures, which is still cloudy, not fully developed. Then, without another word, Cyril casts off the rope and Bill pushes the raft out into the current.

Adrenaline sears through Neil's veins, enlivening his legs, twitching his hands. Until now it has felt like a game, with Phee and Sleet, with Trevor and Joyce, even with Bill and Cyril. But now that he has a covered raft and a place to sleep and the piano is securely lashed down, there is no doubting that he has committed to this journey.

'Don't look so terrified,' Bill calls after him. 'Take some risks.'

Soon the raft drifts out to join the main canal. 'New things are not necessarily bad things, just unknown,' Bill calls. 'If I was any younger I would come with you.'

Neil waves, watching the two men turn from the quay and walk towards the hut.

'Pancakes for breakfast, and coffee,' he hears Bill tell Cyril, and Neil feels the blood drain from his face. It did seem a huge stack of food but he didn't stop to consider that it might be to share! Should he call out an apology, or even paddle back and apologise in person? Neil hesitates, but the raft is caught in the current that is quickly pulling him towards the main canal, and the leaves and willow branches are closing behind him and the reclamation yard is already out of sight.

'I feel awful,' he tells Bushy-Mush, who is sniffing at the bag Bill gave him, and his cheeks grow even hotter. The Polaroid has developed now and in it his face is beaming, with a look of real love towards Bill. Bill, on the other hand, stands passively, almost blank. What did he call these pictures – happiness banknotes?

'Oh crap!' Neil declares. Why does he always see these things after they happen?

A couple of hard thrusts with his improvised paddle bring the raft to the towpath, and he leaps ashore and loops the mooring rope around his shoulder, pulling the raft behind him. The exertion feels good, takes his mind off his thoughtlessness.

After a while, his shoulder feels sore where the rope has rubbed. He shifts it to the other shoulder but this pulls the raft off course. Maybe if he adjusted the rudder it would help. He sets the rudder at an angle that will steer the raft out towards the middle of the canal and then tries again, but it's difficult to get the setting just right, and the tendency is for the raft either to want to steer right away from the bank, or to come slowly back towards it, eventually colliding with the mud and sticking fast.

His solution is to tie two ropes to the rudder, feeding one past the cabin one way and one the other way. Then he forms a loop with the main mooring rope and slips this over his head, positioning it around his chest. Now he can pull and have a steering rope in each hand. It is crude and he feels weighed down with ropes but, for now, it works.

After an hour or so, his thigh muscles have developed a dull ache. The raft is not light. Sometimes the current is swift, but it is not consistent and an hour or two later it might be barely moving. The sun glitters on the surface, reflecting back distorted trees and blue skies between rain-laced clouds.

'Someone, somewhere, is opening and closing locks to pass and they have no idea that their actions are affecting you and me here, Bushy-Mush,' Neil says, watching a dragonfly that seems to be attracted to his shirt. 'If they open a gate above us, the water has to go somewhere, even if we are miles away.' He has always liked the look of the locks, with their massive gates that regulate the flow into or out of the chambers – a brilliant solution to the problem of moving boats up and down gradients.

Bushy-Mush, exhausted from spending the morning running up and down the towpath, is curled up asleep. His annoying, incessant barking has been almost entirely absent today.

'What did Cyril say to you?' Neil asks his little friend, but Bushy-Mush doesn't even open an eye.

There was something about Cyril that Neil liked. 'When we've finished this quest we'll go back and see them,' he tells his canine companion. 'Find out more about Cyril and his mill.'

Walking backward, instead of forward, with the rope across his back, uses a different set of muscles. It's a bit slower than walking forward but he is still making progress. He has time to notice the flying insects in the hedgerows, the indentations his heels make in the hardening mud, the ripples the raft leaves behind and the ever-changing sky, high up, winds forever forming and reforming the patterns in the clouds.

'Just steady progress, don't think of the distance,' he tells himself as one leg begins to quiver with the strain. Far behind him on the canal, a black dot appears: a canal boat. As it approaches, it looks wide, not like one of the touristy narrowboats.

'I'll keep pulling until it draws level with that oak tree back there,' Neil challenges himself, and he digs in with his heels. 'I can't believe I ate all the pancakes ...' Dig, pull, dig, pull. 'What was I thinking?' Dig, pull. 'Or, more to the point, why was I not thinking?' Pull, dig, adjust rope.

The raft has its own momentum and the current has become swifter, matching his walking pace. There is little resistance now. 'Okay, so it looks like it will be easy to keep going until that black dot reaches the oak tree, so when it gets to where the cows are lying down in that field …' Step, pull, slack rope, step, step.

'A banknote for happiness.' Neil has wedged the Polaroid picture in the handle of one of the drawers that makes up the wall of the cabin so that he can see it from the towpath. This side of the raft looks awesome. A stack of drawers and not one opens! Wooden knobs, brass drop handles, T-handles, cup handles: the array brings a smile to his face. 'All for the fun of doing it!' His eyes are drawn to the Polaroid photo again. 'Bill's bank of happiness.'

Bushy-Mush wakes and after a brief stretch he jumps across to the bank and trots beside Neil.

'You were happy there, too, weren't you? Cyril making animals happy, Bill making people happy.' He sighs. 'I only make you happy, Bushy-Mush.' He intends his comment to be a joke, to amuse himself, but it rings a little too true.

He watches the black dot of the canal boat grow bigger and then pass the cows lying down in the field.

'To the gap in the fence, then,' he says to himself; he wants to push himself even though it is hurting. His back is chafed, his legs are aching, but it feels only right that he should be sore. 'I suppose I gave Bill a drawing.'

The black spot is close enough now that Neil can identify it as an old iron coal barge. There was a photograph of one of these vessels on the pub wall for years. Underneath, a little window in the mount said that it was a coal barge, built in 1890 by the Yorkshire Ironworks Company. It had massive holds piled high with tons and tons of coal.

The shape of the barge is very attractive, low and fat; normally, such a sight would absorb him, but he has slipped into a strange mood that is tinged with disappointment at himself, and it feels all too familiar. It reminds him of his fights with Kim, when he knew she was right but kept going anyway, just so he would not feel so wrong, so he would not feel criticised.

Adjusting the rope, he concedes that he cannot pull the raft much longer without a rest. He lets the rope go slack and takes a step every few seconds to keep up with the raft's momentum.

The wide, black canal boat is upon him. The engine revs change; the motor idles and its pace slows. The man at the back has a black leather cowboy hat on and a worn leather jacket. By the time they are within speaking distance, the huge boat has very little momentum left.

'Hey,' the captain says, grinning and revealing very white teeth. Under his hat, his hair is dark brown and he has remarkably green eyes.

'Hey,' Neil replies.

'Going nowhere fast like that. Want a tow?'

'Sure.'

'I'll tow, you make the coffee. I can take you as far as Wigan. How far are you going?' His skin is very tanned, and he looks as if he spends all day every day outside. Neil throws him a line and the man ties it to a robust black cleat. Offering Neil his forearm, he grasps Neil's elbow and pulls him aboard.

'Wigan'll do fine, going to London,' Neil says, and Bushy-Mush, alone on the raft, starts to whine.

'Get the dog, then,' the man says briskly, and Neil hauls on the towline to close the gap so that Bushy-Mush can jump aboard the barge. 'Is that a piano under that tarp? You play?' The man nods towards the odd shape.

He can't be much older than Neil himself, perhaps mid to late twenties, and yet there is something aged about him, a wisdom, evidence of a hard life, something that Neil cannot put his finger on; he finds himself recoiling but at the same time intrigued.

'No, I don't play,' he says, and once again he wonders how to explain the situation, what role to cast himself in. 'It belongs to a girl, a friend. Drifting down to her on the canals seemed like a good way to deliver it.'

'Ah, you'll love it,' the captain of the barge says. 'I've been on the water four years, wouldn't change a thing.' He tells Neil his name is Pat. 'No girl's waiting anywhere for me, though. I'm married to my boat now,' Pat adds. 'And a more faithful and fulfilling partnership I have never had.'

His voice is light, but Neil sees something dark pass over Pat's face.

'So,' Pat continues. 'Coffee. You'll find the stove to the left and the mugs hanging by the window.'

The whistling of a kettle can be heard from the interior so Neil takes his cue and trips down the five steps into a room bigger than the whole of his and Kimberly's tiny flat. The cavernous space that used to hold the coal is now a very comfortable sitting room, with windows above him in what used to be the openings to the hold, where the cargo was poured in and scooped out. There's so much light that it feels like being outside even whilst he is enjoying the warmth of inside. It is magnificent. Neil looks around for traces of who this man is, like the photos Trevor and Joyce had on their walls, but, although the space is comfortable and homely, there is nothing that feels really personal. What really interests him, though, is how a man who is more or less the same age as himself can own such an amazing boat! Maybe he inherited it.

Neil looks back up the steps, where he can see Pat's legs.

'And he in turn is probably wondering why a person his age has nothing but a raft and a piano to his name!' Neil says to himself, and snorts, before concentrating on making coffee.

Maybe if he had done something other than the book factory since he left college he might have made something of himself ... It isn't just that opportunities don't exist for young artists in Greater Lotherton, though; what really pushed him into inaction was what happened in London at the end of the third year at college.

Before then, he never needed prompting to pick up a paintbrush – he made art for art's sake. But after the disaster at the exhibition, it all changed. He continued to sketch of course, at every opportunity, but just couldn't raise the enthusiasm to develop these ideas through to a finished piece.

They'd all been working on their entries to the exhibition for months – everyone at college – although none of them really believed they'd be selected. Only twenty artists were included each year and they were chosen from entrants from all over the country. So the odds were pretty slim, and when it was revealed that someone from their little college had won a place in the exhibition, the news buzzed around the campus in no time.

Neil didn't expect for a second that it would be his name that was called out, but he went with Sleet to hear the announcement anyway, just out of curiosity.

'You jammy git!' Sleet exclaimed when Neil was called up, and soon after that everything began to change.

Even before the exhibition – before he'd even been down to London to see the space – his whole frame of reference had begun to change. Art was no longer just a calling, a passion, something he couldn't help involving himself in. Now it was also a career, a vocation, a responsibility.

Important critics would be at the opening night, and he represented the college now. There were rumours that someone from Saatchi & Saatchi would be there.

His win altered how he viewed his work, too. He began to see real value in even the smallest sketches that he did – often, they were the most free – and he suggested to his tutors that he exhibited those instead of his big pieces. They advised against it. His sizeable pieces were more impressive, they said. If only he had stuck with his gut instinct, how different things might have turned out.

His space was ready for him when he arrived at the London gallery to hang his work, with his name in foot-tall letters – Neil Campbell-Blair. The fascia board looked like it was screwed in well to the wall, and no one told him there was a weight limit; nor was it he who had erected the display screens in front. His pieces were heavy, three-dimensional sculptures, and as they finished hanging the last one disaster struck. Neil had the impression of watching in slow motion as they let go of the final sculpture and the weight of it ripped the screws out of the wall. The weighty work twisted as it fell, the fascia board still attached, and as he watched he could see what was going to happen, as if time had slowed down even further, but he could do nothing. Corner first, his large work, and then the fascia board, crashed into his pile of canvases, slicing through a large portion of the past three years' worth of work that was lying on the floor, waiting to be hung.

It was as if someone was digging his insides out with a spoon. The other artists seemed to expect him to shout or cry or something, some of them stepping towards him to offer comfort, others shying away, trying to avoid any scene that might be made. But his only outward reaction was to shrug his shoulders.

The domino effect ensured that every last one of his pieces was damaged. Yet all he could think was that this was destiny and that perhaps he wasn't meant to succeed. Wasn't that what Dad always said, anyway? That it wasn't real life, that art was just for kids, and a game, and that he should get a proper job like Sleet, who by then was already working for his own dad?

Besides, Neil reflects, as he finishes making the coffee, people like him, who come from a backwater like Greater Lotherton, do not become artists and make a living at it. The best he can achieve, if he is lucky, will be to paint watercolours and print them as local postcards – maybe do a calendar once in a while. That is the reality, and deep down he knows that his dad may be right, and that that – yes, that – is why he has not found the energy to do anything he is really satisfied with for the last two years, nothing he feels has any real value.

Broken dreams. Who would have thought they could be so crippling?

But if he can't be an artist, what will he do with his life? How is one supposed to know what one wants? Some people just seem lucky and have interests that lie in a realistic line of work, but for everyone else, for him, how to decide? It's not that there isn't any choice. No, that's the problem – there's a whole world of choices out there, and he feels caught like a rabbit in the headlights, frozen by choice and scared to try again. Which, of course, is ridiculous.

'That coffee anywhere near ready?' Pat calls down.

Neil rubs a hand over his face, wipes away his tears on his sleeve and, with a big sniff, takes the coffee up and sits at the stern.

The great barge slides effortlessly through the water.

'Have you been living on this beauty long?' Neil asks.

'Four years now.'

'How did you come by her?' Neil pats the wooden handrail that sweeps around the stern.

'Found her sunk in the mud. She'd been for sale but no one wanted her. I said I'd take her on, gave the man a pound.' Pat smiles.

'A pound. You got lucky!' Neil looks over the boat again.

'No, I saw an opportunity. Once she had sunk he wasn't going to sell her. Stuck in the mud like that, he had a problem, and he was lucky I didn't ask him to pay me the pound.' Pat chortles and takes a long sip of coffee.

'But to get her from something sunk in mud to this stage must have been an expensive business?' Neil knows he is fishing, but he is curious.

Pat settles on his seat. 'You know what I liked to do as a kid?' He doesn't wait for a response. 'I liked to play the lute.'

This makes Neil smile.

'Sounds funny, doesn't it?' He grins. 'The kids at school thought so too. They were all learning the guitar, and one day the guitar teacher brought his lute. He was a good player, too, and the sound it made, amazing.' Pat takes on a faraway sort of look. 'Anyway, the guitar teacher was happy to teach me separately and, I think, up to a point he took the place of my dad. I never had one, you see. Mother never told my father about me and he went on his way.'

'Oh.' Neil is not sure what else to say to this.

'Anyway, father figure or not, he taught me the lute and I became quite good.'

'Ah, so you played the lute to make money to fix this boat?' Neil jumps in.

'No!' Pat laughs. 'I'm not that good. I learnt to play the lute, you see, but I also learnt something much more important. I played from the age of eight until I left school at eighteen. By that time I was good enough to be offered a place at music college, but I couldn't take it. I had something else I needed to do first. But that's another story.'

He pauses to blow across the top of his cup. 'But the point is, what it taught me was how much you can achieve with just a little bit of effort each day. And a little bit the next day, but consistently, you know. That's how I fixed this boat. Took me two years, a little bit each day, but I knew, from learning the lute, that if I kept going I would get there and the result would be amazing.'

'It is amazing,' Neil agrees. Pat adjusts the rudder slightly and falls silent. The water glides past, the engine grumbling quietly.

They pass fields and farms, and clouds blow over the sun and away again leaving the sky a beautiful blue.

In the distance, an obstruction lies across the canal, and as they draw nearer Neil smiles and his legs begins to jiggle. It is a lock! The first on his journey. Pat cuts the throttle and steers to the side, then he puts the engine in reverse and they come to a standstill.

He jumps off on nimble legs and ties up before Neil has even put his coffee cup down.

'Always best to take in the fenders,' he volunteers, pulling them up from the towpath side and throwing them on board. Neil, leaving his coffee cup where he was sitting, pulls the fenders up on the other side. By the time he has finished, Pat is cranking a handle in the lock's old mechanism.

Pat explains why they took the fenders in. 'The canal walls warp over time, there's many a tight lock. Mind you, that's not the only problem. Having not been on the water long yourself, you wouldn't believe how often boats capsize in the locks.'

Neil thinks he is making a joke and laughs. Bushy-Mush gives a bark, jumps ashore and runs off into the bushes.

'I'm serious,' Pat says. 'Look here.'

He points behind the lock gate and Neil jumps off the boat to see what Pat is indicating.

'See that? That's the sill, and the gates close up to it to create a seal. But when the lock fills, like it will do when I turn this handle some more, it gets covered over. Then you draw your boat in, and if you're not careful you might leave the tail end over the sill, and when you empty the water out, your back end gets caught, grounded on it. The nose of the boat begins to be lowered and by the time you try to right it, close the lock off, fill it again from the top, the whole boat has tipped. If you've got bow doors and they're open, you'll take on water and you'll be surprised how quickly these things can sink. Thirty seconds, I'd give it. If you're inside, the water pressure could keep the doors from opening until the whole thing is full of water and anyone inside is a goner. So, yes, keep your eye on the sill. You'd be amazed how many people do sink their boats over the summer months.'

Pat begins to turn a handle again. 'Oh, and make sure you're moored up well before you let the water in the lock. You see how she's being pulled?'

Neil looks at Pat's boat, and at the lines, which are now taut. The raft is pulling against the tow rope too. Water rushes into the lock until the level inside is the same as the higher level of the canal, and Pat's iron barge is brought into the chamber.

Pat shows Neil how to lean his weight against the massive beam that opens the gate, his backside and hands against the smooth wood, his feet pushing back against the iron treads sunk into the ground. The water resists the huge wooden gate, which swings open slowly.

The barge and the raft will not both fit into the chamber at the same time.

'We'll have to do it in two shifts,' Pat says. 'That's going to lose me time.' He frowns, and looks at his watch. 'I was going to get a sleep in before Wigan. What do you reckon – after these locks can you take the tiller for a couple of hours while I sleep?'

'Sure,' Neil says without any real thought, and then he wonders – if it is so easy to sink a boat going through a lock, what other dangers lurk? But he keeps his concerns to himself. After all, a tow from Pat's barge will save many hours of backbreaking labour and will help him make good progress.

The canal boat goes through, and they repeat the process for the raft, filling the lock with water, letting the raft into the chamber, and then emptying the water, so that the raft descends with it, like going down in a lift.

Once both vessels are through, Neil jumps on board, ready to take the helm.

'Er, we need to leave the lock as we found it, mate,' Pat tells him. 'The gates need closing.'

Neil jumps off again. Bushy-Mush appears, loitering around his ankles.

Neil decides he likes Pat. He likes how laid-back he is – easy-going. He also makes Neil feel like his equal, which of course he is not. He has been on the dole for the last two years and during that time, he has to admit, Kim was doing more than her share around the house. When did he ever cook dinner, make the bed, take the clothes to the launderette? Whereas Pat has been living independently on his boat for years ...

Neil frowns. Something doesn't fit about Pat's story. If he had to do something before he went to music college, why has he been floating about on this boat for the past few years? Why did he spend his time doing it up in the first place? Why not just do whatever it was he had to do and then get on with his life? Maybe they have more in common than he thinks ...

'So what was it you needed to do before going to music college, or has everything changed now, with your life on the canal?' Neil tries to sound casual.

'My life on the canal is what I have to do. Or rather, it is the only way I can think of to do what I need to do,' Pat says.

This riddle sounds like an excuse.

'You need space?' Neil tries to sound like he understands.

'No, I need to find my dad,' Pat says.

Neil stammers and coughs, not sure how to reply to this. 'You need his permission or something to go to music college?' he asks, aware it is a stupid question.

'Not quite. But music is art, right? It's all about exploration and expression and questioning yourself – and, having never met my dad, I felt I needed to find him.' Pat yawns.

'Ah, I get you, but how does the canal fit in with that?' Neil doesn't really understand but he wants to smooth the conversation, keep it going, learn more.

'My mum knows two things about my dad. She knows that he likes motorbikes and that he loves the canal, and he lives near it, somewhere. He's from round here, so it seemed like the best chance to find him.'

He yawns again. 'I'm going to take that sleep now. You all right with that?' But before Neil can answer, he has passed over control of the tiller and skipped down the steps into the cabin.

Chapter 11

It's not long before Neil can hear gentle snoring from below.

He looks straight ahead, legs rigid, white knuckles wrapped around the tiller. He raises his eyebrows to keep his eyes open wide to take everything in, checking the distance to the banks, on the lookout for what's in front, what's behind, the weight of the responsibility like an iron rod down his spine. But there is only flat, calm water and the smooth sides of the canal bank, and soon he settles back, master of the big black barge. Hanging on a nail by the cabin doors is Pat's worn and misshapen black leather cowboy hat. It suits the macho look of the broad-beamed former coal boat, and he puts it on and lets one hip sink, crosses one leg in front of the other and puts a hand in his front jeans pocket.

'I'm a pirate now,' Neil tells Bushy-Mush, who is leaning over the edge, watching the coots that are bobbing in their wake. The sound they make is that of a child's hand horn: parp parp from the bigger ones, peep peep from the chicks. Neil likes their company.

After the first half hour or so, it turns out that steering the huge vessel is actually quite a boring occupation. There is nothing to it: watch and steer, no corners, no curves, just a light touch to keep the vessel on course. It leaves time to muse, and recent events revisit him unbidden. He ponders Bill and his Polaroids of happiness. He cannot help but chuckle at the thought of all those smiling faces, and then a new and yet more obvious idea comes to him and he is surprised at himself for not thinking of it at some point in the last two years.

'You know what, Bushy-Mush,' he exclaims, 'I get what Bill is doing now.'

The dog looks up at him blankly, tongue lolling out.

'It's simple! Happiness is a by-product, not a product. You cannot control what and who is around you to make yourself happy, but you can do stuff that makes other people happy. You have all the control over that, and the by-product of making other people happy is the satisfaction of doing it. Seeing them smile, it makes you happy.'

Bushy-Mush has lost interest so Neil says to himself, 'The long and the short of it is, if I had concentrated more on making Kim happy, I would have been happy. Or happier, at any rate …'

Something plops into the water behind the barge, but by the time Neil has turned to see what it was it has disappeared into the depths, leaving just a series of expanding circular ripples on the surface. Perhaps it was a fish. The motion of the surface is hypnotising. There is so much nature to watch, it could occupy him for hours. He will sketch some of it from memory when he gets the chance.

A gentle rain starts to fall – not the drenching kind, just a light shower. Each drop creates a ring in the still water beside the boat. The rings spread out further and further, softer and softer, until they are gone. They are a delight to watch, especially as the sun is still out and its rays catch one side of each ring, lighting it up brightly in contrast to the darker side. How do the rings go through one another so effortlessly where they meet, without distorting? There is so much he does not know. The patterns they make, the variations as they cross over and cross over again: if that could be captured, what a fine piece of art that would make.

Bushy-Mush has left the coots and is now sitting on the roof at the front, keeping a lookout. He barks once and turns to look at Neil. Up ahead, something is blocking the canal: another lock.

Neil glances below at Pat, sprawled on the sofa, mouth hanging open. His sunken eyes have taken on a bluish tinge, and he is deeply asleep. Maybe Neil can manage the lock on his own; it might even make Pat happy. It is, of course, possible that Pat was giving him a tutorial at the last lock in the hope that he would not need to be woken, isn't it? Settling the cowboy hat more firmly on his head, Neil decides that he can do this.

The ropes are secured, and Neil has checked carefully to see how far the sill inside the lock extends underwater. The raft will wait its turn outside the lock, as before. This time it is not a single lock, but a set of three, stepping down in stages. He will have to take the big boat through all three and come back for the raft; there is no other way. With the handle Pat used at the last lock, Neil opens the sluice gates and water streams into the lock basin, and he watches the level slowly rise. Both vessels tug at their lines, drawn towards the lock by the flow of water.

Once the first lock is finally open, Neil very carefully moves Pat's boat slowly into the chamber, making sure he is well clear of the sill. He closes the gate and empties the chamber, all the time wondering if the sound of the rushing water will wake Pat. Better to get the boat through the locks without mishap so that it is a fait accompli when Pat emerges.

He checks carefully for anything he is not aware of, anything he has missed. What if there is something he needs to check on but doesn't know about? Maybe it is a stupid thing to do; the boat is not his, he is taking a risk. This barge is a hundred years old! What if he damages it, or the lock itself?

'Oh cripes,' he says, deciding that the best thing to do is to backtrack. But the boat is in the lock now, and what if the reverse revving of the engine to get it back out is enough to wake Pat – then what would be said?

He decides to push on, taking every stage as slowly as he can, rushing nothing, and, to his immense relief, an hour and a half later the big iron barge chugs out of the bottom lock in one piece without a scratch. It has taken what feels like forever, and now he has it all to do again with the raft.

It is tempting to hurry the procedure with his own vessel, but the pace has settled into his bones: the stillness in the water, the parp parp of the coots, and the swooping of a kingfisher that has come to join them remind him of all there is to be gained in the moment. He takes the process slowly, twice going down to check the mooring on the big black barge. Finally, the lock gates are shut just as he found them, the barge and the raft are recoupled, and Bushy-Mush is on the roof at the front of the big boat as they slide away to continue their journey. Neil very quietly whistles a sea shanty he has heard somewhere to himself, and he changes the words slightly in his head:

'We'll heave him up and away we'll go

'Way, ho, Kim-me-darling-ho!

We'll heave him up and away we'll go

We're all bound over to London-o!

We'll heave him up from down below

'Way, ho, Kim-me-darling-ho!

That is where the cocks do crow

We're all bound over to London-o!

An' if we drown while we are young,

Way, ho, Kim-me-darling-ho!

It's better to drown than to wait to be hung,

We're all bound over to London -o!'

He cannot remember any more of the verses, and besides, he is just making it all nonsense, using Kim's name and adding in London, so he continues to hum and his mind becomes blank and time loses all meaning until he is left simply with the shifting of the clouds and the slow drifting of the hills and the comings and goings of the ducks and swans. Fields yield to woods and back again, and towns appear in the distance, loom large and then fall away behind them. When a second light shower begins to fall, it is not unpleasant, and when it stops and the sun reappears he is treated to a rainbow. Very slowly, the light begins to fade as the sun slithers down the sky.

Bushy-Mush whines once, and the whine turns into a yawn, but the yawn is just a reaction to the whine and the whine is a sign that he is hungry. So is Neil. The sack that Bill gave him is on the raft behind them. He can wait, but he is thinking of Bushy-Mush.

From inside the boat the whistle of snoring stops and is soon replaced with the whistle of a kettle boiling. Pat is awake. Now it is Neil's turn to yawn; he has not realised how much he has been concentrating to keep the boat on course. He is suddenly exhausted.

'Suits you.' Pat emerges up the steps and indicates the cowboy hat that Neil is still wearing.

Neil can feel his cheeks glow, and he takes it off.

'No, really,' says Pat. 'It suits you, leave it on.'

So Neil does, mostly out of politeness and to hide his glowing cheeks. Pat holds two mugs of coffee in one hand and two plates of beans on toast, balanced precariously, in the other. He puts Neil's coffee and plate down and produces a couple of cold, wrinkled sausages that look decidedly unappetising to Neil. Bushy-Mush, on the other hand, is delighted, and he swallows one whole and takes the second to the bow of the boat. where he chews on it, wagging his tail. Pat laughs at him and then rubs his eyes.

'Where the heck are we?'

'No idea.' Neil shrugs.

Pat slurps his coffee and puts the mug down before refocusing his eyes, looking about him for clues.

'Hang on,' he says, 'if we are where I think we are, that means that you … How long did I sleep?'

Neil drinks from his own mug and looks away, up the towpath. There is a chance Pat will be angry with him for going through the locks alone. He would have every right to be angry, but then he did leave him in charge, novice though he is.

'So you took us through Three Locks, eh?' Pat says.

Neil swallows hard. He shouldn't have done it.

'Yeah, well, I got it through okay,' he begins defensively.

'Of course you did, never imagined you wouldn't.' Pat gives him a wink and makes a clicking noise in the side of his mouth and then tucks into his food.

Neil smiles and takes a firmer grip of the tiller. Pat spoke as though he was talking to someone who would always be capable. But yes, why not? When Neil approached the job of getting through the locks methodically, broke it into smaller chunks, a step at a time, and took it slowly, he got a taste of what he is capable of. Maybe he is capable of convincing Kim that–

But his thoughts are interrupted: Pat has finished eating, and he takes the helm so that Neil can eat his own food, which is lukewarm now.

'It's another few hours to Wigan. You might want to take a nap yourself,' Pat says. He flicks a switch, and lights come on at the front of the boat, lighting up the way like headlights on a car. Neil yawns and realises that he is in fact very tired.

'There's a sofa right there.' Pat points with his empty plate. Neil takes the hint, and he carries the plates down below, washes them up, and flops onto the sofa to close his eyes, just for twenty minutes or so.

When he opens his eyes it is under a strange-looking roof, in another alien place, and he experiences the familiar struggle to recall where he fell asleep this time. It is the width of the room that jogs his memory and, sitting up and rubbing his eyes, he wonders how long he has been asleep. Up the steps, he is most surprised to see blue skies. Has he really slept through until morning? Really? He finds his feet and staggers up the steps. Pat looks drawn.

'Another two minutes,' Pat says, and he passes control of the tiller to Neil, who is not sure if he means he needs another two minutes' sleep or something else. He watches Pat patter downstairs and then settles in for another long haul at the helm. But Pat returns immediately with the black cowboy hat.

'Here.' He puts it on Neil's head. 'You earned that yesterday. See? You could do more than you think, eh? It's all just trial and practice.' And Pat smiles, revealing a missing tooth on one side, and Neil gets the strangest feeling that he has known him forever and will know him forever. He rubs his hand over his chest but the warm feeling that is making him smile is inside.

'Let's tie up over there.' Pat points at a space on the bank and reduces the revs. Neil steers and Pat controls the throttle, and when they come to the bank, instead of hopping ashore, Pat casts off the Pianoraft.

'There you go,' he says. 'You want that waterway there. That's the Downland Canal. Follow it down to the the Midland Canal, then you want the Lower-Midland and then the Oxford Canal, or maybe the Grand Union on to the river Thames. I'm not sure about that bit, but you'll figure it out. Say hello to your girl for me.'

He passes the rope to Neil, who draws the raft in close to the stern of the barge and jumps across. 'Your raft will handle like a doddle after this big beast.' Pat slaps the iron side of his own boat.

And with that, he pushes the throttle forward and steams away. Bushy-Mush jumps off at the last minute, and Pat glances back one more time and calls, 'Find me next time you're up this way.'

Neil smiles to himself, but it seems strange to see Pat motoring away. He would like to spend more time with him at some point. Perhaps their paths will cross again.

'Nice bloke,' he tells Bushy-Mush. He puts a hand up to his hat and settles it more firmly on his head and, walking with the rolling gait of a cowboy, he begins to pull his raft along the towpath.

Chapter 12

Neil had imagined that where the canals slipped through the centres of the towns the surroundings would be grim: dirty ribbons of water, greasy passageways blocked by half-sunk shopping trolleys and disused industrial buildings looming on either side. Certainly, he did not picture the open space that he finds himself in, with its neat, wide grass verges on either side of the canal. A car park behind an office block on the opposite bank is about as industrial as it gets. He had thought he might resent the concrete and the tarmac, the roof tiles and the street lights, but he finds he is comforted by these familiar sights after his recent days in the countryside.

Then again, although the lack of industry might be more pleasant than what he has been anticipating, from a practical point of view he had hoped there would be places along the way, right by the canal – industrial units, storage yards where he could get work and make a living as he went whilst keeping the Pianoraft in sight. His breath quickens, and for a moment he can hear his pulse in his ears.

'You'll be fine,' he tells himself. 'Take it a step at a time.'

He needs to get his bearings and double-check Pat's directions before making a plan, but his first job is to tie up so he can check the contents of the bag that Bill gave him. Maybe there is enough food for a few days. He takes the bag out onto the towpath and shakes it to disgorge its contents.

'A sleeping bag,' he tells Bushy-Mush, who sniffs at it warily. Bits of white fluff escape from a hole in one corner. A sleeping bag is going to be useful. Bushy-Mush seems very interested in a rather stained green cushion that has also fallen out of the bag. He snaps at it and gives it a good shake with his teeth.

'Leave it,' Neil commands, but Bushy-Mush growls at him and shakes it again.

'Leave. It.' Neil makes a grab and Bushy-Mush lets him take hold of the opposite corner but does not let go. The feisty animal pulls backward, head down, rear end up. 'Oh, have it, then,' says Neil at last and he lets go.

Bushy-Mush worries the pillow for a minute but quickly loses interest in favour of the new things Neil has found.

'So what are these?' Neil examines two foil packages. One contains chapatis, the other, onion bhajis. There is also half a loaf of sliced bread that has mould growing on one end, an apple, a tin mug, a fork and a penknife, and a couple of blankets.

'Very useful.' Neil puts the knife in his pocket. 'But not much to eat, and we can't drink the canal water.'

Well, Neil considers, there should be some money in the bank that was set aside for next month's rent – but that's not going be enough to get him to London. He will have to find work at some point.

'No panic,' he tells Bushy-Mush, and he puts his hand in his back pocket to feel for his bank card, but there's nothing there. 'Oh!' he says and checks the other back pocket. With growing concern, hasty and grasping fingers check his front pockets, and then the back ones again, but the card is in none of them. He looks on the ground around him: nothing.

Did he put it somewhere, hide it on the raft? With a bound he is on board. There is nothing on deck except the piano, and he lifts up the tarp. Maybe he put it down on the keys. The tarp slithers off but there is no card. Inside the cabin there is only the mattress and the chair with his clothes dumped on the seat. His jumper is flung into one corner, his jeans in another, but no card anywhere. He turns around to survey the whole room and then becomes still, his eyes transfixed.

'Bushy-Mush!' He sinks to his knees and wails. 'You stupid, stupid dog.'

In the middle of the mattress is the card, mis shapen and perforated with teeth marks. Bushy-Mush appears, tail wagging, stinking of onion bhaji. 'You stupid little–' Neil begins, but the little dog's eyes are wide as he licks his lips and lets his tongue hang out. He looks like he is smiling.

'So ridiculously happy,' Neil mutters through closed teeth. He gives the dog the smallest of reassuring strokes before looking at the card again. How long will it take them to replace it? Well, that's a dumb question. They have nowhere to send a replacement, no address. He can hardly ask the bank to send his replacement card to 'The Pianoraft, somewhere on the Downland Canal'!

He sits and stares out through the wall of reclaimed windows, watching the surface of the water, where a group of ducks swim past without a care in the world. Bushy-Mush pads round in a circle on the bed and curls up. On the far bank, long grasses have bent over and now trail in the slow-moving current.

'Okay.' He talks out loud, to keep calm and to slow his racing heart. 'It's not raining, and I have shelter if it does. I'm not hungry, so there's no immediate threat. Right.'

This approach seems to be working, and he feels a little less alarmed by the loss of his card.

'The next place we end up in, I will find work because I have to, and it's as simple as that.' He takes a few deep breaths and watches the water flow. His gaze turns to a stare; his mind is blank, time is lost.

Has he been sitting for a minute or an hour? He has no idea, nor does he care. With lazy legs he steps onto the bank, scrunches up the foil packages that the chapatis and onion bhajis were wrapped in, and takes up the mooring rope.

Slowly, he pulls the raft along the bank to where the canal splits. Straight ahead, the waterway leads to the west coast; the other way heads south, along the Downland Canal, which winds its way, eventually, to London.

He guides the raft round the bend and into the Downland Canal. This new waterway follows the road, and the traffic noise is irritating. Where fields once were, housing estates now loom. It all feels very urban and Neil now experiences a feeling of resentment after the days he has spent in the peace and quiet of the countryside.

The towpath is now parallel with another, paved path that runs beside the road, and for some distance there is nothing to separate them. Neil finds himself walking next to businessmen in suits and women with prams. It must be common for them to see canal folk with their boats along here, because at first glance they pay him no heed. But then they look again, their gazes drawn by the raft and the many handles on the obsolete drawer fronts. Some point at the raft and comment to their companions. Neil feels that if he does not hurry along this section, it will only be a matter of time before someone talks to him, and he's not ready for that yet. He wants to be quiet now; he has to find a place inside himself where he can trust he will survive without his bank card, forgive Bushy-Mush his sins and make sense of what he is doing.

'I have no idea what I am doing,' he tells himself. 'I have not a clue what I'm embarking on. But I have a purpose and a reason.' His lips move and he draws strength from this monologue. 'So, stuff you, life, for taking away my bank card!' Out loud he says, 'You can keep your onion bhajis too. You're not going to win that easily.'

A man with a newspaper under his arm, walking by the side of the road, looks over at him. 'You tell it like it is, mate,' he calls. 'Who needs onion bhajis anyway?'

'Exactly!' Neil replies, and they walk abreast for a little way, in silence, until the two paths curve in opposite directions and the man nods a goodbye. The noise of the traffic fades and the canal heads towards fields once again.

Neil is happy to be back in the countryside, but his stomach grumbles now and he is equally relieved when they approach the next town, which smells tantalisingly of grilled food, fresh bread and chips. He's been towing the raft for the past three hours; a rest is deserved! Just up ahead, the canal passes the edge of a park and there is a canteen and a queue for the hotdogs it serves. Bushy-Mush scrounges in his own canine way from those seated at the picnic tables to the side of the canteen. Neil counts what money he has and considers whether it makes sense to buy a hotdog or to save his cash and buy a bag of rice or something from a supermarket further ahead. Unlike Bushy, he cannot beg, or pick things out of bins – that is not the man he wants to be.

'Listen to me, with my pompous airs. "Not the man I want to be", as if I have a choice.' He whistles to Bushy-Mush, who staggers slowly back to the raft, his stomach full. Neil makes the raft fast to the bank and joins the queue.

'Burger or hotdog?' the man serving asks him, his voice lacking any expression.

'Either,' Neil replies.

The man exhales and his shoulders drop as if he is exhausted with life, or customers, or both.

'But …' Neil tries to smile. 'Can I earn it? I could wash up, take the rubbish somewhere, work for you for a couple of hours.' The man rolls his eyes at this, but Neil presses on, aware of the people behind him in the queue. 'You see, I'm on that raft.' He points and the man follows his finger, 'and my dog ate my bankcard and if–'

'Save your breath,' the man says wearily but not unkindly. 'It's not my van,' he explains, 'and I have to account for every slice of bread, every squirt of tomato ketchup. Every burger has to tally with the amount in the till.'

'Oh, okay, sorry I asked,' Neil says, and he looks at the man again. His skin is grey, his eyes are lifeless. Neil is so glad he is not him, but he would like to draw him. He pays a pound for a bag of chips and immediately regrets this – a bag of rice would have cost the same, and he could have boiled it up on the little pot-bellied stove, and it would have kept him going for days.

He wanders back to the bank, weighing his options.

He could go further into the town, find work somewhere, but it's not ideal, not if the raft and the piano are to stay safe. A placard by the canal describes the town and the mills, and shows a map of the waterway, indicating another town not far away. Maybe something will turn up there.

As they pass through the town centre, Neil pulling and feeling stronger for the chips, and Bushy-Mush standing sentinel on the raft in front of the piano, the canal cuts right up against tall mill buildings. The water is discoloured here, and although there are no half-submerged shopping trolleys, Neil does spot an old oil drum floating near the opposite bank. The mill buildings tower over him, all dirty stone and broken windows: little black pupils into a time gone by. It is a piece of history, preserved by indifference, and Neil feels the urge to capture it. Tying up the raft, he takes out his sketchbook, but before drawing the mill he draws a cartoon of Pat and then a serious picture of the man in the canteen. Neil wishes he had his charcoal with him, to make his features jump out of the blank page. In pencil, the drawing takes a while, and although he is quite pleased with the result, the mill is calling, and he feels compelled to commit that to paper. He has no idea how long it takes to finishes his sketches, but nor does he care. When he is satisfied, he puts them back on the raft and begins to walk again. As they draw close to a wooden bridge across the canal ahead of them, which was presumably built for the mill workers in days gone by, Bushy-Mush stands, alert, ears forward, clearly sensing something that Neil cannot detect.

'What is it, boy?' Neil says, but as they draw near to the bridge he can just make out a quiet squeaking, and there, by the water, under the bridge, is a kitten, bedraggled and shivering.

Neil's initial response is despair – he can barely feed himself, let alone take on the responsibility for this tiny animal! But he knows what he must do and he leans down to pick it up. Before his fingers touch the kitten's matted fur, though, Bushy-Mush, who has jumped from the raft, decides the kitten needs a wash and roughly licks it.

'Gently, mate, this guy's even smaller than you.'

He looks at the kitten more closely, noting its long fur, and noting too that it is female. 'How did you get there, my friend?' he says. 'Look at you, all shaking and scared.'

Working on instinct, he stuffs the kitten inside his T-shirt and jumper, settles the black cowboy hat more firmly on his head and, taking up the ropes again, continues to pull. The kitten curls up against his warm skin and he can feel rather than hear her purring. He starts to hum and then sing:

'When I was one I was just begun,

when we were two, we had just set out anew.

Now we are three it's not only me, but when we'll be four …'

His mind drifts to thoughts of Kimberly, and he finishes '… I will be so much more.' He hopes whoever wrote the original will not disapprove of him altering the poem. The kitten in his shirt is very still; she has stopped shaking but she continues to purr. The tiny creature, whose life is dependent on him now, gives him strength and he pulls for another two or maybe three hours through the ever-changing countryside. Trees line their way again, and where the trees stop, the fields spread away into the distance, revealing pretty country pubs and little stone bridges, each change so gradual it is as if it has always been. In some places, Neil sees large, expensive houses by the water's edge and, beside one, idly strolling through the grounds, a man in a white trilby hat waves to Neil, who is wearing his black leather cowboy hat, as if they are old friends.

The towpath widens and flattens out, telling him he is nearing a town, maybe even the city of Rolby itself. After another twenty minutes or so, the canal passes under a very wide steel bridge with cars travelling at speed across it, and he suspects it is a motorway. The general noise around him suggests dense living conditions, the hum of traffic and people, and he is thankful that they are mostly hidden by bushes and neat rows of council houses.

'Definitely a city,' he tells himself, and he strokes the bump in his jumper to reassure the kitten all is well. Bushy-Mush has pushed the door open on the raft and gone inside the cabin, no doubt to fill the mattress with dog hairs and find things to chew on.

At one point, the towpath stops abruptly and the canal narrows. Steel walls contain the water on either side, and, looking over the side of these, Neil can see that he is now suspended on a viaduct that crosses a river below.

'A bridge of water crossing a river of water!' he exclaims. 'Well I never.'

As there is no towpath on this section, he climbs aboard the raft and, clinging on to the side of the bridge, pulls himself across, grasping the girders. Worried he is going to squash the kitten, he puts her inside the raft where, as predicted, Bushy-Mush is asleep in the middle of the bed. The kitten snuggles up to the dog and Neil returns to the extraordinary situation.

'Who would have thought?' he says to himself, and his stomach rumbles, but not in affirmation. Neil stands in awe of the ingenuity of the workers of a time gone by. He would like to know more about the history of the canals. He looks back at the bridge they have just crossed, tempted to stop to make a sketch, but his hunger is gnawing at him now and he must push on and look for an opportunity.

On the other side of the river, despite being on the edge of a city, the canal continues to be tree-lined and pleasant; it shocks Neil that the waterway is so hidden from the hubbub he can hear all around him.

'Nature is just continuing, ducks are floating, insects humming, trees and bushes growing, brambles brambling – it's amazing!' he tells the breeze.

He has walked a long way today – all day, in fact – and the raft is not as light as it was, even if it does float better since Bill added the extra barrels. His legs ache and he acknowledges that he must rest soon. The line of a track curves to accompany the towpath, a low fence separating the two. A whistle sounds, and then a noise like that of a hundred stampeding horses heads towards him and a train blurs past, passengers looking but not seeing, the last carriage all dark. The train stirs up the air behind it, creating a vortex that whips up the leaves and deposits a silence in its wake. He walks a little further but finally, at a spot that looks no different from any other, Neil ties the raft up to a tree. It is very unlikely that anyone will use the towpath, and if they do and they cannot negotiate stepping over a rope, they can always knock on the door.

'Knock on the door.' He chuckles and looks at the many drawer fronts. 'It really is art,' he says, his eyes already closing even though the sky is not yet dark. Yawning, he curls up with Bushy-Mush and the kitten.

Chapter 13

Bushy-Mush's sharp yapping filters through the layers of sleep, dragging Neil into wakefulness before he is ready. Neil turns over, pulls a jumper over his eyes and tries to recapture his dreams, but there is another noise: a chewing, nattering sound, more irritating even than Bushy-Mush. Neil forces one eye open but his vision is restricted by a fuzzy white substance. He raises his head slightly, and the fuzz comes into focus to reveal the tail end of a tiny kitten, who is curled up next to his face, grooming her most intimate parts, and sounding like she is sucking saliva through a straw.

'Oh, do you have to!' Neil turns over to face the other way, but it's no better. Now Bushy-Mush can be heard clearly through the thin wall of the cabin, whining and howling out on the bank.

'Oh, for goodness' sake.' Neil sighs, thoughts of sleep abandoned, and wriggles out of his sleeping bag, pulling on his jeans. He eyes his trousers critically, noting the stains and grime they've picked up in the few days he's been living aboard the raft. He'll need to find a launderette, and sooner rather than later. Out on deck, blinking in the morning sun, he yawns and finds Bushy-Mush proudly standing over a dead rat.

'Well, good for you, mate,' Neil says, rubbing his face with the palm of his hand. It is too early for Neil to eat – he has never understood how people wake up hungry – but later, at some point, he is going to be ravenously hungry, and what will he do then? The longest he has ever been without food has been a day and that was when he was ill as a child. He could probably manage with one meal a day, but less than that? Even the thought of 'less than that' starts him panicking. Maybe he will have to catch a rabbit, cook it over an open fire like he has read about in books.

He can see three rabbits right now up in the fields above the canal, lolloping slowly in the morning ground mist, grey shadows on a sage blanket. One of the animals tears off across the field, and Neil watches it go, aware he does not have a clue how he would catch one, and he dismisses the idea. Besides, he is not a caveman: he does not have the guts for what would have to be done before cooking the poor creature. Food is going to become a big problem if he doesn't think of something.

A quick survey of his surroundings reveals no people, no houses and no roads anywhere in sight, but nevertheless he still chooses a bush to go behind and keeps a lookout to remain discreet. 'No, I am no caveman,' he repeats, and he wipes his hands down his jeans.

'Come on, Bushy,' he calls, and steps back on board, where he finds little white Fuzzy-Pants, curled up asleep again. She is going to need food soon, too. Well, he can do nothing about any of it out here in the countryside; best to get pulling.

Today it doesn't take Neil so long to get into the rhythm after he sets off. Soon, however, his muscles complain that yesterday was too much. There's no option though – today's priority is finding food for Fuzzy-Pants, as well as for himself, and he will walk as far as he must. On the horizon, across the fields, he can see a collection of buildings – barns, maybe, but no sign of a town. He needs to get to the next town – not that he can presume he will find work wherever there are people but at least food actually exists there.

The towpath here is mostly grass with a thin strip of mud down the middle, and it seems little used – perhaps worn smoother every few days by a dog walker or two. Hedges flank the path on both sides, untrimmed, wild, full of birds and their song, separating the waterway from the fields and the hills beyond them, topped with emerald trees and crowned with a layer of cream clouds. The day promises to be beautiful, the high heavens a delicate blue. Neil's feet find a tempo and the miles pass.

Gradually, the familiar signs of civilisation begin to appear. The towpath widens, and the hedges are trimmed back, and round the next bend Neil is presented with a row of neatly moored canal boats with thin ribbons of smoke rising from their chimneys. The boats are moored to the towpath that Neil is walking along, and they present a barrier – the only way to pass them is to hop aboard the raft and trust that the current will carry him past. Many of the occupants of the boats are out on deck, enjoying the sunshine, and they smile and call out a hello as he passes. One or two give a gentle push with their boathooks to keep him going.

Beyond the last in the line of canal boats, the towpath is paved and much wider, and soon there is a hum of unseen cars. A row of houses springs up on the right, and a road begins to follow the canal's course on the left. They pass under a bridge, which rumbles and shakes with the weight of the traffic passing overhead and then, like a gust of wind on a hot day, the left bank opens out into a park in which there stands a clean white building. A banner strung over the entrance declares that the building is a school of the arts, and a part of Neil has the sensation that he has come home. The area in front of the building, all the way down to the canal, is full of students as well as dog walkers and passers-by.

'Hey, you play that?' A man with a wide smile and baggy trousers springs from nowhere, takes hold of the raft's tow rope and helps Neil pull. The man seems slightly too old to be a student.

'Er, no.' Neil lets go, rubs his wrists, which have become stiff, and then stretches.

'Is it tuned?' the man asks, 'or is it like an art piece, a statement?'

It would be nice if he had started the raft as an art project, but to claim that this was his motivation would make him feel a bit of a fraud. On the other hand, if it does have any validity as an art piece, then who is he to disregard that? He has always loved installation artists such as Cornelia Parker and Sakir Gökçebag, who really stir his thinking, but he has never thought that he could be equal to them; he doesn't have the vision. Equally, in the other direction, he doesn't have much time for Tracy Emin and her *Bed* or Carl André's *Bricks*. But maybe he and the raft are somewhere between the two. After all, this is not the first time it has been suggested that the raft is art. And if he wants it to be called art, then why not? Call it art if it makes people think. If it stimulates the mind, then it is art.

Neil hedges his bets. 'Both. A statement and art.'

The man stops pulling, eyes on the piano, taking in the construction of the raft, clearly intrigued. Neil looks the man up and down. He has the self-confidence of the 'cool' students at art college, but he is a little too old to be a student now, and where once a smooth brow was bound to dominate there is a permanent little frown, a knot of skin between his eyes. But he has an open face and when he does grin it is broad, open and real. He moves like a dancer, as if he is aware of his limbs.

'May I?' the man asks, and barely waits for Neil to nod his permission before hopping on board. He plays a chord or two, grins even more widely, and breaks into an embellished version of 'Roll Out The Barrel', or some such tune. Neil has no ear for music, which Kim found amusing and teased him about regularly, but even he can tell that the piano is somewhat out of tune, and he frowns. Presumably the damp is the cause, but there's nothing to be done. The man gives the ditty a musically humorous and clichéd ending.

'Hoy!' He lifts one hand off with a flourish and a group of women in raincoats who have gathered to listen, handbags over their arms, break into ragged applause. The piano player gives a little bow and bounces back ashore.

'My name's Jez. Yours?'

'Neil.'

'And the dog?' He squats.

'Bushy-Mush is the dog and I've got a hungry kitten on board called Fuzzy-Pants.'

'Ha, Fuzzy-Pants. Hey, Jasper!' He calls over to a tall, gangly man with red hair, a large nose, and a coffee cup in each hand, who greets them with a smile.

'Here you go.' Jasper hands one of the cups to Jez.

'Ah, that's not okay, is it?' Jasper looks at Neil, hands him the other cup and turns to survey the raft.

Jez puts down his coffee and marches off down the towpath, and Neil wonders if he said something wrong.

Neil peers, a little taken aback, into his own steaming cup.

'Hey, a piano, cool,' Jasper says. 'What's the story?'

And so the story is told again;

'It's art, a piece about the role of determination and persistence in relationships. I'm floating the piano down to London.'

Jasper examines the raft as if what Neil has said has real validity. 'Nice one,' he remarks.

Jez returns with a third coffee, three croissants, a roll of bread for Bushy-Mush and a piece of corned beef wrapped in silver foil for Fuzzy-Pants, which he hands to Neil. The little kitten attacks this latter item with such relish that Neil fears she might just throw it all back up. The corned beef is gone in under a minute, and the cat starts to clean herself again, vigorously and noisily, making quite disgusting little noises as she bites at fleas or some other invisible irritant.

'So how long have you been on the quest to end all quests?' Jez asks, flakes of pastry on his lips. Neil chews on a croissant and tries to remember the days, but they blur into each other. He tears off a piece and feeds it to Bushy-Mush.

'No idea,' he says, aware that he is playing to the audience. 'Four days, four months ... could be four years. I've given myself twenty-five years to succeed but lack of dosh might stop that.'

'Ah, funding,' says Jasper, nodding wisely. 'But it's art! You should apply for a grant.' He dips his croissant into his coffee.

'Just set out, didn't think about it,' Neil says, eyeing what's left of Jasper's breakfast. He could eat it all over again.

'Come on, Jasp, this is our thing. This is what we're good at. Besides, it will save us the fare to Ruttingham.' Jez sounds excited, encouraging. He takes aim and tosses his empty cup into a nearby bin. 'Goal!' he shouts as it lands.

'Forty–love,' Jasper replies with a grin, and Neil feels a bit lost. At art college there was a cool set of students, full of banter and witticisms, who created art pieces that made him gasp. That group went out and got drunk every night and rarely turned up to lectures. Neil and Sleet did not fit in with that crowd; instead, they read books, talked art, and more often than not stayed in with a can or two of cheap lager. These two guys, Jez and Jasper, are definitely of the 'cool' sort, the sort Kimberly also used to tell him about, who studied Documentary and Film-making alongside her at her 'proper' university. Jez even looks a little like a picture Kim had of a fellow student she met whilst she was there. She refused to throw the picture away, whilst insisting he was only a friend. What was his name? Peregrine, or Montgomery, something like that? – certainly not a Neil. Soon enough, Neil feels sure, Jez and Jasper are going to recognise that he, Neil, is not one of them; they'll say something teasing, maybe even derisive, and they will be gone. But at least he got some breakfast out of it.

Jez jumps onto the raft again and plays a loud trill.

'Ladies and gentlemen,' he announces to the people passing by, 'it gives me great pleasure to start work on the tale of Neil and Kimberly, known to all who know them as Nimbly. But that is only when they are on land. When they are aboard their raft, we call them Keil.'

Two students and a man with a dog stop to stare, but no one laughs, and Neil lowers his gaze and puts his hand on his forehead. Some of the passing students loiter, clutching their bags or books across their chests and whispering to each other.

'Neil is our hero,' Jez continues, playing a short staccato collection of brash chords, 'and

Kimberly …' He stops and addresses Neil. 'Hey, she needs a surname … What's her surname?'

'Holliday,' Neil answers, but the question feels intrusive and he becomes aware of the crowd that is gathering.

'And Kimberly Holliday …' Jez plays a cascade of notes and adorns them with triplets and grace notes. It is quite beautiful. 'Is our heroine!' He plays the cascade again. 'Who takes herself to London.' He sings these words and adds another rush of chords at the end, before breaking into a melody that Neil recognises as a hymn – or a nursery rhyme, perhaps. Jez sings in a high voice,

'I need to seek my fortune, Neil …

They offered me a very fine deal, Neil …

How does the idea appeal, Neil?'

Jez stops and leaves a dramatic pause. A few more students gather. The women with handbags have arranged themselves on a nearby bench. Jez lowers his voice to continue,

'I find the idea very grim, Kim …

I think I would sink while you would swim, Kim …

I certainly feel out on a limb, Kim …'

At this point, Jasper steps forward, takes his jumper off and puts it over his head so that the arms fall down either side of his face. Stroking and fussing

169

at the woolly arms as if they are his hair, he puts his knees together and flutters his eyelashes. Jez plays the cascade of chords to introduce him. Jasper takes on Kimberly's role, adopting a high-pitched voice:

'Ah, your heart is made of steel, Neil …

I beg to you to come to heel, Neil …'

The women on the bench laugh at this but Neil feels his cheeks flush. Jasper is oblivious to Neil's discomfort as he finishes,

'If you don't come now there'll be no appeal, Neil!'

And the tall gangly redhead takes a little bow and waves his arms, encouraging the sizeable crowd that has now gathered.

Jez plays the serious, brash chords that he started with, and sings in a low voice,

'Then go, Kim, for your life is a Holliday!

Then go, Kim, let London lead you astray!

Then go, Kim, but what will you take today?'

Neil looks up. He has been examining his hands to keep his cheeks from burning any hotter, but this last sentence makes no sense. Jez and Jasper both look around them as if they have lost something. Jasper leaps ashore, and takes an umbrella from one of the women on the bench and a book from a student and the black cowboy hat from Neil's head.

Jez picks up the steering plank, a tightly coiled bit of rope and one of Neil's shoes, which Bushy-Mush has been chewing on despite Neil's attempts to stop him.

'Will you take your shoe?' Jez calls, throwing the shoe to Jasper.

'I will not!' Jasper replies in a high-pitched voice and tosses the shoe back.

'Take your shoe and give me my umbrella,' Jez demands, throwing the shoe again. Jasper throws the umbrella and Jez catches it. Immediately, the umbrella is thrown back, as is the shoe, both of the men declaring they do not want the items, and it is quickly apparent that Jez and Jasper are in territory that is not only very familiar to them but in which they thrive.

'And I believe this plank of wood is yours,' And the steering plank is now in the mix.

'And this book is yours.' Four objects now sail across the gap from raft to path, Jez and Jasper juggling with ease and competence, illustrating their tale of Neil and Kim.

Neil, the attention now focused away from him, finds he is smiling. The tightly coiled rope is included and the cowboy hat sails through the air and the six objects are juggled back and forth, Jasper throwing one under his leg once in a while, Jez taking an object out of the flow and balancing it on his head, one item after the other until it is the plank that remains. The book is thrown back to the student, who catches it, and Jez pretends to throw the umbrella at the women on the bench point first, but catches it by the handle at the last minute and returns it to its owner with a bow. The black cowboy hat finds its way back onto Neil's head, and the juggling act is over. A buzz travels through the crowd, who are waiting for what will come next.

Jez turns back to the piano and plays another flourish of dark chords. He grins at the crowd, making eye contact with as many as he can.

'Alas and alack,' he begins, 'what have I doney?

Kimberly was my only sunny.

I must go find my little bunny

For this I'm afraid I need some … money!'

He looks at the keys of the piano and breaks into an amazing piece of boogie-woogie; the audience start to clap, and Jasper takes the umbrella again and balances it on his chin. Jasper snatches the cowboy hat off Neil's head and holds it out to the audience, upside down. Most of the students start to wander off, now that the performance has reached the stage at which they are expected to put their hands in their pockets, but Neil can hear a surprising number of coins clinking their way into the hat. Jez builds his piece to a crescendo, crashes the last two chords and leaps from the raft to the shore as the crowd cheer and shout. A little girl approaches him and gives him a coin, and he takes off his shoe and pops it in and then walks along the towpath, one shoe on, the other held out, in the opposite direction to Jasper, collecting offerings as the people begin to disperse. The three ladies on the bench stand, Jasper gives back the umbrella, and they walk off.

Neil looks around. It's only a minute or two since Jez stopped playing, but aside from one or two of the students who are still hanging around, peering at the raft, there is almost no trace that anything just happened. And yet something amazing did just happen.

Jez pours the contents of his shoe into the black hat and Jez hands it to Neil.

'So, how did we do?' Jez's smile is even wider than before as he sits cross-legged on the paved floor. Bushy-Mush decides his lap will make a very nice bed and he settles down for a sleep, Jez lifting his arms to allow the little animal to do this. Neil pushes his finger about in the money.

'So many pound coins! You must have made over thirty quid.' Neil can hear the incredulity in his own voice.

'Ah well, it will do. All right for the first performance. What do you think, Jasper, shall this be our way to Ruttingham?'

'Best ask the captain,' Jasper replies, and they both look at Neil.

'What, you want a lift?' Neil says.

'We can stop at every town and village we pass, put on a little performance, pay our way in pocket money and sandwiches. What do you say?' Jez asks, with a broad grin that creases his eyes.

'We'll be a bit crowded.' Neil wonders where they will all sleep.

'Ah, if we stop where there are places with pubs we'll get a bed all right. We'll manage – what do you say?'

A little thrill of excitement bubbles across Neil's chest.

'All right.' He wonders if it's difficult to learn to juggle.

Chapter 14

'Right, we'll get our stuff then,' Jez announces, and he and Jasper stride purposefully towards the arts building. They re-emerge a few minutes later carrying a good deal more stuff than Neil anticipated, which they store on the deck of the raft, behind the piano, and they cover the lot with the tarpaulin. Neil's curiosity is aroused by a padded black bag, flat and round at one end, thin at the other, but he doesn't enquire as to its contents.

Once they are satisfied that their belongings are secure, Jez suggests he and Jasper play paper, scissors, stone to determine who will pull first, and Jasper loses. Neil and Jez sit on the raft whilst Jasper tows, and the art school, the students and the setting for Jasper and Jez's fantastical performance all drift slowly off into the distance.

Neil looks back at the spot and asks, 'Is that what you do, then?'

'It is now, yes, but technically we're actors,' Jez says, his voice relaxed, easy. 'I kept bumping into Jasper at auditions. We always seemed to be going for the same roles. Auditioning is ninety per cent waiting so there's lots of time to get to know people.'

He sighs and strokes Bushy-Mush's soft ears, and is still for a second. 'Anyway.' He perks up. 'We both kept getting shortlisted, which meant more waiting and – I can't remember who started it, but one of us threw something at the other.'

'You threw your empty drinks can at me,' Jasper calls from the bank.

'And you caught it,' Jez calls back, a taunting tone in his voice, and Neil feels it could all kick off again, the banter, the juggling, the music, but Jasper is busy pulling the raft and Jez turns to Neil again.

'And from there it just became what we did when we were waiting at auditions. The other actors seemed to like it, and we started making up little plays around the juggling. The other actors would make suggestions, they really got into it. Anyway, we must have been to about a hundred of these auditions, and it was always "don't call us, we'll call you". I was about to give up the whole entertainment and acting thing–'

'Me too!' calls Jasper from the bank.

'–when we were caught juggling some stage props,' Jez continues.

'We thought we were going be in so much trouble,' Jasper says.

176

'Instead, it turned out there was someone there who had something to do with Glastonbury, and he asked us to do a slot – you know, juggling, putting on an act.'

'Wow!' Neil looks from Jez to Jasper. Kim went to Glastonbury when she was at college and loved it, then talked about it non-stop for the first year they were together, saying they should get tickets for next summer. But it was a lot of money, and not just the entry price: there would have been the travelling, too, and the food. It was far more than they could realistically afford, but, more than that, Neil found he felt slightly afraid. Afraid of the number of people, the size of the place, and not really knowing a lot about music.

'You've been to Glastonbury, right?' Jez asks, but he doesn't wait for an answer. 'They had us in the circus and theatre field.'

Neil had thought the festival was all about music, but now he pictures a striped circus tent full of girls spinning on ropes, acrobats and tightrope walkers. A vision of a series of sculptures forms in his mind. They could be kinetic, or balanced in some way. Creations filled with colour flash, a myriad of hues to reflect the circus, but toned down to suggest age, a time gone by. It has been years, literally, since he has had ideas like this – art for art's sake. He reaches for his sketchbook.

'So we created a play for Glastonbury, based on people drinking too much, falling over, throwing bottles at each other – we kind of made it a bit moral, the "need to take care" sort of thing. We even had a stretcher and paramedics' uniforms, and we would drag someone out of the crowd, take them to hospital, you know... And they loved it. We've been invited back every year since.'

He looks over at Neil's sketchbook. 'I like that.' Neil has roughly sketched a man on a tightrope, almost off balance, limbs elongated to accentuate the lines.

'Jasper can slack-rope walk,' Jez adds. 'I unicycle.' This last piece of information explains the padded black bag, round and flat at one end and thin at the other.

'Hey, Jasper, we could add a bit about Kim struggling in London, use the slack rope to show her trials. What is she doing in London, did you say, Neil?'

'She's got into television, Channel Doc. She wants to make documentaries.'

'Oh, okay. Well, that opens up a whole world of possibilities. We could involve the unicycle, have her doing a documentary about bicycle wheels being stolen so there are only single-wheeled bikes in London. Something like that.'

'We could juggle her TV microphone with bike spanners. Let's see if we can't pick up an old bike wheel on our way,' Jasper adds.

Neil begins to see their idea and transforms his sketch accordingly, adding a second long-limbed figure stretching out towards the first. To this figure he adds a microphone, but it looks like an ice cream cone so he changes it to an oversized bunch of flowers. Kimberly loved these sketches of his. Maybe he'll give her this one when he gets to London.

Neil carries on sketching, listening to Jez and Jasper developing their theme, adding ideas, discarding others, outlining a script, helping each other with rhymes for the spoken parts. After a while, Jez takes over pulling the raft from Jasper, but the talking doesn't stop. Jasper sits at the piano, trying out tunes to go with the script. He is just as good as Jez.

The hours pass quickly as the two plot and Neil draws, also sketching the ever-changing landscape, the flat fields that become rolling hills with woodland. Woodland turns into farmland, with soil tilled, waiting for crops to grow, and scrubland with neither man nor beast roaming. The hedgerows that border the towpath change, hawthorn to elderflower to stunted trees tangled with ivy, then trees so tall and majestic they form a cathedral arching over the canal.

Nature is splitting her seams in the abundance of spring, Neil considers, and it jolts him when Jez calls 'Land ahoy!' and Jez and Jasper stand to see over the cabin roof towards a small town in the distance.

'We'll find lunch there, I reckon, and we'll try out the new show,' Jasper says.

Boats are moored on either side of the canal, as they seem always to be on the approach to a town, and the raft slows almost to a stop as Jez is forced to stop towing. Neil feels it would not be right to use the moored boats to pull themselves along by, but Jez has no such hesitation; he grips wherever is useful, and they start to move again. None of the occupants of the moored boats seem to mind, and some lend a hand.

'You need a pole,' Jez says, 'then you could punt these bits.'

'We'll find somewhere to set up by the canal,' says Jasper. 'The whole thing won't work as well without the raft and the piano.'

A child is running along the towpath, waving, and Neil waves back. There's a couple walking their dog up the path, and gardens, rather than open fields, behind the trees that line the towpath. Up ahead, a group of people lean over the railing of a bridge that spans the canal. They wave and chatter excitedly as the raft makes its slow way towards them. There's a flash as they pass under the bridge, and a man with a camera calls to them.

'Where are you tying up? Can I do an interview?'

Neil looks at Jez who looks at Jasper who looks at Neil.

'You famous or something?' Neil asks.

'I was just about to ask you the same thing,' Jez replies. 'Is there somewhere to tie up?' he calls back up to the man on the bridge.

'Victoria Park.' The man points in the direction they are travelling. 'Can we say I'll see you there?'

Jez shrugs, bemused, and the man takes another photograph and packs his camera away.

'What's going on?' Neil asks.

'Search me,' Jez replies.

Another ten minutes or so brings them firmly into the town, where the towpath is paved, and the houses give way to grey, ugly office buildings. Between the offices is a patch of green with swings and slides and picnic benches. The man from the bridge is waiting for them by a bollard.

'Hi, guys,' he calls, raising his camera. 'Smile!'

As they approach the bank, he slings his Nikon over his shoulder and extends a hand.

'Ian, culture section, *Rolby Evening Press*. Which one of you is Neil?' He rummages in a pocket and brings out a Dictaphone. Both Jasper and Jez point to Neil.

'I heard about the raft and your performance today from my daughter. She's at the college over in Bywater. She loved the performance, by the way, but she loved the raft even more. So it's art, right? Can you explain it?'

He points the recorder at Neil, who feels his throat tighten. Sleet would be great at this – he would be in his element and would make up a whole stream of nonsense. Jez looks on expectantly, one eyebrow raised, which just makes Neil's tongue stick to the roof of his mouth all the more. What did he say to Jasper and Jez when they first met up? It was so easy to talk to them. Didn't he say that it was a piece about the role of persistence and something else in relationships? He has forgotten. His tutors defined art as something that is created to express ideas or feelings, and installation art as a piece designed to transform the perception of a space. There is no lie there, then, as it is definitely designed to express his feelings to Kim where he would fail with words.

'It's a piece about love.' Jez takes over and Neil exhales and his shoulders drop, which allows his tongue to loosen a little. He does not want to be the stammering, voiceless one.

'I'm trying to get to London, take Kim's piano to her.' Neil forces the words through his dry mouth.

'Ah!' Ian exclaims as if he understands everything now. 'So it is a piece about commitment and dedication.'

'And persistence,' Neil says.

'How long do you think it will take to get there?' Ian asks.

Jasper speaks up. 'Neil has given himself twenty-five years.'

Jez joins in. 'Neil is offering his time to demonstrate his commitment, so this is a piece about time being our most precious commodity …'

It is like being back at college, where he would produce work and Sleet would give it significance by spouting nonsense, creating meaning out of nothing.

'What is there but time?' Jez says, and Neil studies his face to see if he is serious.

'And you are …?' Ian asks.

'Me and Jasper there, we're the jugglers and performers extraordinaire that your daughter saw back at Bywater. In fact, you're just in time,' Jez announces, bowing low to a small group of people who have gathered to see what the raft is and who is being interviewed.

'Ladies and gentlemen,' Jez calls out in a booming voice, sounding not unlike a ringmaster from a circus, 'gather round to meet Neil, captain of the Pianoraft, a unique construction, the likes of which you'll never see again, dedicated to love and man's ceaseless battle against the cruel sands of time!'

Neil pulls the front of his hat down so his eyes are hidden. Jasper ties a rope to a lamp post and back to the raft. It hangs slack.

'But wait!' Jez has captured the attention of the group, and passers-by are stopping to see what's going on. 'Where is the piano, I hear you ask!'

No one has asked, but Jez leaps on board nonetheless and pulls back the tarpaulin with a flourish to reveal the piano. His fingers flow across the keyboard and the familiar trills of Kimberly's theme ring out across the canal.

Meanwhile, Jasper rummages in the bags stored behind the piano and pulls out a long, frilly pink dress, a pink umbrella and a blonde wig and, after donning this costume, hops nimbly onto the slack rope. Using the pink umbrella for balance, he acts out Kimberly's struggle in London, feeding the pigeons at Trafalgar Square, saluting the guards at Buckingham Palace, following the narrative that Jez relates. The crowd swells and Ian sits beside Neil.

'This is really going to capture the readers' imagination,' he says. 'Are you guys going to stick together all the way to London?'

'I don't think so.' Neil feels more comfortable without the microphone in his face and the focus elsewhere. Jasper is still wobbling on the slack rope, and Jez begins the juggling act, tossing implements across to him from the raft. Amongst all this, he mounts the unicycle, using it to illustrate Neil's dithering, his legs pedalling backward and then forward, playing the part of someone who cannot make a decision. Although it hurts Neil a little to see himself represented in this way, he cannot deny that it is accurate – and extremely funny.

'Well, they are a great act,' says Ian, 'but the story for me, you know, for the arts column, is the raft. I think I'd like to run it as an ongoing piece, if you're okay with that?'

Neil isn't clear what Ian means by this, but he is flattered by the attention. 'Sure,' he says.

'Great, have you got a phone with you?'

'It's out of battery and I have no charger.' Neil frowns. Jasper has engaged a boy in the crowd, and he instructs him to snatch Neil's hat from his head and bring it to him on the slack rope.

'Well, look, I don't see why you should pay the bill anyway,' Ian continues, 'so I'll get a phone and a solar charger, how does that sound? If you could text me each day with a short piece about one thing that has happened, thoughts you've had, adjustments you've made to the raft or yourself. Maybe describe people you meet, or send a picture of a drawing you've done, you know, something like that. Oh, and don't worry about the wording, I'll polish it up into something readable. I just really think people are going love it. What do you say?'

Neil doesn't answer immediately. He likes the freedom of having nothing specific he needs to do each day. Having to remember to write something and check in sounds restricting.

'Actually, I'm not sure it is going to fit in with–' he begins, but Ian butts in,

'Of course, we can pay you. You have a bank account, I take it?'

Jez is back at the piano, and the crowd clap along the rhythm. Neil explains about Bushy-Mush chewing up his bank card, but Ian is not fazed by this.

'Give the bank a call,' he says. 'They can send a new card out to the address they have on record, and you must know someone who can pick it up and forward it to you at the next town?'

Neil had not thought of this, and it seems so simple. Sleet will find a way to get into the flat and pick up the new card.

Jez now has the crowd singing along now and Jasper passes round the hat.

I'll get the phone out to you today.' Ian takes out his camera once more and snaps a couple of portraits of Neil and some general shots of the raft, the crowd and the jugglers. 'I'll write a one-off piece about your juggling friends, too,' he says, and with a wave he moves off, taking photographs of the crowd as he goes.

The crowd aren't keen to disperse; they seem to want more, but Jez has clearly finished and Jasper is coiling up his slack rope. Some of the audience chat, and a couple of teenage boys eye the unicycle. Jez lets them try it out and they laugh at each other's attempts to balance on the single wheel.

'What did you think?' Jez asks Neil.

'Brilliant!'

'Has the newspaperman gone?' Jasper asks.

'Yes, but he says he's going to write a piece about you guys.' He feels reluctant to say that Ian was mostly interested in him, and the raft. Jasper counts up the money.

'You want to stay in a bed and breakfast tonight?' he says. 'We've done really well.' He puts the cowboy hat back on Neil's head.

'Yup,' Jez says emphatically.

Chapter 15

A little way down the canal, just back from the water's edge, a sign on the side of a pretty stone house declares that it is The Duck Inn. Despite its name, which Jasper cannot resist saying a few times very quickly, The Duck Inn is a welcoming, old-fashioned pub, with horse brasses on the wall and a fire burning in the grate. It's the sort of place where the locals claim the same worn wooden chairs each night and the beer is served in tankards. The food is unimaginative but the portions are generous, and Jasper, Jez and Neil relive the day as they tuck in hungrily. Bushy-Mush tries to impress a red setter and Fuzzy-Pants sits on Neil's lap, begging for scraps. No one seems to mind the animals being there. After a couple of halves of a very pleasant local cider, Jez's eyes narrow as he spies the landlord drying glasses with a tea towel.

'Hey, landlord.' His words sound a little slurred. 'I bet you I can balance a tea towel on my nose.'

The landlord looks at him suspiciously and exchanges glances with the regulars at the bar. 'We've got a right one here, Charlie,' he says to one of the locals, and clears away the plates.

'I'm serious,' Jez says, sounding more drunk than his two halves of cider would account for. Neil checks Jasper's reaction to this – is it one of their acts, or can Jez really not hold his drink?

'If I can,' Jez continues, slurring heavily, 'then the three of us get a free drink, what do you say?'

'Sounds like you couldn't even balance on your own two feet,' calls another of the locals. Jez has got the attention of the place.

'Ah, give the lads a drink each if he can do it,' says the man with the red setter.

There's a general hum of interest, and the landlord stands, undecided.

'I'll tell you what, let's increase the bet,' Jez says. 'You have rooms, right? Well, we want to stay the night, so if I can do it we get breakfast for free – all three of us?' Jez is clearly working the place, challenging the landlord on his home turf.

'Who thinks he can do it?' the landlord asks those assembled. There's much laughter and noise now – the regulars appear to be loving this diversion.

'Not a chance!' one calls out.

'It won't count if you just lay the cloth on your face,' says another.

'No, I'll balance it,' Jez assures him.

'I'll lay a quid you can't do it,' a stout man with a red face joins in.

'That's fair,' the landlord says, looking relieved. 'Put your money where your mouth is. I'll run a book, and you can take bets to cover the price of your breakfast.'

'Okay, who's a taker then?' Jez turns to face the room.

The locals seem keen for the entertainment, and it's not long before a stack of pound coins is piled up on the bar. Jasper fishes in his own pocket to match the bets, and the landlord checks that the amounts match up, noting which of the regulars has placed a bet. Neil watches the boys closely. Jasper appears calm and Neil begins to suspect that this is something they have done before. When all the bets have been laid, the landlord announces that the book is closed and a hush falls over the pub.

'Right, here you are, then,' the landlord says, holding the tea towel up in the air for all to see, before presenting it to Jez. 'And,' he continues, laughing, 'it's my opinion that our cider is more than a match for you and has fuddled your brain.' He looks around at the men, who have now gathered round the table, and they nod in agreement. 'So I'll add a bet of my own. A bed for the night if you win, and you clear up the place if you lose. That means wiping down all the tables, all the glasses in the dishwasher, mop the floor, dry the glasses and …' He pauses for effect. 'Tomorrow morning you help out in the kitchen with breakfast. Is it a deal?' He sounds confident now, backed up by his regulars, who murmur their approval.

Jez glances at Jasper, and Neil thinks he can see concern in their eyes. Jasper shrugs his shoulders, as if to say, 'What have we got ourselves into?' The landlord folds his arms and grins.

'Not so cocky now, lad?' He laughs, and his laughter is echoed around the room.

'Er, okay,' Jez replies in a quiet voice. 'Best give me a shot of something to calm my nerves. Oh, and a freshly laundered tea towel.'

The landlord fills a shot glass, and Neil can see Jez's head tip back, the glint of light on glass and then the slam of shot glass onto the bar.

'Right, give me some room.' Jez says, inspecting the fresh tea towel that the landlord hands him. Neil can hear the ringmaster's tone in his voice, all traces of drunkenness gone. The men shuffle back, leaving a space in the centre of the room, and Jez clears the central table of glasses and dries it carefully. Then, with all the flair and showmanship he could possibly bring to such an act, he rolls the tea towel into a long sausage, drawing out the procedure, building up the tension in the room. He wipes imaginary sweat off his brow and glances nervously at Jasper, who nods encouragingly. When Jez tries to lift the tea towel sausage off the table and up to his nose the inevitable happens, and it collapses on itself.

'Bit off more than you can chew, if you ask me,' Jasper says quietly from the sidelines. Neil feels a sense of panic. Is he serious? It seems he is.

'I'll double my bet,' someone shouts out, and he slams another pound on the counter. Jasper matches it.

'Me too,' another says. Jasper quietly matches all the new bets, and the room is alive again with the buzz of voices and laughter.

'I'll make it two beds against you clearing out the backyard tomorrow,' the landlord adds.

'Done,' Jez agrees, but his voice is unsteady. The room grows quiet.

He rolls the tea towel again, slowly, carefully, but again it crumples. There are a few murmurs around the room, people cough, take a drink from their glasses; a little chattering starts.

Jez slaps his hands together and rubs them against each other hard. He has quite a presence. Once more he rolls the tea towel, and now the room is silent, as if it has been agreed without it being stated that this is his third and final attempt. This time, after he has rolled the tea towel, and before he picks it up off the table, Jez takes each end and pulls with a quick, short snapping motion. He then pushes one end and gently lifts the other, and the tea towel comes off the table stiff and rod-like. There's an intake of breath around the room. With slow and careful motions Jez lifts the tea towel so that it is vertical, and balances it on his nose, smoothly, as though he has practised it a thousand times. Carefully, slowly, he removes his hands and sure enough the tea towel is balanced on his nose. There's a moment's silence, and then the pub explodes with clapping and cheers.

Jez stays absolutely still, the tea towel straight up from the end of his nose, arms out to his sides, for thirty seconds, and then he relaxes, allows the cloth to fall, catches it, throws the cloth in the air, catches it again and bows deeply. The other drinkers applaud and slap Jez on the back. Jasper slides the mountain of coins off the bar top and into Neil's hat.

The pub is humming with admiration and excitement, but Neil watches the landlord to gauge his reaction. He has been beaten on his home ground – will he be a sore loser?

'So, a free room?' Jez asks the landlord as more people come in to the pub, presumably attracted by the laughter.

'And cheap at the price!' The landlord grins and pours him a pint ahead of the queuing customers.

Hesitant at first, one of the locals asks Jez to teach him the trick. Neil feels sure Jez will keep it a secret but is delighted when he shows first one and then another man how to snap the tea towel so that it remains rigid. The landlord hands out more tea towels and soon everyone is having a go, with varying degrees of success.

193

After much hilarity, more beers are ordered and the locals settle back into their seats and the quiet conversations are resumed.

An earnest youth steps into the pub and looks around nervously. It is obvious that this person is not here to drink. He scuttles to the bar, a box in his hand.

'S'cuse me,' he says to the landlord. 'There's a raft out there on the canal and I'm looking for the man who is on it, a Mister' – he reads the label on the box – 'a Mister Neil Pianoraft?' The landlord looks blank.

'Er, that might be me,' Neil steps forward.

'You'll have to sign for it.' The nervous courier offers his pen.

'What you got?' Jasper asks as the courier leaves.

'That journalist, Ian, asked me to give him my position every day, text what I've been doing. It's a phone and a solar charger.' Neil examines the box.

Jasper pours the money from the hat into his pockets and replaces the hat on Neil's head. Neil looks out of the window, where he can see the raft, dimly lit by the pub's lights.

'How does he do that?' Neil asks. Jez is sitting at a table with a group of locals, showing them a coin trick and laughing as if he has known them all his life.

'Some men are like peacocks,' Jasper says. 'They like the attention. And some don't. If you like it, you do the things that bring it to you, and if you don't, you do the things that keep yourself unseen. You are a ninja, my friend – you seek the shadows, search out the dim corners, keep your face from the light.'

Jasper turns to go and talk to Jez, leaving Neil to contemplate his words. In this moment, it occurs to Neil that the real reason he didn't properly check his wall space or his stand at the London exhibition was precisely *because* he suspected that it would not take the weight of his pieces. His crashing stand, the annihilation of his exhibition, ensured that the light that was focused on him faded and died before it could fully illuminate him: he had courted failure so that he could stay safely hidden.

'Oh.' The sound he manages to utter doesn't come close to expressing the feelings stirred up in him by this realisation. And, he reluctantly admits to himself, that isn't the only time he has tried to stay hidden. Did he not use Sleet's loud humour to hide behind before and during college, and his own beautiful Kimberly's shining light ever since, to ensure that he remained unnoticed? His chest feels like it is collapsing.

'You all right, you've gone very white?' Jasper asks.

195

'You think a ninja can become a butterfly?' Neil asks. He is trying to inject humour into his voice, but it feels like the most important question he has ever asked.

'Ha ha,' Jasper starts to laugh but then stops and looks thoughtful. 'Isn't there a moth that appears dark but when it spreads its wings it has a bright red underside? That could be you, couldn't it? If you spread your wings. You want another drink?'

That night, alone with the animals on the raft, guarding Kim's piano while Jez and Jasper sleep in their free beds, Neil dreams he is a moth. In the dream he is trying to fly out of the dark and up to the light, but every time he spreads his wings a bigger moth steps on the ends of them, pinning them down. In his moth brain he knows that if he could get his wings open fully the scarlet undersides would distract the other moth long enough for Neil to fly, but try as he might he cannot get his wings to open because of the big moth's feet. He knows that if he pulls too hard the big moth will tumble backward and fly no more.

Neil wakes up sweating. Bushy-Mush and Fuzzy-Pants lift their heads at the disturbance but soon settle back to sleep.

'Blimey, that was freaky,' he whispers. The mist over the water's surface glows eerily in the grey half-light of the predawn. It does not help to dispel his dreams. It is not often he remembers his dreams at all, but when he does they seem so real, so meaningful. He recalls a similar dream from a long time ago, in which he wanted to run but his coat was stuck in a door, and he couldn't open the door because he didn't have the key. He told Kimberly about it in the morning because it had upset him.

'Oh, my poor baby,' she said, and she wrapped her arms around his head. 'You will run – one day you will run, my love.'

'Yes, but why did I have such a dream?' he asked.

'We have dreams to sort stuff out, don't we … It's not me, is it? I'm not the door that stopped you running, am I?' She sounded so worried.

'No, of course not,' he was quick to answer, but he wasn't sure.

'What sort of door was it?' she asked and then he realised it was the front door of the first house he could remember living in. He remembered watching his dad paint it. It seemed to take him days and days, sanding and sanding the bright yellow paint, through to the red layer below, the colours emerging and then the paint disappearing altogether before the smell of wood filled his nostrils. Then the day of painting arrived and Dad let him help. Neil was allowed to prise the top off the new tin of paint. He could remember the excitement he felt in anticipation of the vibrant colour that would be revealed when the lid came off, and the crashing disappointment at the ugly shade of brown his father had chosen. Something beautiful was extinguished for Neil with the loss of the bright yellow door. He refused to help paint it brown, and Mum was upset at his rudeness.

'It's Dad's door,' he said, and Kimberly put her arms around him and rocked him gently.

He looks out at the pale horizon, and in that moment a sliver of sun emerges over the hill, a shard of orange slicing through the grey.

'So, is it Dad who will tumble and never fly if I spread my wings and show my true colours?' Neil arranges the stained green cushion behind his back so he can sit up in his warm bed, looking out of the window-wall at the sunrise, and takes out his sketchbook and a pencil.

'He never liked art,' he tells the blank page. 'Seemed to think it impossible, or wrong, even, to make a life from art.'

Bushy-Mush raises his head and thumps his tail on the boards.

'What if I did succeed, Dad? What would you have to say then?' He sketches the outline of The Duck Inn. 'Would you fall and never fly again?'

Bushy-Mush curls up again and goes back to sleep.

The light over the pub doorway casts misty shadows. Neil shades with his pencil, then uses his rubber, creating white forms from black. He wishes he had colours with him now, but he continues without and finishes the drawing. When he is satisfied he has captured the essence of the scene, he tucks his sketchbook away and wonders what he will do until Jez and Jasper are awake.

At the end of his mattress is the phone, still in the box. He should work out how to put it on to charge. For a moment his breathing quickens: what if he cannot work out how to use it?

'Come on, Neil, you took a hundred-year-old barge through three locks! You can figure out how to use a solar charger for a phone.'

It turns out it is as simple as plugging the charger into the phone and leaving the panel in the sun. The phone is already charged but he cannot think of anything to text Ian. This new phone is much fancier than the basic one he is used to, and it can do all manner of things – connect to the Internet and play music, and it has a touchscreen. These things do not really interest him, but the built-in camera does. The mist over the water is just beautiful, and he videos it, the vapour rising and swirling off the surface. It would be amazing to record his journey, so that when he convinces Kim that they are good together he can share it with her.

'I don't know if this has sound, Kim,' he says to the phone, 'but if it does I just wanted to say that this is for you. I wish you were here with me, on this amazing adventure. It would be so much better if you

were here to share it with me. I miss you so much.'
He clicks the video off when his voice starts to waver.

Chapter 16

Breakfast at the pub is a hearty affair and the landlord seems glad of their company. He chats to Jez, asking where he learnt his skills. Jez is vague in his replies. It seems he just picked up a bit here and there, and Neil thinks of Pat and his lute playing at school. Presumably, with enough hard work and practice, it's possible to do anything you put your mind to. But surely some things, like being a brain surgeon, would require his entire life to learn. So by the time he was capable, he would be dead, or his hands would shake too much. And with some things, like playing basketball, for example, there are physical limitations. But even there – wasn't there a little guy with the Harlem Globetrotters, who was only five feet two or something, with a strange name – something like Too Tall?

'You still dreaming?' The landlord nudges him. 'I said do you want more coffee?'

'Oh, yes, thank you,' Neil says.

After a moment's silence, he ventures, 'Jez?', and then he feels shy and wishes he hadn't.

'Yeah, buddy?' says Jez through a mouthful of bacon, and Neil feels himself go red. All eyes are on him now, and it seems easier to finish.

'Can you teach me to juggle?'

'Sure,' Jez replies and casually butters more toast. After breakfast, Jasper clears the table and tidies the kitchen. With a little stab of guilt, Neil thinks of all the times he left the kitchen in a mess when he lived with Kim. Then Jasper offers to help clean the backyard of the pub.

'But you won your bet!' the landlord says as Jez stands by Jasper, his sleeves rolled up.

'Ah, but we had no idea your beds were going to be that comfortable,' Jez teases.

'Well, the truth is, just a few barrels need moving and that sort of thing.'

'Come on, then.' Jez heads for the door.

They have the yard clear and tidy within half an hour and go inside to wash their hands.

Jasper dries his hands down the front of his jeans and then fumbles about in his jacket pocket and pulls out three chiffon handkerchiefs.

Without a word, he begins to juggle them. They move slowly through the air, floating rather than falling, and he has all the time in the world to catch them. Neil watches closely. Jasper makes it look so easy.

'There you go.' Jasper stops and hands the three scarves to Neil. He starts confidently, but one scarf flutters to the floor. He tries again, more hesitantly this time, but it's not much better.

'Right.' The landlord goes to the fridge. 'Sandwiches for three and some bits for the dog.' He takes foil-wrapped parcels out and hands them around.

'Cheers.' Jez takes the packages. Neil admires the ease with which Jez seems to live his life, give and take, no fuss.

They draw straws to decide who will be first to tow the raft, and Jez draws the short straw.

Neil stands next to the piano, opposite Jasper, and he practises with the chiffon scarves as Jez pulls. He almost has it when one falls into the water. He is quick to retrieve it, but now it is waterlogged he can no longer practise. He spreads it out on the piano stool to dry.

'Ah well.' Jasper says. 'You can try with beanbags when we stop.'

The canal winds its way through open countryside, and they have taken two turns each in towing the raft before finally there are signs of civilisation – the familiar clipped hedges by the side of the towpath, and then canal boats moored to the bank, before houses appear by the side of the canal.

'About another hour, I reckon,' Neil says, 'and we'll be in the town.'

'Fancy putting on a show when we get there?' Jez asks Jasper.

'We don't need to.' Jasper jangles his bulging pockets and points to the foil-wrapped sandwiches on the piano top.

'We could take a break, get a coffee.'

The town looms closer. There appears to be a school with railings almost up to the water's edge. It's lunchtime and there are children running and screeching in the playground, hair and coats flying behind them. When they spot the raft, first one and then the others stop their games to stare and wave, pressing themselves up against the railings.

'Surely they see boats every day?' Jasper says.

The teacher on duty, coffee cup in hand, comes over to see what's going on, and waves too.

'Just friendly, then,' Jez says. 'Maybe it's a game they play.'

'Play us a tune,' one of the bigger children shouts as they draw closer, and Jasper is quick to oblige, turning nursery rhymes into tunes that remind Neil of *Tom and Jerry* cartoons; he can almost picture the cat chasing the mouse. The smaller children jump up and down with excitement and shriek when he stops.

Jez, who is towing the raft at this point, smiles but continues his pace, keeping close to the water's edge to avoid the dog walkers and joggers who are also using the path. Most wish him a cheerful 'Hello' and smile as if they are old friends. A man jogging on the other side calls a cheery 'Morning!' to them all.

'Is this town just a little bit odd or is it me?' he asks Jasper.

Jez seems as bemused as he is. 'If it's not odd then it's the friendliest town I've ever been in!'

A couple lean over the edge of an old stone bridge and wave as the raft passes under it.

'Very friendly,' Jasper says through his teeth as he puts on a smile.

Ahead are a series of large low buildings, set back a little from the water, facing each other. There are parking spaces between the shops, and in one of these, as close as it is possible to get to the canal, is a large van with blacked-out windows. There's something serious – official, perhaps – about the van, and about the group of people standing in front of it, all looking in the direction of the raft. A man in an oversized padded jacket balances something on his shoulder, and as they draw nearer they see it is a camera.

'Neil?' the man next to the cameraman calls out. He is holding a large fluffy microphone. Jasper points at Neil.

'This might be an opportunity to open your wings,' he whispers.

Neil swallows. 'I'm Neil.' His voice sounds croaky.

'Alan Parkins, Midland Radio,' the man announces, holding the microphone out as far as he can over the water.

A woman in a pink suit bustles forward.

'West Midlands Television,' she says. Her microphone has a pink fluffy top and the cameraman shuffles forward to stand by her side, panning along the length of the raft.

'Neil, is the art piece a protest?' asks the man from Midland Radio.

'Is it a proclamation of love?' the woman in pink gushes.

Another man separates himself from the group and starts to take pictures, snapping here and there, focusing his long lens by zooming in and out. Jez has stopped towing the raft now and stands to one side as the throng of reporters and photographers push forward onto the towpath, trying to get as close as possible.

'Can I come on?' the pink woman asks, and without waiting for a reply she tries to step over. Bushy-Mush yaps furiously, and she steps back onto the shore, looking a little flustered.

'Best you go ashore,' Jasper says quietly to Neil. 'Make up a load of nonsense for them, keep them happy.' He nudges Neil's elbow. It's not a push exactly, but it's the encouragement Neil needs, and he steps across onto dry land.

The reporters gather round to take his photo, and passers-by stop to look, curious. Slowly the little crowd of people on the towpath grows, to the point where they are blocking the way.

'So, Neil,' the pink-suited woman purrs into her fluffy-topped microphone, 'we all saw the photos and read the piece in the *Rolby Evening Press*. What the people want to know is' – she refers to her notes, shuffling the pages – 'does Kimberly Holliday know that you are on this quest to declare your love to her?'

'Er, well, no,' Neil says. 'I mean, I tried to call her, but – well, it went to voicemail.' He looks back nervously, to the safety of the raft. Jasper's elbows are tucked into his sides and he flaps with his forearms, mouthing the word 'fly'.

'So she has no idea that you are making this gesture? How do you see that working out?' the television presenter asks.

'Is the raft a protest against modern life?' The man with the grey fluffy microphone jostles the television woman. Neil feels more comfortable with this question than the one about Kim, but either way no answer forms itself. What would Jasper say, or Sleet? That's it – he should pretend he is Sleet. *If I were Sleet, what would I say?*

'The raft is about the natural way of things,' he starts, not quite sure where he is going with this. 'About turning away from the modern world.' Neil tries the words out to see if there is any ring of truth about them, if they even make sense. The reporters look at him earnestly, and one or two note down his words. Several mobile phones are held out to him. They seem to be taking his reply seriously, and this gives Neil a sense of confidence.

'And the piano?' the man presses.

'The piano is – er, the melody of our lives that we take with us wherever we go.' Sleet would be proud of that reply! 'To show we need no modern appliances, no electricity to keep the music in our hearts playing.' Neil can feel somehow that he is on the right lines now, that this is the right sort of response, and he stands a little taller, and grins.

Jasper has folded his arms and there is a big grin across his face too. Jez gives him the thumbs up.

'And the girl – Miss Holliday?' the woman in the pink suit asks, looking down at her clipboard again. 'What is her connection to the art piece?'

'Well …' Neil momentarily loses his momentum. Questions about Kim seem to throw him off guard. He takes his time to consider. 'The truth is that, without Kim, none of it makes sense. Not the raft, or her piano, and the melodies of our lives can be discordant and tuneless without …'

He hesitates and he can feel the heat rise from his neck. 'Without love,' he finishes quietly, looking at the ground. This has become too personal, and he feels off balance again.

'So it is her piano?' the man from the radio asks.

Neil looks up again. 'Yes, I'm delivering it.'

'It says here you are taking twenty-five years to do this,' Miss Pink Fluffy-Mic says, reading from a newspaper cutting on her clipboard. 'Do you think Kim might be a bit tired of waiting by the time you arrive?' She smirks as she says this, and winks at the camera.

'Is there a time limit on the love in your life?' Neil retorts, and her cheeks turn a bright red that clashes with the pink of her suit. She turns to camera with a forced smile.

'And that's all from me, Chrissa, reporting on the Pianoraft and the love story of Neil and Kim. Now back to the studio.' She doesn't say anything else to Neil but she looks daggers at him as she storms off back to the black van, mouthing something to herself.

The reporter from the radio chortles and steps into the space she has left.

'Is there any meaning in the drawers, do they open?' he asks, inspecting the raft.

'I, er, well …' Neil's mind is cast back to school, a trip to the British Museum where he was mesmerised by the icon gallery, the painted faces and the gold backgrounds. Bill's hut had the same atmosphere as the icon room, almost as though the hut itself was a three-dimensional icon dedicated to all the different people in Bill's life! Drawing this parallel makes Neil feel he better understands Bill and what he was trying to do.

He takes a deep breath and looks the reporter in the eye. 'An art piece can mean different things to different people, don't you agree? We each take from a work what we need at the time, and it can be healing – cathartic – to one person, or energising and confrontational to another. It doesn't really matter what I have to say about the Pianoraft. It's how you interpret it that gives it meaning.'

He takes a breath, and is half surprised to find that he has more to say. 'Mixed into this piece is my commitment to Kimberly, and I'm taking the piano to her to make her happy. In the process I have cut free of all ties to make this journey, and my craft, my vessel, is made up of discarded pieces of other people's lives.'

Now it is his turn to look at the raft. 'What did those drawers once hold? Love letters? Socks? Bills? We fill our drawers with items that are of great importance. I mean, where would we be without socks?'

This raises a titter from the crowd.

'And yet we discard them with such ease. Maybe if we thought about things more. Maybe if the things we did in life took more effort–'

'Like going to London on a raft?' The man asks.

Neil does not stop to answer, instead concluding '–we would be more grateful for all that we have, and not give it up too easily.'

'So you're saying that what is unwanted by one man could be the saving of another?' the man asks.

'If that is what it means to you.'

'Can I have your autograph?' A boy who might be seven or eight holds out a pen and a sheet of paper, his mother's hand on his shoulder.

This catches Neil off guard. The mother all but rolls her eyes at him.

'Oh, yes, sure – sorry, mate. What's your name?'

'Tom. Well, I want to be Tom, but everyone calls me Tommy.' He has a slight lisp.

Neil speaks as he writes. 'To Tom, may you find your own raft to float away on, love Neil.'

It seems to take ages to get away from the spot, but eventually they are saved by the arrival of a pleasure boat with a banner down its side offering thirty-minute rides. The man on board declares, loudly, that he is a local tour guide, and he tries to attract the attention of the television crew.

'Midland Cruises, thirty minutes to feed the ducks, see the sights and listen to the history of the local landscape.'

It is a well-rehearsed patter. He turns to Jez and says more quietly, 'I read about this thing in the paper. I'm going down the canal a few miles to do some maintenance. You want a tow?'

Jez, Jasper and Neil agree to press on, and they accept the offer of a tow. Neil cannot be sure, but it seems like the current might be against them on this section, and this makes the offer that much more welcome. Mostly though it will be useful to have a little time alone to reassess their situation. Even Jez seems thrown by the ongoing attention on the banks of the town.

The cruise boat is a long, motor-driven vessel and the helm is at the front, so once they get going there is no way to talk to the man.

'Well, when I said you should fly,' Jasper says to Neil, 'I didn't expect you to turn into Icarus!' Jasper sits on the piano stool, Neil stands to use the makeshift rudder and Jez sits on the floor, legs stretched out, ankles crossed, slouching back on his hands.

'Oh, did I make a mess of it?' Neil shifts his weight from foot to foot.

'No, mate, but if you keep this up you'll be on the front page of *The Sun* before you know it!' Jasper cackles at his own joke.

'Well, it won't do us any harm if he does appear in a national paper,' Jez says, and he waves back at a group of people on a metal footbridge that passes over their heads.

The buildings begin to thin out and the land either side of the canal gives way to fields again, and they watch the water pass, and the swallows wheel and dive to drink from the canal's surface, each lost in his own thoughts.

Chapter 17

When the revs of the cruise boat suddenly drop and the raft's speed through the water starts to slow, Neil feels slightly disappointed. It has been a relief to be sitting on deck, watching the water flow past, not having to worry about whose turn it was to tow and not being bothered by the crowds of reporters.

The cruise boat slides neatly up to the bank in front of a wooden hut with a hand-painted sign declaring *Midland Cruises*. Here, the towpath has been boarded over with bare wooden boards. A pile of fenders are heaped next to the hut, along with a rusting engine and a single wooden chair. Although the day is bright, the place seems grey, waterlogged. The cruise boat captain unties the tow rope, coils it neatly and passes it across to Jasper.

'All the best,' he says, and he gives a sloppy salute as Jasper pushes the raft away to the side to catch the drifting current, and they slowly inch past the boat. The man walks up the inside of his boat, keeping pace with them.

'Say hello to Kim for me,' he says as he reaches the bows, and touches another limp hand to his forehead.

There are fields either side, and the canal curves away in the distance, an idyllic panorama before them. They all seem happy just to drift and Neil is glad of the slower pace, which gives him the time to turn over recent events in his mind. Idly, he speculates on what, if anything, will come of today's media interest. A paragraph in the paper, perhaps, buried near the end, before the sports pages? Mum might cut it out, and Dad will splutter and snort about how their son is wasting his life. A spasm grips his stomach. Maybe Dad has a point. Would Kim be more impressed with him if he just got a job? But where? – in London? She might take it the wrong way and feel he is stalking her. He chuckles to himself quietly, playing out in his mind a brief fantasy of stalking Kim through the streets of London, and the picture in his head turns into a board game, with Kim always two squares ahead … What was he thinking before that? Oh yes – if he got a job back home, how would that help? How would she even know? It was more pleasant thinking about chasing her through the streets, Kim screaming with laughter, looking back, encouraging him, hiding in doorways, jumping out on him and then running away.

A group of coots come to investigate the raft. Bushy-Mush wags his tail, sniffing in their general direction and standing right on the edge of the raft.

'So, Neil' – it's Jez who finally breaks the silence – 'you'll be on local telly tonight.'

They fall silent again, absorbing this thought.

'Yes,' Jasper says lazily, 'you flew a little there, my friend.'

'I had no idea what to say.' Neil can feel the heat in his neck rising again. 'I just talked a lot of nonsense.'

'You were just finding your stride,' Jasper encourages.

'It'll sell a few newspapers anyway,' says Jez. 'Your fifteen minutes of fame! Andy Warhol, I think ...'

Silence again. Neil watches the coots, trying to avoid thinking about the press. Jasper lies on his back, gazing up at the clouds, and Jez closes his eyes. Neil focuses on the sound of the birds in the hedgerows. He takes out the phone and shoots a quick video of a small bird on a branch, possibly a wren, and then pans down to the coots in the water. It is the sounds he is trying to capture, but just at that moment something smallish bobs downstream and he pans towards it, and as it comes closer he identifies it as a wellington boot, part filled with water, floating upright.

'Look, Kim,' he says quietly, near to the phone. 'Coots with boots. But listen. Can you hear it?' He lifts the phone a little higher. 'The sounds of nature, the endless song that is played all around us if we listen.'

'I think I'll pull for a bit,' Jasper says, and he jumps ashore with the tow rope. Neil decides to video this, too, watching Jasper's back as he strains against the rope, building up the raft's momentum. Jez is now snoring quietly, Bushy-Mush by his side, and there, scratching at the door of the cabin, is Fuzzy-Pants. Jez opens the door for the tiny cat, and she steps out tentatively. Neil clicks on his phone again to capture her nervous exploration of the raft, the terror of seeing the coots so close, her interest in the tow rope as it slackens and dips in the water and then tightens, water pinging off its surface, each time Jasper takes a step. Clumps of weeds float past now and again and Fuzzy-Pants watches these with mistrust. Eventually, when she has toured the circumference of the raft twice, she comes up to Neil, purring and rubbing her cheeks against his foot.

Neil clicks off the phone and leaves it to charge on top of the piano. Stooping, he picks up the kitten and pushes her nose into his face, her soft fur against his skin like silk. 'You're going to love this little creature, Kim,' he whispers, letting the breeze take his words. Out of the blue, his stomach twists. What if she has moved on, found someone else? But then, it has not been so long, a week at the most – or maybe a little longer, but not long enough for her to have moved on, surely? The thought is beyond what he can bear, and he tries to direct his thoughts elsewhere. He takes over from Jasper so he can concentrate on the physical effort of pulling the raft.

Jez relieves him of duty a few miles down the path. Ahead, there is nothing but countryside as far as they can see and the day is passing.

'We need to find somewhere to stay tonight,' Jez says, and they all agree to take another turn pulling. They finish off the foil-wrapped sandwiches, which barely seem to touch the sides, and Jez points out what they are all thinking – that, as well as a bed for the night, they need to find somewhere they can get a substantial meal.

But night begins to fall before any signs of civilisation have been spotted, and there's nothing for it but to spend the night on board the raft. The rocking chair is expelled from the cabin and the double mattress is unfolded and allowed to fill the internal space. The three of them fight for space.

Neil wakes up looking at the nose of a stranger. The nose is long and defined, with a soft fuzz above the thin upper lips, and the closed eyes have almost reddish-blonde eyelashes.

He scrabbles backward in shock, and immediately bumps up against a heavy object that groans at him.

'What the heck?' he hisses, and the memory of last night slowly returns.

Jasper and Jez are still fast asleep. Neil is tempted to let his head sink back into the jumper he is using as a pillow, but then Bushy-Mush starts scratching at the door. Careful not to wake the others, Neil untangles himself from his sleeping bag and yawns, stretching, his hands hitting the walls of the tiny cabin. Outside, eyes still half-shut, he stretches properly, easing the knots out of the muscles in his back. It was dark when they tied up last night, and as he opens his eyes Neil looks around to see just where they are. The sight that greets him is the last thing he expected, and he stumbles back in surprise.

'What the ...' He trips up as he steps back into the cabin, falls on his backside, rolls over and pushes the door shut with his foot.

'Guys!' he hisses at the two sleeping men. Fuzzy-Pants is curled up on Jasper's head, like a furry hat. 'Guys!' he says with more urgency, but neither of them moves.

On hands and knees he opens the door a crack and peeks out. They are still there, and they look up as his head appears, cameras trained on the raft.

'Neil?' one calls, but Neil closes the door firmly again. Bushy-Mush scratches to come in and he opens the door again for a moment.

'Neil? Can we just have a quick word?' It's a different voice from the first one, softer. Neil leaves the door open just a crack and peers out.

There are three TV cameras out there, but not handheld ones like yesterday: these are on stands and look like they mean business. There are also several men with microphones, and behind them are a throng of photographers, some on stepladders. It is the most bizarre sight he has ever seen, and it looks so out of place on the grassy bank, with nothing but trees and fields either side.

'Neil?' the soft voice continues. 'I've got you some coffee here.'

The man with the soft voice turns and snaps his fingers at a girl who hastily passes him a cardboard cup, which he holds out towards the raft like an offering. Neil wishes Kimberly was here, and with this thought he takes out his phone and films the reporters, opening the door a little further for a better shot.

Several voices call out his name and he pans across the group.

'Neil.' The soft-spoken man leans forward and puts the coffee on the edge of the raft.

'Are we the art now?' He smiles and there is humour in his voice but the question sounds serious. 'Is there an overall motivation for your art,' he continues, 'or do you work with individual inspirations?'

Neil takes the coffee and retreats into the cabin.

With his back to the wall, knees pulled up to his chest, he sips the hot brew.

'What was that noise?' Jez stirs.

'There's a bloody army of press out there.'

'Really?' Jez is suddenly awake, sitting up.

'Television cameras, newspapers, radio, the whole lot.'

'Hey, Jasper. Wake up. It's show time.' Jez nudges Jasper, who protests and rolls over, then slowly surfaces.

Chapter 18

'Are you going to perform for them?' Neil asks, his mouth hanging open. He would love to have as much nerve.

'You don't mind, do you?' says Jez, frowning slightly. 'I mean, I realise they're here to film the raft but, hey, I don't see you desperate to hog the limelight so I thought we may as well promote the act. It will get us more work if we can say we've been on national telly.'

'Be my guest.' Neil exhales his tension. 'I'd much rather they were looking at you than me.'

'I thought you were going to spread your wings?' Jasper says, yawning.

'Not that bloody wide!'

Jasper tuts and then smiles, shaking his head. Jez hands him the blonde wig, which Neil finds amusing because Kimberly is dark-haired. He is curious to see how they will perform the act for the press. Maybe they will juggle with the microphones; after all, taking things from the crowd is part of the act.

The reporters seem to know Jasper's name and someone calls Jez 'Jeremy' but he does not respond. The cameras film the performance, and they juggle microphones and clipboards, and at the end both Jez and Jasper give interviews with ease and confidence. But when they have finished, the cameras do not roll away, and the attention is focused on Neil again. He backs away a step.

'Is it true that Saatchi & Saatchi are interested in the piece?' one of the reporters asks.

'Where on earth did you hear that?' Neil asks, disguising his surprise with a laugh.

'It was posted on the Pianoraft Facebook page.'

'What the ...' Neil begins.

'Are all the artworks displayed on your social media pages recent works?' asks a woman with her hair tied back in an unforgiving bun.

'My artwork?' Neil says, and then narrows his eyes. There is only one person who has access to his portfolio – Sleet!

'So are you saying that Saatchi & Saatchi have *not* made you an offer?' The first man presses for an answer.

Neil wonders if he should be angry at Sleet but he finds himself smiling. He puts his hand to his mouth to suppress a laugh, then rubs at his chin to cover this action.

'I wouldn't know,' he says finally. 'I leave all that stuff to my manager.' Sleet will be amused if they refer to him as Neil's manager. He should mention his name. 'My manager, Sleet. Er ... Mr Sleet.'

Jez catches his eye, looking quizzical. Jasper stares at his feet, arms crossed, hiding a smirk.

'Will there be pop-up exhibitions of your work en route?' the woman with the bun asks.

'Like I said, best ask Mr Sleet.' Neil is beginning to enjoy himself now.

'Can you stand a little to your left so I can get a shot of you with the piano, please?'

Neil obliges and ten or so flashes blind him. He blinks.

When they finally cast off, the press follow them for a while, but soon, one by one, they fall away, and at last the raft is alone again with nothing but open countryside and the sound of their growling bellies. No discussion is required when they finally spot a pub in the distance on the edge of the waterway. As they tie up, Neil half wonders what sort of a reception they will receive, but to his relief no one even looks at them. Well, almost no one. The landlord's wife steps behind the bar and, with her back to the counter, she nudges her husband and points to something in a folded newspaper she is holding, and then they turn in unison, trying, but failing, to look natural.

That evening they stop at another pub, which provides food and beds. Jez and Jasper encourage Neil to take a room too, but he knows he will only spend the night worrying about the raft, the animals, and Kim's piano.

The next day starts cloudy and grey and drizzling and no one wants to pull the raft. As they linger over their toast and coffee, Neil watches a man tie up a small pleasure cruiser. He strides into the pub and straight up to their table.

'Morning!' he says in a jolly voice. 'Saw you on the telly last night. The missus says she wants a piano delivering to her now!' He laughs. 'I did a bit of juggling back in the day. Nothing serious, just for fun. Anyway, I thought I'd do a spot of fishing today and the missus said to give you a tow if I were to see you, and seeing you I am, so, well – you want a tow?'

The cruiser is only small and the engine is very noisy, but the boys are all grateful for the tow. The captain of the cruiser seems to be happy to take them as far as the next town.

'I'll leave you here, then, if that's okay?' he says, almost apologetic.

'We appreciate it, thanks,' Neil says, and the man waves and grins and manoeuvres his boat around to return the way he came.

'We could do with a few more like him, save us having to pull.' Jez watches the noisy boat disappear.

The sun breaks through at last, and Neil pulls off his extra jumpers. It wasn't exactly cold last night on the raft but then again he did have on four layers of clothing. It makes sense to collect wood along the way for the little pot-bellied stove that Cyril and Bill installed.

'Good idea,' says Jasper when Neil suggests it, and he scans the banks on either side. There are a few straggly bushes but no trees, no fallen branches.

'Hey, guys!' Jez is at the front of the raft. 'The heavens must have heard me. Here comes another one.'

Neil and Jasper pop their heads around the side of the cabin, and sure enough, another small pleasure cruiser is heading towards them. The couple on board are waving excitedly.

'Hey, hey, hey!' the man calls as the boat draws nearer. He seems very excited. 'Saw you on the telly last night.'

He cuts the engine. The raft bobs with the boat's wake and Neil makes a grab for his phone, which is charging on top of the piano again, and puts it into his pocket before it meets a watery end.

'Carol here said you'd be hungry,' the man says, and Carol waves and grins and holds up a Pyrex dish covered with foil. 'Lucky blighters, it's her shepherd's pie!' The man laughs.

'Dennis,' Carol says, 'pass it across. Do you have any forks, boys?'

Dennis hands over the dish, which is still warm, almost too hot for Neil's cold fingers.

'Forks,' Carol says and looks Neil in the eyes.

'This is very kind of you,' he says, taking the cutlery.

'My son's an artist.' She says this as if she is sharing a secret and sniffs, and Neil sees the rims under her eyes glisten.

'He is, that!' Dennis exclaims and his chest puffs out but quickly deflates. 'Working in Hong Kong. Very famous out there, we hear.'

'Yes,' Carol agrees. 'But we do miss him.' She sighs.

'Ah, sons – temperamental things, sons, but they always love their mothers.' Jez winks at Carol.

'This smells good.' Neil peels the foil off the top of the dish.

'Yes, well, you boys tuck in and we'll give you a tow down the way a bit. We only live at the next town but every bit counts, right? We cannot have the lovely Kimberly waiting twenty-five years.' Dennis winks at Carol now. 'Oh, and give them the paper, love,' he adds.

'They've probably seen it.' Colour comes to her cheeks.

'How would they have seen it out here? Have you seen the paper today?'

When the boys shake their heads, Carol seems delighted and hands across not one but two papers.

'Right, we should get underway,' Dennis declares.

Carol and Dennis sit arm in arm at the helm of their little motor boat in matching green waterproofs, talking quietly to themselves; there is a little laugher once in a while from Carol, a little squeeze round her shoulders from Dennis.

Jez, Jasper and Neil gather round the dish on the floor, sitting cross-legged with a fork each. Bushy-Mush sticks his nose in the dish, and Neil shoves him away and gives him a portion. Fuzzy-Pants mews until she is let out of the cabin, and she shares with Bushy-Mush. The mashed potatoes on top of the dish have been fluffed into peaks that are browned to crispy perfection. A little melted butter has been drizzled over the top. The rich smells of garlic and stock set saliva running in Neil's mouth and without hesitation they attack the dish until there is nothing left. Bushy-Mush and Fuzzy-Pants lick the dish clean.

'God, that was good.' Jez lies back and looks up at the sky, which has mostly cleared now, the white fluffy clouds banished to the horizon.

'Could do with a coffee now,' Jasper says.

'Hey.' Jasper pulls one of the newspapers from under the empty dish. 'It says here that there is a Facebook page for the Pianoraft and someone called Mr Sleet has set up a donations fund to keep you going. That's the guy you mentioned to the press yesterday, isn't it? I thought you had just made him up! So who is he, this Mr Sleet?'

Neil laughs out loud.

'We've been mates since art college,' he explains. 'This whole thing is right up his street. He loves to make up stories, wind people up.'

'So will he sting you, then? Will he pocket the money?' Jez asks.

'Doubt it.'

Neil has never considered whether Sleet is trustworthy before. Sure, when all they had to worry about was a fiver between them, it was never in question. There was a time when Sleet's dad owed him a day's pay, and it was given to Sleet to give to him, and Sleet bought a six-pack of beer with some of it on his way over. They drank the beers, Sleet gave him the remainder of the money, and, if memory serves, didn't he pay back the amount he had spent on the beers the next day? Yes, he stood the price of fish and chips for them both the next day to make it even.

'Nah, he'll stash it away somewhere.' The thought is an uncomfortable one; he doesn't want other people's money. 'What does it say?'

Jasper shakes the paper flat and folds the page over.

'Blah, blah blah … ah, here we go …' He reads aloud.

The artist travelling to London on a raft, known only as Neil, revealed to us yesterday the name of his manager, and we caught up with this Mr Sleet at his home in Greater Lotherton. Mr Sleet told us, 'The journey on the raft is a process that will turn an ordinary piano into a unique artistic statement. The trials and hardships of the journey will be etched into the patina that is becoming imprinted into the very essence of the instrument.' He also claims, 'The resonance of the timbre will echo this exacting undertaking and all who hear the piano played will be able to relate to it as its very sound will mirror the hardship that is life's tortured path.'

Jasper pauses and lifts his chin, looking down his nose, attempting to look cool – or what he thinks of as cool – and as he reads on he adopts an accent that might possibly pass for American.

It is a performance piece, and only if the Pianoraft makes it to London can it fulfil its nature. This journey of tribulation reflects all our lives, our trials and relationships, the storms we endure, and the calm waters too. Mr Sleet is promising that anyone who contributes, no matter how small their contribution, will have their name etched into the side of the Pianoraft to mark their own personal journey.

Jasper pauses. 'I think I like this Sleet friend of yours, he sounds like he's swallowed a dictionary.'

Jez is looking at the other paper. 'You and me get a mention here,' he says to Jasper. 'I wish we could have added our contact details.'

'If anyone wants to find us it's not hard,' Jasper says, still skimming the paper. He laughs, 'Listen to this. This is Sleet who is talking, clever toad …'

The Pianoraft is an important piece of social history. That an artist would make such an epic journey to highlight how one can make one's point in a peaceful way, in these modern times when our televisions and our collective focus seem to be permanently tuned into war and terrorism, must be chronicled in our art history journals. It is therefore completely reasonable that Saatchi & Saatchi would show an interest.

Jasper rolls onto his back, laughing. Jez has put his paper down to take the one Jasper was reading from so he can read it for himself.

'Cleverly said, eh?' Jasper sits up again. 'He never states that Saachti & Saachti have actually approached him, or you, or whoever, but he makes it sound like they have. Oh' – Jasper's hand covers his mouth – 'unless they have!' He looks wide-eyed at Neil.

'Nah.' Neil dismisses the idea, and then pauses before shaking his head. 'Nah, they would have come to the raft like the press did if they had. It's just Sleet being Sleet!'

'Hey, listen to this. This is the *Daily Post*.' It's Jez's turn to read.

The Pianoraft Facebook page has been inundated with posts from women all wanting the piano to be delivered to them. This journey of Kimberly's piano on a raft being pulled from one end of the country to the other by her lover is an act of devotion that has not been seen since DiMaggio's flowers for Marilyn Monroe or King Edward's abdication for Wallis Simpson. It has captivated the hearts of young and old alike.

Jasper and Neil both laugh at this.

'Excellent.' Jasper gets the word out between chortles.

Neil shakes his head at Sleet's mischief. Jez is chuckling away to himself as he scans the paper for more comments.

'And here is *The Star*'s piece, entitled "Barmy Boat Boy's Kim Canal Crusade" …'

Not since Tracy Emin's Bed has the wool been so firmly pulled over Britain's eyes! In a case of the emperor's new clothing, a hodgepodge of wood strapped together with string is polluting our historic waterways on a doomed trip from the North to the capital in the name of art.

All three of them burst into laughter in unison.

Carol has turned around to see what is amusing them. What must they look like – three madmen on a raft! And with this thought Neil remembers how Jez and Jasper had seemed to him when he first met them. They came across as elite beings who had never had to struggle in life, possessors of self-worth and self-belief who did well wherever they were and whatever they were doing.

Men of courage and high expectation. People who lived life lightly – and now, here he is, laughing with them. He laughs even harder.

Chapter 19

Carol's and Dennis's village is a picturesque little place, with the canal snaking through a quintessential landscape of rolling hills and fields, weeping willows on either bank, their long sinuous branches trailing in the water. Swans glide gracefully ahead of the boat, and on this sunny afternoon there are plenty of dog walkers on the towpath, and families enjoying a day out.

There's a pretty stone bridge over the canal and the inevitable country pub. Just past the pub is a small landing stage to which two or three boats are moored, and Dennis steers towards this.

A couple on one of the boats look up and wave as they approach.

Carol waves back. 'Hello Jean, Bert!'

'Ahoy, Carol, kettle's just boiled,' Jean calls, and she disappears from view into the cabin. She returns after a minute or two with a tray of mugs and a pot of coffee. Dennis pulls in behind them, and mugs are handed out and names passed round, and Neil gets the impression that this is no chance meeting.

'Jean has a son too,' Carol says. 'David.'

'Ah, David.' Dennis says and shakes his head. Neil feels uneasy – not another artist son, surely?

'David is not an artist like our Stephen,' Carol says, and looks at Jean as if it is her turn to speak.

'His wife recently left him,' Jean says hurriedly, and her cheeks flush red. She looks at Neil directly with what he can only describe as hope in her eyes, as if there were something he could do about her son's plight.

'Jean was round at ours when we saw the Pianoraft on the news,' Carol says.

'Your gesture to your girl.' Jean sounds very breathy as she speaks. 'It gave me such hope – hope that maybe David can do something to make amends to his wife, for the children's sake if nothing else!'

Bert is silent on the matter, looking earnestly into his coffee. Neil casts a sideways glance at Jasper, but Jasper looks at the ground; he is making eye contact with no one. Jez is contemplating the sky. Neil slows down his drinking to make his coffee last.

'Well, that was a good cup of Java.' Dennis breaks the silence. 'Thank you, Jean, and here is your prize.' And he hands over the tow rope to the raft.

The pleasantries and accompanying laughter are tight and uncomfortable. Coffee mugs are handed back, fond farewells are exchanged by Jean and

Carol, and Dennis gives Bert's boat a shove away from the shore with his foot.

Jean and Bert take them quite a distance with no conversation or demands and then wish them a blessed onward journey and leave them to drift.

As they motor away, Neil allows the ensuing quiet to envelop him, and he revels in the slower rhythm. What on earth had Carol and Dennis and Jean and Bert thought he could do about their sons? Presumably he was just standing in for Carol's son. Maybe doing something for Neil was as close as she could get to caring for her Stephen ... But Jean? She had looked at him as if he had answers to her son's situation. That was creepy – stressful, even. It reminded him of a time when his parents had friends round for dinner, a married couple, and he got stuck washing up with the woman. That had been so awkward. She asked him about how men think and whether he thought her husband still loved her. He waffled somewhat, but then she asked him directly, 'What would keep you faithful in a marriage?' So embarrassing. What does he know about marriage?

A picture of Kim in a white dress flashes though his mind. She runs to him, jumps, her legs wrapping around his waist, her hands around his neck, her head thrown back, and he spins her around to make her laugh.

Bushy-Mush licks his face, waking him from his daydream, but he is still not ready to do any more than drift. He needs time to process the interest the raft is generating and the focus this is putting on him. Also, since when have people started being so kind? It is quite unsettling to have to recalibrate his view of the world so fundamentally. Jez and Jasper are also sitting in silence; maybe they are having similar thoughts, as they all seem to be content with the slow motion and the silence.

Drifting at this slow speed, with no engine noise, causing no disturbance, they almost become a part of the landscape. Birds swoop past unafraid, and Neil spots a water rat on the bank. Cows lazily chew their cud in one field, and in the next, sheep pluck at the grass. Clouds form and disappear as the sun grows stronger. Neil is down to just his T-shirt and jeans. In the distance, the sound of an engine can be heard, getting slowly louder as it comes up behind him.

'Ahoy, Pianoraft,' a voice greets them as the canal boat draws level. The helmsman calls, 'I bring greetings from the Midland and Valley Canal Boat Association,' and introduces himself as Clive. He has ruddy cheeks and a slightly uncared-for look that suggests he is single. Neil tries to store the man's name away, but it feels as if he has met so many new people over the past few days, heard so many new names. Bill and Cyril he will never forget, of course, and he has made up his mind to visit them when he is next at home.

'At home,' he whispers to himself. 'Where is home now?'

He leaves his thoughts behind to shake the hand Clive offers across the gap between their crafts. Clive strikes up a conversation with Jasper and Neil uses the moment to take out his phone and surreptitiously take a picture of their new acquaintance. He types in *Clive* as he saves it. The other photos he has taken are mostly landscapes and waterscapes, but when he comes across one of Jean and Bert he labels this with their names too, and he does the same with one of Carol and Dennis. And whilst he has his phone out, he might as well send an update.

'So you'll be able to tell us exactly where we are?' he asks Clive.

'About ten miles as the crow flies to Ruttingham,' Clive says. He is all smiles and fidgeting energy.

'You're kidding!' Jasper exclaims.

'Wow!' Jez blurts out.

'Oh!' Neil puts his hand across his stomach. He feels as if he has been punched. Ruttingham is Jez and Jasper's destination, and although they've not been with him long, the thought of them leaving the raft, and Neil continuing alone, comes as a shock.

Clive takes up the rope, puts his boat into gear and they are off again. The motor of his boat is quiet and he has made the tow rope short: it's clear that he wants to talk.

'You guys are doing amazing things to raise the profile of canals in this country.' He speaks to them across the watery gap. 'It's about time the waterways were appreciated more.' Clive raises his voice a little to be heard over the noise of his engine but there is no need. 'It's crazy to think we were so reliant on the canals until the early sixties, and now they are used for nothing but pleasure.'

'What happened in the sixties?' Jasper asks.

'The big freeze of sixty-two! Canal boats were trapped, unable to move for the ice all over the country for six long weeks in the winter of sixty-two, and nothing could be delivered. Fascinating, isn't it, history?' He grins at them and Jez agrees that it is. 'I don't know why I've wasted so much time,' Clive says.

'Wasted time on what?' Jez asks.

'Accountancy. Been an accountant all my working life but finally made the break.'

'Oh, you mean to just live on the boat?' Neil asks.

'Oh no! To train to be a teacher – history, that's the stuff.' His eyes flash and his whole countenance becomes more animated. 'Like the sixty-two freeze – fascinating. Back then, they depended on the canals to deliver materials needed for industry – coal, building materials and all that sort of thing. But when the waterways froze, goods that had been delivered week after week for generations failed to arrive. Coal for the power stations, chemicals for export, boats to carry away the daily household and factory rubbish – all were trapped in remote canals.'

'My mum was born in sixty-two,' Jez remarks.

'Well, she was too late to see the canal in its heyday.'

Clive keeps one eye on the water ahead as he talks, his hand resting lightly on the tiller. Neil can see him as a teacher in a tweed jacket at the front of a class.

'By the nineteen-sixties, canal transport was already finding it difficult to compete with road and rail, but at the end of those six weeks the canal trade was dead. Gone, kaput!'

The kids are going to love him, Neil decides.

'Trucks, and trains, even though they were more expensive, were faster and more reliable, and the big freeze gave them a chance to prove it. The railway company also bought up as much of the canal network as they could – bought it and then allowed it to fall into disrepair. And that was it – the canals were never allowed to recover. I wonder how many times in history you can pinpoint the exact point when an industry collapsed.' Clive whistles through his teeth and looks ahead.

'But if canal boats were used to haul everything, there must have been loads of them. What happened to them all?' Neil asks. He is thinking of Pat's wide black coal barge. It was so big and there must have been so many of them. Where did they all go?

'I've heard tell that many boats were scuttled in a lake in the Midlands somewhere. Some were sunk to support the sides of some of the bigger docks.'

He clicks the revs down on his motor and the noise of the engine drops to a purr.

'Of course, some were converted to pleasure boats later on, or houseboats. But here's the thing' – he almost jumps from foot to foot in his excitement – 'lengths of towpath that had always been closed to the public for safety reasons – you know, because there was so much trade, haulage, things being lifted on and off boats, which had been considered dangerous … Well, these were opened up as rights of way, making the towpaths what they are today.'

He pauses and looks up, a faraway look on his face, as if picturing the joy on people's faces when they first gained access to these rights of way. Then he looks back at Neil.

'You guys want to come aboard, by the way? There's no reason to stay huddled on your raft, unless you want to, of course.'

He slows his boat even more and they all transfer, leaving only Fuzzy-Pants on the raft, curled up asleep on the mattress in the cabin.

Jez and Jasper seem appreciative of the extra legroom on Clive's boat. Jez uses the toilet. Clive puts the kettle on and talks almost non-stop. He seems to know everything there is to know about the canal network and is an enthusiastic and entertaining speaker. Late in the afternoon, a sign welcomes them to Ruttingham.

Neil puts a hand across his stomach again. He recognises the feeling as fear. Once Jez and Jasper leave to carry on their lives, he will be alone, miles and miles from anyone he knows: just him, two animals and the piano. 'Madness!' he mutters.

'You okay?' Clive asks, pausing in his monologue.

'Yeah! I was just thinking, this is where Jasper and Jez were heading. It's going to be lonely without them.' Exposing himself like this, admitting his concerns, his need for other people, feels risky.

'Ah, you'll be fine.' Jez says. 'You're on a mission.'

'We'll catch up with you at some point,' Jasper assures him, nodding sincerely.

Neil tries to give the impression that he is fine, that their departure has no emotional impact on him after all. He smiles and nods in return. But a little knot has gripped his stomach, his mouth has dried up and his nose feels blocked all of a sudden. The journey started with Sleet, and then there was Phee. No sooner was she gone than Joyce and Trevor turned up, and they were replaced by Bill and Cyril, and then Pat. He has not actually been alone for much of the trip so far. He pushes the black cowboy hat more firmly on his head and looks ahead at the outline of Ruttingham, a jagged horizon. Just up ahead, before they reach the city, the canal divides into two.

'So, I'm going off to the left here, which will take me as near to the centre of Ruttingham as possible,' Clive explains. 'But you'll want to go right, which takes you round the city, to the south.'

Clive speaks as if he is addressing them all, but Neil knows it is only he who will be heading right. Jez and Jasper will want the centre, for sure.

Bushy-Mush is on Jez's knee again. The canal divide comes closer. Does he have any reason to go into the town centre, or would that just be putting off the continuation of his journey – the part he must do alone? But why shouldn't he go to the centre just because he wants to?

'The way to the left, into Ruttingham, is basically a very convoluted dead end,' Clive adds, which makes Neil's mind up for him. He is not about to be pulled all the way into the town only to find he must tow himself all the way out again – that would be nuts.

'Best you cut me loose then.' His brave words sound hollow to his own ears.

'Right, mate,' Jasper responds. 'When you get back to civilisation, look us up, we've got a web page. I want an invite, right? To wherever you are. We've got to meet Kim and this Sleet bloke.'

Jasper then grabs him and gives him a hug. It feels quite alien. Dad never hugs him and Sleet is a real hands-off kind of guy. But however foreign it feels, it also feels good, and he is sorry when Jasper lets go. Jez pulls him in next, and there is real affection and warmth in his embrace, which surprises Neil and reminds him how little he really knows these guys. He really hopes he does see them again.

The tow rope to the Pianoraft is pulled in and Neil crosses over whilst they are still on the move. Bushy-Mush makes the leap without hesitation.

'I'll miss that dog,' Jez says. He throws Neil the tow rope, and the raft is independent again. Neil watches as Clive steers his canal boat off to the left. Jasper and Jez wave. Neil takes hold of his rudder and steers himself to the right until finally a bush and then a tree obscure his friends from view.

'Oh crapola,' Neil mutters, contemplating his new isolation.

The landscape ahead is not beautiful. There is a hedge down one side and rows of disused warehouses down the other. Further along, industrial bridges cross overhead, and on the opposite towpath he can see an abandoned shopping trolley lying on its side.

The raft is losing momentum but the canal here appears to have some current, so he takes out his phone and presses the button to record the view of the urban decay.

'Hey, Kim,' he says, close to the phone. 'I've just left my friends and I'm alone again. I wish you were here.'

He clicks the phone off, only to click it on again. 'That's me all over, eh?' He chuckles. 'Selfishly wanting you here just to keep me company … But that's not the only reason. I wish you were here just to experience this with me.'

He takes a breath and turns the camera on himself. 'I've been thinking about love and partnerships since all the stuff Sleet said to the press. Did you read any of it? Typical Sleet baloney. But it's made me think. What is it about being in a relationship that is so important? I think it's that when we are alone, life just doesn't have such value. I think it's about witnessing someone's life, and having someone witness yours. If we have a witness, it gives all we do perspective, makes it real, gives it value. It's a bit dramatic, but imagine if everyone else in the whole world was to disappear, leaving you alone. What would you do with your time? What would be the point of experiencing or creating anything if you were completely alone? I really think there would be no point, that we need others to give our lives meaning. I know one thing for sure – you give my life meaning. I miss you so much!'

The battery light flashes and Neil clicks the phone off and sets it charging. He believes every word he said but he still cannot reconcile himself to the image of him and Kimberly in London. Treeless roads, the hum of traffic, the rush of the city. Much as he loves her, the idea of living in such a place is hell.

'Why London?' he asks the absent Kim. But he knows why. She is ambitious, she always was, and London will fulfil her dreams. If he wants a relationship with her, he must accept all of her – the striving, hard-headed part of her as well as the fun-loving, giggly, childlike Kim that he loves so much.

More for something to do than to make progress, he jumps onto the towpath and begins to haul the raft. The current is quite fast so the pulling is easy, and he sets off at a good pace. After a few minutes, Bushy-Mush leaps to join him and the two of them stride out through the backwaters of the city, along a transportation highway that smells of drains;

they slip by, unseen, behind buildings that are no longer used or wanted.

By the time night falls, he has reached the far side of the city. The houses here have gardens, and the towpath shows all the signs of being a well-used walkway, but at this time of night no one is about. The houses, set back from the canal, form ominous silhouettes, but the lit windows, the slits of light between drawn curtains, offer more comfort and they cast their light onto the gardens below. The world is closing up, ready for sleep.

For some reason, the idea of mooring up here, in suburbia, feels too exposed, so Neil breaks the rule he made on his first night, or was it his second, about not mooring under bridges where he cannot be seen and pulls the raft out of sight, then ties up and closes the door on the world behind him. He gets the stove going, makes a cup of tea and curls up with Bushy-Mush against his back and Fuzzy-Pants curled up against the warmth of his head like a hat.

Chapter 20

The morning is warmer than it has been for the last few days. Fuzzy-Pants is noisily grooming herself and Bushy-Mush is quietly chewing on a rubber chicken that Jez and Jasper must have forgotten to pack into their prop bag. He stops as soon as he realises Neil is awake, looks up guiltily and wags his tail to ingratiate himself.

Neil feels in his pockets for his phone to make an early morning video for Kim.

'Damn,' he curses. He must have left it outside, on top of the piano. Hopefully the dew will not have done it any harm – that is, if it is still there. Without even pulling on his trousers, he opens the door to retrieve it.

'Oh!' he exclaims, backing into the cabin again and closing the door. A young couple are sitting on the towpath, holding hands, legs crossed, their backs against the bridge wall. Hastily he pulls on his trousers and opens the door again just a crack.

'Morning,' the young woman – not more than a girl, really – says through a wide sunny smile. Her red jumper looks like something someone once gave her at Christmas for a joke, it is so bright. The two are standing now, the man fidgeting and hopping from foot to foot.

'Hi.' Neil opens the door a little wider and looks up and down the towpath for some explanation as to why these people are standing outside his front door. It's not raining so they are not sheltering. There is a temptation to ask 'Can I help you?' but he resists.

'Er, um, this is Denise and I am Tristan and – well, they sent us first. I am student union rep, you see, so it was agreed that I would be the appropriate candidate to introduce the group, and so in that role here I am ... I, er, mean here *we* are, obviously, because there are two of us. Well, the point is that we think you've got it right and we fully support you and the others will be here soon ... So that's it, really, so – right, yes.' He trails off, looking down at his shoes and shuffling. He is in black, head to foot, including his bobble hat.

'Sorry?' Neil rubs his eyes. Bushy-Mush scratches at the door behind him, pushes through the gap and runs out with the rubber chicken in his mouth. He hops across onto the bank and lays it at the feet of the couple and looks at them, wagging his tail expectantly.

'What Tristan meant to say is ...' Denise begins. Tristan glares at her, and looks like he is going to say something, but then he shuts his mouth. He seems to be barely out of his teens, with his smooth chin and his awkward manner.

Denise continues. 'The raft is a protest against aggressive forms of communication, to show that peaceful dialogue is a better way to resolve conflicts, despite what the media and society would have us believe.'

'What? Oh, yeah, right.' Neil yawns noisily. 'Thanks. What time is it anyway? It's a bit early for a walk, isn't it?' But the pair are not walking, they are sitting. *Were* sitting. He frowns.

'Oh, it's early, and we're not walking – not yet, anyway. We're here to support you. It's important,' Denise says.

Neil is only half listening. His phone is still on top of the piano, and it's still working, if a little damp from the dew. He wipes it dry with his sleeve and checks the time. It isn't even six yet. Some of what the girl has said makes contact with his brain.

'Support me? What do you mean?' he asks.

'Oh, you know, solidarity and all that.' The boy jiggles about with nervous energy.

'Right,' Neil says, and he slips back inside. Fuzzy-Pants is now asleep on her back, belly exposed, crucified in her comfort. Neil flops down beside her.

'There's a pair of nutters outside,' he whispers to her and tickles her soft underfur, making her limbs stretch out even further. Jasper would say something light and funny about the two outside if he was still here, and Jez might juggle for them. Certainly he would entertain them, get them laughing. Neil chuckles at this thought, a chuckle that fades as a wave of loneliness hollows out his stomach. They both had the gift of making everything scintillating and fun. Look at the way they embraced the media!

'Well, at least the media people have gone.' Fuzzy-Pants is purring very loudly. 'Which is good,' he adds. The nugget of loneliness tightens and moves from his gut to his chest as it renames itself 'rejection'. Maybe he is not so glad that the media response was so short-lived; a tiny place in his core liked the attention, enjoyed the unfamiliar feeling of being someone important.

'So, we are past Ruttingham.' He tries to envisage a map of England. 'Isn't that about halfway to London?' he asks the kitten, who is now curled up tightly – a ball of fur, her nose tucked in, her tail over the top.

Outside, the couple have been joined by another couple about the same age.

'Morning!' the new pair twitter in harmony.

'Got a map?' Neil asks.

'Sure.' The new boy takes out his phone, his thumbs moving quickly over the keyboard. 'Where do you want a map of?'

'England.'

'Sure.' Neil steps across onto the bank and the boy moves so they can stand side by side and look at his phone. 'There's Ruttingham.'

'Can you zoom out?'

'Sure. There's London.'

Neil peers at the screen, searching for Greater Lotherton. 'Zoom out again,' he says and then he sees it, and traces his journey to Ruttingham and then on to London.

'What you looking for?'

'Just seeing how far I've come and how far there is to go. I'm more than halfway.'

'Yeah, you should have told the papers when you started out. Can you imagine how many people would have joined the trail by now?' the boy says, pocketing his phone. 'Any chance I can pull first?'

This request bothers Neil. With Jez and Jasper gone, he had almost, despite his loneliness, been looking forward to the challenge of being self-reliant and resilient; having braced himself for a solo journey from here to London, making videos for Kim, with his feet finding their rhythm and nothing but birds for company, this new, uninvited company bothers him. It's flattering, but he also feels slightly invaded, in the same quickening heartbeat. The conflict passes in a second and the comforting safe feeling of having someone else around wins and, falling back into familiar grooves, he smiles.

'Sure.' Neil unties, and the two couples talked excitedly.

'Here come Dusty and John and the rest,' Denise with the bright red jumper says.

Sure enough, coming down the towpath towards them, small rucksacks on their backs, walking shoes on their feet, is a whole gang of people, all looking remarkably like the two couples already there. Scrubbed faces, neat new clothes, tidy.

'Who the heck are you guys?' Neil blurts out. He hadn't meant to ask, but the shock of so many people all coming towards him so early in the morning – well, it's just not normal.

'Hi' – 'Hi' – 'Hi' – 'Hi' – 'Hi'– 'Hi'- 'Hi' … As they all greet each other, they sound not unlike a jazz choir.

'We are' – Tristan takes centre stage – 'first-year philosophy students at Ruttingham Uni.'

'What you're doing is really important,' someone from near the back of the group says.

'Right,' Neil replies, looking from one shiny face to the next, each as sincere as the last. 'Right,' he says again, beginning to understand who they are and their motive. His college days are not so far in the past that he has forgotten how right he thought his opinions were, or how at that age he thought the world needed to wake up. He felt so passionate about everything then. The slightly geeky art students and the philosophy students always hung about in the same places, the same corner of the library, the same seats in the student union bar, preaching to the converted about truth and beauty. Pulling a raft along a canal is conceptually ambitious enough to be the perfect field trip for all of these guys – while at the same time extending their practical horizons.

'Well, say cheese.' He takes his phone out and holds it up. The group tightens and they all smile. 'Thanks.'

He types *Ruttingham Uni*. 'Well, er ...' He points to the boy who was there first, the one in black.

'Tristan,' Denise prompts him.

'Yeah, Tristan is pulling first, and after that you decide between you. And if you have no objection I need to spend some time inside.'

'No', 'Fine', 'Of course','Absolutely', 'Yes', 'I understand' and several other permissions are granted him, but he does not hear them all because he has stepped back onto the raft and closed the door behind him. Once inside, he throws himself on the bed, and within five minutes he is lulled to sleep by the movement of the raft being towed and the quiet chatter of the group on the towpath.

After a deep and dreamless sleep, he awakens with a yawn; he knows by now, even on waking, that he is on the raft, but he panics at the movement, concerned that he has come adrift. But then he hears the chatter, which seems louder than before, and the memory of first-year philosophy students comes flooding back.

'Oh yeah.' He addresses Fuzzy-Pants, who is stretching and yawning. 'A group of life enthusiasts.'

In his first year at college he felt as he imagines the philosophy students do now. He also felt that way for most of his second year, too, but by the time he was firmly in the third year, the reality hit him that the course would indeed come to an end, and the prospect of stepping into the real world loomed large. Sleet went through the same struggle, and between them they became very good at being cynical and condescending. At the time, he started to think about and miss Kim and so he wrote to her, twice, but she never replied. Sleet said that she was probably still wrapped up in 'Life, Enthusiasm and Naivety', or, as they condensed it, LEN for short. LEN became a thing between him and Sleet, and they used it widely as an arrogant put-down for the young, green and naive. They applied it to anyone, really, who was not self-aware or who seemed to be having too much fun.

'You can tell his name is LEN' – and for girls, LENA. Not that the 'A' meant anything; they just thought they were being clever giving it a sort of Latin or Greek female ending; they didn't really know which.

The real purpose of this cynicism was that it kept them separate; it excused them from the mainstream and the cool who, in their opinion, were all far more LEN than they were. Of course, it is easy for Neil to see now that forming this cynical group of two was a defence against their fear of the future, and that of course everyone in their year felt as they did.

'So arrogant,' Neil says to himself. He takes out his phone and clicks it to video.

'Hi, Kim. You know you never really had any time for Sleet, and that was sometimes a big divide between you and me? Well, I think I kind of get what you were saying about him now. About him being childish and short-sighted. Don't get me wrong, I still think he has a lot of good points – you know, he makes me laugh, he is loyal, he doesn't shirk work. But I do understand what you didn't like about him and, well, to be fair to Sleet, I don't think it was just him, I think I am …' He pauses. 'I *was* like that too. Anyway, that's all, I just wanted you to know. Meanwhile, you've got to see who has joined me pulling the raft this morning.'

With the phone camera still going, he scrambles off the bed and opens the door, pointing the camera towards the bank. The group of philosophy students has been joined by others, but these look very different. Some wear coarsely knitted, brightly coloured jumpers; one lady is in a tweed suit, several have on green waterproof coats, and in amongst them are a variety of dogs, some on leashes but the scruffier ones running free. Also, skipping along, holding parental hands, are several children, some with dreadlocked hair. Most are laughing, bouncing as they walk. The slightly older, grubbier-looking children run ahead.

'What the heck?' he mutters. One or two of the group spot him and there is a little cheer. Some of them punch the sky. A woman in an anorak, a baby papoosed on her back, trots towards him, holding out a foil packet.'

'Vegan falafels,' she says and passes it to him.

'Er, thanks.'

Tristan is no longer pulling the raft. A very tall man with long hair has taken up the rope. Tristan breaks free of the group and walks alongside the gently moving raft, as close as he can to Neil.

'I have organised a system using the alphabetical order of our given names to choose the next person to pull, so we all get a go. But what I thought might work would be if we attached another rope to that rope and then we could all just hold it in a long line and pull together, or maybe many ropes leading like umbilical cords to each of us, what do you think?'

'I haven't the faintest idea,' Neil admits and opens the falafels enough to smell them. Bushy-Mush is immediately at his ankles.

'How did you envisage it?' Tristan presses.

'Envisage what?'

'All of us.' Tristan sounds confused and a little exasperated by this answer. 'You must have realised, when you took the decision to make such an epic journey to raise awareness that our focus should be more on loving our fellow man than on war, that you were going to create a huge following, that you were going to be on the six o'clock news.'

'You're kidding me. You're not saying the raft was on the six o'clock news, on TV, are you?

'Of course, and then again at nine on all channels. The people have been waiting for something like this – you know they have. You knew there would be this big response, didn't you? I mean, that's the point, isn't it? Why else would you make London, the seat of government, your finish point?'

'Because Kim lives there,' Neil replies.

'Oh. So there really is a real-life Kim then? She's not just a symbolic identity?'

'No, there really is a Kim.'

'Ah, so you work together? She's organising the PR in London?'

Neil takes a really hard look at Tristan, and in the younger man's eyes he can see his earnestness, his hope, his belief – and he falters. To crush that would be cruel; he just can't do it.

'She is, how can I say … I know, she is my muse.' He feels ever so slightly triumphant at this.

'Ah, your muse! I see, yes, that makes sense. So that makes the whole thing so much more real,' Tristan blurts out.

'Yes, to make it more real.' Neil does his best not to laugh. Tristan seems satisfied and rejoins the group and Neil can hear him repeat the words 'Kim' and 'muse'.

Chapter 21

The members of the group walk on and on and just don't seem to tire. When the children get fractious, earthy-looking mothers take parcels from their rucksacks and feed them. Strong fathers give shoulder rides.

At one point the group bursts into song – a popular melody that Neil doesn't much like. Soon after this, one of the group asks if they can actually play the piano, and from then on a continuous serenade is played by one walker or another. Even the children have an exploratory bash at the keys, and then one mother plays a medley of nursery rhymes, which has young and old alike singing along. She is followed by a talented teenager, who demonstrates his skills with Chopin as he floats on glassy waters.

Since daybreak they have passed two villages and three waterside pubs. At each place a few of the group have left, but more have joined, and at each place a new camera crew or journalist has been lying in wait, looking for the perfect picture, an interview, a new angle. With all the comings and goings, Neil has become faceless, one of the masses. He has learnt to merge with the crowd. Most of those walking along the towpath do not realise who he is, and a woman explains to him in hushed tones that Neil is inside the raft's cabin – meditating, apparently.

As they pass under a bridge, Ian from the *Rolby Evening Press*, who gave him the solar-charged phone, trots down the stone steps that lead to the towpath. Neil hangs back, breaks away from the main bunch. Ian will recognise him and is bound to call him by name, reveal his identity, and at the moment Neil is enjoying the anonymity.

'Hi, Neil,' Ian greets him. 'Thanks for your daily updates, the column is on the front page now.'

Neil smiles but his eyes flick to the group ahead.

'I have a few questions, if you don't mind.' Ian rummages in his bag and takes out a notebook, from which he fires off a list of questions in a sharp, slightly high-pitched voice. He asks about Neil's college days, posing personal questions about his childhood, his friendship with Sleet and Kim, and then he waits for an answer, arm extended, Dictaphone in his hand, too close to Neil's face for comfort. Still Ian waits. Neil does not speak. Ian looks at the little recorder and then at Neil, and slowly he retracts his arm, finally clicking off the tiny machine and putting it in his pocket.

'Did your boss pressure you to ask all that?' Neil finally says. He has slowed his pace to drop quite a long way behind the raft and the crowd now.

'Yes – well, no. Well, sort of. It's a big deal, being on the front page. It looks like I might get promotion, which would really help with my daughter's tuition fees.' He sounds like himself again.

'Oh yes – she's at art school, you said.'

'Second year, and even though she is really careful with money, and she has a part-time job, she's still needed to take out a student loan. It's just madness, coming out of university with a loan that will cripple her for years to come. Where's the advantage in that?'

It's a subject Neil would rather not think about. It was the only way for him to attend college when Dad refused to support him.

'You're living in a dream world!' Dad said. Mum sighed, and put a plate of beans on toast in front of Neil. 'Get a job,' his father continued. 'Get yourself stable, then draw all you like in your spare time, but to go to college to do art, it's just your typical modern-day fantasy world that they are encouraging kids to live in and it will end with a lot of disappointed and unemployable youths.'

Neil had thought that was the end of the speech, but just as his dad was about to open the door that separated their living quarters from the pub, he added, 'You're not Michael Sleet-McBride, you know, and mixing with the likes of him is only giving you airs and graces you can't keep up with.'

Then he opened the door. The hall carpet changed colour under the orange light that flooded in, the quiet of their kitchen echoed with the laughter of the customers, and the smell of Neil's beans was replaced with the stench of beer that drifted in from the bar.

When his dad shut the door behind him it was as if another world had been closed off to Neil. Usually, he wanted to be in that other world, but this time he preferred to stay at home with Mum.

She stood up stiffly, went to the cupboard where she kept the tinned food and then sat beside him and pressed a tightly curled roll of notes into his hand.

'A little bit from the shopping money each week adds up over time,' she said. 'Don't let your father see.' And she curled his fingers around the money and gave his fist a little squeeze.

It was a hundred and fifty pounds and he stretched it as far as he could. The moment he got to college, he took on two part-time jobs and slept on the floor of Sleet's room until the landlord caught him. Then he did a tour of friends' sofas. Sleet, lucky sod, had everything paid for him by his parents: a nice room, money for food, even a beer allowance – at least, that was what he called it. The envelope he took it from each month said *Miscellaneous* in his mother's swirling handwriting. It arrived in a package with another two envelopes marked *Food* and *Laundry*. But there's no such thing as a free lunch and now, of course, poor old Sleet feels obliged to pay it back by working for his dad.

'I have a loan that is crippling me into inertia,' Neil says, and then he blinks at his own words. Is that the truth or is he just feeding Ian for his front-page story?

'Really?' Ian replies with his press voice, raising the end of the word to leave space for Neil to say more.

'I had no choice but to study art. I felt like I was compelled by something. I had no choice, but I also had no money. I worked two jobs, slept on friends' floors and still came out of it shackled to a massive student loan.' He takes another breath, 'It seems like there is no point in getting a job now unless the wage is enough to start to repay the loan, so when I think about work the whole issue just appears too massive to think about and I freeze.'

He continues to wonder if what he is saying is honest or if he is playing up to Ian's desire for a story. The discomfort he feels, however, tells him it is possibly true. Is that what has held him back these last two years?

'So is the Pianoraft a way to pay off that debt?' Ian asks.

'How do you mean?'

'Well, it's become a big thing, on local TV, national TV, and in the papers. It's becoming the art piece of the year.'

'I don't get it. Why is there so much interest? All I am doing is floating a piano to London down the canals. I never really intended it to become an art piece.'

'You want my honest answer, Neil?' Ian says, and Neil suspects that this is the way he speaks to his daughter. He sounds adult, compassionate, gentle.

'Yes, I really do.'

'I think you've got lucky, or rather *we* have got lucky, seeing as it was my first article that started all this off. I think there wasn't much happening in the way of news one day and the whole romantic idea of someone making such a quest for his love just struck the right chord in people at the right moment.' He takes a step or two, looking at the ground. 'And, if I might be so bold as to offer you some advice ...?'

'Yes, sure.' Neil is always glad of advice.

'Run with this for all it's worth. This could be your golden ticket. Milk it. Play it. Use it. Because one thing is for sure, if it pays you dividends you won't regret it, but if you do nothing and it comes to nothing, at some point in your life you will probably regret that you never grabbed the opportunity.'

'Hmmm.' Neil is silent for a moment. 'My friend Sleet,' he begins, after a pause, and then he starts again. 'My manager, Sleet, is very good at that sort of thing, but I find it really hard to be insincere. If it doesn't feel right inside of me I cannot do it.'

'Well, something felt right inside of you to start this whole thing, so stick with that, kid.'

Neil would have liked a dad like Ian. His upper lip curls as he thinks of his own father.

'Okay, Ian,' he smiles. 'What can I give you to help with your front page?'

'I just need something that no one else has.'

'Are you in touch with Sleet?'

'Only through social media. People are donating left, right and centre, you know, and he's keeping an online tally. Actually, if it keeps going like this you'll be able to repay your loan pretty soon, just from the donations. Now, there's an idea. Shall I suggest it to Sleet? It would give him a nice total to aim for!'

'I don't feel at all comfortable with people donating. I mean, I'm not a charity, and I've done nothing to deserve their money. It's just wrong.' There is passion in Neil's voice.

'Maybe it's not about you,' Ian replies. The teenager on the piano has stopped playing Chopin and the chattering of the group seems louder. One of the dogs is barking at Bushy-Mush, who is running around, getting under people's feet. He is too fast for the barking dog to catch him.

'What do you mean?'

'You are giving people hope, kid! Simple as that. The Pianoraft has become a symbol. It reminds people that there's more to life than money and greed. That it's fine to take your time. That relationships, and romance, are worth focusing on. If someone sends you a pound, it's not about you getting the pound – it's about that person feeling like they have done something to keep this thing going.' Ian zips up his jacket; a cloud has passed over the sun.

'Really?' Neil says. He takes his jumper from around his waist and puts it on as Bushy-Mush comes running at him, gallops in a circle around his ankles and runs off again, a collie with a handkerchief collar chasing after him.

'Really.' Ian is emphatic. 'And, unfortunately, sooner or later, other news will come along and sink the Pianoraft story and then your moment in the spotlight will be done, so grab all you can out of it now, because you will make a lot of people happy if you do.'

Neil likes the idea of making people happy. It gives him a little buzz, like he has downed a lager too quickly after a walk in the sun.

'So what do you need to help with the column?' he asks.

'Give me a scoop. Will you ask Kim to marry you when you see her?'

'I don't even know if she will see me yet, so that's a bit of a leap.' Neil swallows and blinks at the same time, his mouth suddenly dry.

'Okay, then – tell me about your time at art school.' Ian takes out his Dictaphone again.

'Sure.'

Neil starts with how going to art school meant that he would be separated from Kim whilst they studied but that they got back together again when they returned to Greater Lotherton. He surprises himself with his narrative; it sounds like a genuine romance story and an empty place opens in his chest that yearns for Kim to fill it.

'That's great,' Ian says when he has finished. 'In the bag, as they say. So if you can, keep updating me each day, and maybe you can let me know how many people are with you at each stage.'

'Sure.'

They walk along side by side as the afternoon turns to evening.

'I've arranged to be picked up at The Mouldy Lettuce pub just up here.' Ian breaks their

270

companionable silence. 'It might be a good place to stop for the night. They say the food is good.'

'What, with all this lot?' Neil smirks.

'Well, if I were you I would slip away. They all seem to think you are in the raft. The rest of the village is off to the left over there, and it's big enough to have another pub. There's also quite a well-known hotel not far from here. I know – I'll book you a room there, and put it on my expense tab.'

'You can't do that!'

'I can! An expense in exchange for the exclusive. Come on.'

Neil casts a last, nervous look back at the raft. There are plenty of people there to keep it safe but its awkward shape, its lack of comfort, feel almost like an extension of himself now, and to be parted is jarring.

'Don't worry about the raft, Neil – it'll be fine. And besides, a little comfort, a hot bath, will fortify you, help you finish this journey.'

It's the thought of a good night's sleep and a hot bath that wins Neil over, and Ian is as good as his word, and his driver waits patiently as he books Neil into the hotel and pays for his evening meal in advance.

The sky is almost black as Ian turns to leave. He hesitates, then with arms held wide he returns and gives Neil a hug, tight and strong and sure.

Neil would definitely like a dad like Ian.

Chapter 22

Neil fills the bath so full it threatens to overflow as he lowers himself into it. As arranged by Ian, his clothes are taken away for cleaning and pressing. In his mud-stained jeans, tatty jumper and black cowboy hat he felt too self-conscious to eat alone in the dining room – well, it was that and the fact that the glasses and the silver, laid out on the tables with their starched white tablecloths, shone just a little too brightly. But alone in his room he ate well and videoed the event for Kimberly. So full is he now that his stomach extends above the waterline. He lifts his beer bottle off the side of the bath.

'To you, Ian. To grabbing the moment – oh, and to having wings, eh, Jasper!' He drinks deeply and lets his head roll back. He is in heaven.

Were it not for a rap at the door and a voice calling 'Laundry service!', he could easily have fallen asleep and woken up in a cold bath in the early hours. Instead, he drips out of the tub, wrapping himself in an oversized towelling robe, to find his clean clothes laid out on his bed, his jeans with a neatly pressed line down the front. Not only has his jumper been cleaned, but the hole under the arm has also been mended. He picks his phone up from the bed and texts Ian.

Warm bath, clean clothes, sprung bed. Thanks mate.

In less than a minute a message comes back.

Boss pleased. Thanks right back at you.

Neil snorts a little appreciative laugh and climbs in between the clean sheets. He doesn't feel in the least worried about not being with the piano now. How many guards does it need? Besides, the piano is well known now; no one's going to bother it. Bushy-Mush is an independent dog and he'll be fine, but he does worry just a little for Fuzzy-Pants as his eyelids flutter closed.

Tap, tap, tap. 'Room service.' Tap, tap. Neil lumbers out of his dreams like a punch-drunk heavyweight boxer. The sheets fight back.

'Sir. Sorry to disturb you, sir, but it is an eleven o'clock checkout.' The voice is apologetic, subservient.

'Oh, er, what time is it?'

'Eleven.' The woman backs out of the door but leaves her trolley, piled high with sheets and towels, as a visual reminder that the room is hers now and he must leave.

'Eleven!' Neil scrambles into his neatly pressed jeans and his jumper, which smells vaguely of lavender. 'Crapola!'

Would they set off without him? No, surely not – they would wait for his command, wouldn't they? After all, it is his raft. But he cannot be certain, and when the lift doors do not immediately open he takes the stairs two at a time. He throws the key on the reception desk and the concierge mutters a surprised, 'Thank you, and did you enjoy your …'

But his words are lost as Neil runs full pelt through the village, his arms pumping, chest heaving, until he can see The Mouldy Lettuce in the distance. It looks deserted. He tells himself that this is nothing to worry about: the raft will be hidden behind the pub, and the crowd, hopefully, will be whittled down to just a few. He slows to a walk, his lungs heaving as he enters the pub garden.

'If you've come for the raft, you're too late,' a man with his shirtsleeves rolled up, collecting empty glasses from the picnic tables, informs him.

'What do you mean, too late?'

'As in too late. They left at eight this morning. There's been a steady stream of people down here to get a glimpse, take a photo or whatever it is they want to do, ever since it was on *Britain's Breakfast* this morning after the news. Did you see it? It was a good shot, showed the pub lovely. Free advertising for me. I imagine I'll be busy all day now.'

But Neil is already at the canal's edge looking up and down.

'That way.' The glass collector points the way the river is flowing. Where Neil left the raft on the towpath, the water is floating with crisp packets and cardboard coffee cups.

'Mucky buggers as well, some of them. Look at the mess, and guess who will clear that lot up.'

The landlord, his hands full of glasses, heaves a sigh. For just a second it crosses Neil's mind to stay to help the man tidy up. After all, it is not the man's mess. But then that would mean leaving Fuzzy-Pants and Bushy-Mush and the piano untended even longer. Fuzzy-Pants will be starving and needing to pee, too. His hand automatically goes to his jeans pocket, where the bacon from his uneaten breakfast is wrapped in serviettes.

'Sorry I can't stay to help,' he says and breaks into a run.

'Why should you, it's not your mess,' the landlord calls after him.

Neil runs until his breath comes in short gasps and his legs feel a little shaky, but there's no sign of the raft. He reluctantly slows to a walk.

'Okay, be sensible. They set off at eight, it's now after eleven. That's three hours, walking at, say, three miles an hour. He stops walking, puts his hand on his knees and bends over to catch his breath. That means the raft is nine miles ahead of him, give or take.

'You all right, laddie?' croaks a voice, quite near to him, which sounds like it might not be all right itself, it's so phlegmy and guttural. The voice coughs, a great hacking noise that scares the birds from the hedges on the edge of the towpath.

Neil straightens up, still out of breath, to meet this new stranger, and immediately any concerns for his own wheezing chest are gone. The man before him has grey hair sticking up at all angles, long in some places, short in others. He is not tall but he is very bulky, and he is enveloped in a herringbone tweed overcoat that drops to his ankles. The coat is shiny at the collar and sleeves and blackened around the knees and hips. A few turns of rough string serve as a belt around the waist, finished with a knot. Protruding below the edge of the coat are what look like rubber boots cut to slip over a pair of brogues with no shine left to them at all.

Neil looks back to the man's face. He has not had a shave recently and his skin is a dirty brown, making it seem tough like leather, the creases permanent. But his eyes are a light blue, and they dance as he looks at Neil and his mouth twitches ready to smile.

'I thought you were going to keel over then.' His grating voice is again at odds with the bird calls in the hedge behind him.

'No, thanks, I'm fine.' Neil looks down the path and takes a few more deep breaths. He needs to keep moving, to catch up.

'You lost something?' The man takes his hands out of his pockets, revealing fraying fingerless mittens. He holds up a cigarette end. 'Got a light?'

'I don't smoke.'

'Ah, wise, very wise. Nine days out of ten, neither do I. But then a nice dog end presents itself, and I say to myself, why not!'

'Sorry, but I have to go.'

'What's your rush?'

'My raft.'

'Raft?'

'Yes, my Pianoraft.'

'Oh! You mean that thing with the drawers and the piano on it that all those people were pulling?'

'Yes, that's it. Look, I'm sorry but I really have to go … Bye.'

'Well, bye if you want, but if you're looking to catch it up you have all the time in the word. Do you have a light?'

'You already asked that. Why do I have all the time in the world?'

'Sixteen Locks. Down that way, five miles. It'll take them a good long time to get through, and that's if nothing is halfway up, coming the other way. I've seen people stuck there up to a day.'

'Really?'

'Really. No light, eh?'

'No, no light.'

The tramp looks longingly at his half cigarette and then returns it and his hands to his pockets and starts to walk the way Neil will be going.

'A whole day, you reckon?'

'Have you been through a lock with your raft?'

'Yes.'

'Remember how long it took?'

'Yes.'

'Times it by sixteen.'

Neil feels all the tension in his shoulders drop and his tight thigh muscles relax. But there is still Fuzzy-Pants.

'And even walking slowly you'll be there in two or three hours, no worries.'

She'll manage – she'll sleep, most likely.

'So why are you floating a piano down the canal? You a musician?'

'Trying to make amends to my girlfriend, Kim. She wanted to move to London, and I wasn't so sure. This is meant to be a big romantic gesture to say sorry and show how important she is to me.'

'Don't blame you, though.'

'I'm Neil, by the way.'

'Honoured to meet you, sir. My name's Quentin.' With the phlegm cleared from his throat, his voice is distinctive, educated.

'Don't blame me for what?'

'Not much relishing the thought of London.' He stops to look around; the hills roll away from them on all sides, dotted with trees, fields lined with hedges, cows lying down, chewing their cud.

'It's the lack of trees and nature and so on, but it's also the fear of being sucked in.'

'Sucked in?' Quentin takes his hands out of his pockets and looks at his cigarette end. 'No light, you said?'

Neil ignores the question this time. The cigarette is returned to the folds of the oversized coat.

'The whole rat race thing, getting up crazy early to run all day and going home late just to afford a house you never spend any time living in.'

'Ah yes,' Quentin says, sounding like a wise old sage. 'The rat race.'

'You must know what I mean? After all, you've opted out of all that?'

'Opted out – I like that. Yes, I suppose I've opted out. So are you saying you want to opt out?'

'Well, no, not like …' He is about to say 'not like you' but realises that this could sound rude, so he finishes with '… not completely.'

'Well, it has to be complete, else you are still in it,' Quentin offers, which makes Neil smile.

'You have a point.'

'So, you think if you went to London you would get a great job and an expensive house and then run in circles to keep your expensive house. You, the man who is floating to London on a pile of sticks with a piano on top?'

Neil cannot help chuckling; the man is funny. 'Not immediately, obviously.'

'So when would you get all that, then?'

'Well, it sneaks up on you, doesn't it?'

'You know what your life is? Your life is merely a combination of the things you are prepared to put up with.'

Neil smiles. It sounds like a joke, but then he runs over the words again.

'You think?'

'I know. When the "worst" I would put up with was a detached house, two kids and a wife, that's what I had. I didn't want more so I didn't work to get more, because I was prepared to put up with what I had. I would have taken more if it had been offered for free, but if it required my work then I didn't want it. The house and family was the "worst" I would put up with. If as a family, for some reason, we ended up in a tiny caravan, I would not have put up with that, so I would have worked to get out, do you see? Our lives are a combination of the worst things we will put up with.'

Now Quentin chuckles as if it is a joke, but Neil is serious.

'I've never thought of it like that.'

'And for you, life without Kim is something you will not put up with, so you are taking her piano to her to win her back. So don't worry about London. If you cannot put up with it, you will do what it takes to change that.'

'But Kim wants it.'

'Then which will you put up with? No London and no Kim? Or London and Kim? Besides, it's all in your head anyway.'

'What's all in my head?' As Neil walks, he looks at Quentin's face, at his dancing blue eyes. He exudes charm.

'The universe is in your head,' Quentin says.

Well, it's either charm or insanity.

'Then I must have a big head,' Neil jokes and takes his cowboy hat off, and then his jumper to sling it around his hips. The sun is heating up the day. He looks at his companion's thick tweed coat. 'Aren't you hot in that coat?'

'Hot, cold, all in your head.'

Neil does not answer. He looks ahead, hoping to see signs of Sixteen Locks and his raft, but the canal stretches into the distance, where it lazily wends left and disappears. They continue to walk in silence. Neil listens to the birds in the hedgerows, and he spots a fox slinking along the perimeter of a field with rabbits dotted here and there that nibble the bright green grass. He can see the openings to their burrows, too, all over the field. The fox doesn't have a chance: the rabbits will be too quick, and they are too close to home.

'You can be free in a jail cell and lonely in a crowd,' Quentin growls. He could be a radio newsreader with that voice. 'Because the universe is in your head.'

'Hm.' Neil is still watching the fox, which is sneaking closer to the rabbits. A rabbit freezes: it looks like it will run, but then it carries on eating. 'You mean you need to look inwardly and get all spiritual?' Another has its head up now, alert.

'No!' Quentin barks loudly and stops walking.

Concerned, Neil turns to face him. Has he offended the old man?

'You look outward. Outward! If you look inward all you see is yourself! I've had a lot of time to think about this.' He starts to walk again.

The fox makes its move and the rabbits run. The fox runs low and hard but the white tails disappear into the holes one by one, plop plop, plop, leaving the cunning one exposed on the hillside. The predator looks uncertain now and slinks between gorse and rocks back to the shelter of the hedges.

'You look outward and you see the people who make you happy, and you work to keep them happy so they stay around. If keeping them happy is uncomfortable for you, so what? That discomfort is in your head! Concentrate more on keeping them happy and you forget discomfort. You forget hot and cold, you forget yourself, and so you turn your discomfort to comfort. The happiness you created outside comes inside – your discomfort has gone and you've done it all from what's in your head.'

'How long have you been on the road?' Neil asks.

'No idea,' Quentin grunts.

Chapter 23

'You must have some idea! Weeks, months, years?'

'Oh, in those terms, definitely years, and quite a few of them. I can remember mostly by the winters. Last winter was mild, and the one before that I found a hut in a wood. It was being used in the daytime by someone who lit the little stove, and they left it at night. Oh that was cosy, a few sacks on top of me. The year before, I made a bivouac. There's a place …' He looks around as if to get his bearings. 'Oh, miles from here, a south-facing hill with this deep dip in it, just right for a man. Well, they coppice those woods so it was easy to find branches long enough to weave a flat roof. You would never have known it was there from the outside. Aye, I might go there this winter, why not.'

'Wouldn't you rather have a home to go to?' Neil would like to ask if he really does have a wife and children, but it feels a little too intrusive.

'Obviously not. Else I would still be there.'

'You have a house, then?'

'House, wife, children. Are you not listening?'

'Well, I thought you were saying that you had a wife and children – you know, somewhere.'

'I used to have children,' Quentin says gravely.

'Oh. What happened?' The question is out before Neil can think through whether it is appropriate to ask.

'They grew up. They are adults now.' Quentin finds this very amusing, his chortles mixed in with a hacking cough.

'Do they know how you live?' The question comes out before Neil can stop himself.

'Meaning what? That if they knew, they would have me inside with a suit on? No thanks, and they know not to try.'

'If it's not too personal a question, I would love to know how you decided to opt out.' Neil tries his best to sound sensitive.

'In an unkind way.' Quentin's head drops forward as he walks.

'Unkind to who?'

'To whom,' Quentin replies, and it takes a second for Neil to realise that he is correcting his grammar.

'To whom?'

'To my wife. Bless her. No warning, you see –
now that's not kind, is it? No warning, and for a while
she had no idea. That was very cruel. But it just hit
me between the eyes.' He gently bounces the heel of
his hand off his forehead. 'It was like you said, I got
sucked in. I was good at my job, and it's always a bad
idea to be good at your job.'

'What was your job?' Neil senses that Quentin
doesn't mind talking about this.

'I was a banker, in the City, London.'

'Really?'

'Really. Savile Row suits, grey with just a hint
of a cream stripe running through the material.
Handmade personalised cufflinks bought by my wife,
and a working day that left me little time to sleep.
But, as I said, I was good at it, made them a ton of
money and they gave me half a ton back. The boys
were at the best schools, Caroline always looked
perfect, the whole nine yards.'

'So what happened?'

'Well, Laurence, my youngest, was in his last
year at Oxford, and Benedict, my older boy, had left
there two years earlier and already landed himself a
great job in New York, and I was getting up to go to
the same job I had done for twenty years. I'd
showered and dressed and I was in the kitchen
making coffee. I always made Caroline a coffee and

took it to her in bed before leaving for work, only this morning I went to the fridge and we were out of milk. Normally we had everything delivered, but I suppose it was left off the list. Anyway, there was no milk and that was it!'

'What do you mean, that was it? You left her because you ran out of milk?'

'Basically, yes.'

'And unbasically?'

'Unbasically is not a word.'

'English is a living language. It's changing all the time.' Neil quotes something he once heard Sleet say. It makes Quentin laugh, and his blue eyes dance.

'Okay,' he says. 'I'll accept that. So, unbasically, I picked up my car keys, intending to drive to the nearest shop, which was just beyond the end of the road, and I popped out of the front door, leaving the kettle boiling. Well, I thought I would only be a minute, but the sun was shining and I looked at my watch – I had the time, so I decided to walk to the shop. Five minutes there and back at most. I bought the milk and started to walk back to the house. Next door had its sprinklers going on the front lawn and it was creating rainbows. Their gardener was clipping the hedges and the cuttings flew up in the air a little before gravity got the better of them. I walked on and in front of our house were the cars, all waxed and shiny, the gravel drive raked smooth by the gardener. He used to rake the drive daily. Ha! Anyway, I was about to go back inside, and then I turned my head and saw the rainbow again, and the leaves being cut, and I pictured my office, the one I had sat in for the last twenty years of my life, and I realised that this tiny snapshot of the rainbow and the leaves was all I would get of nature that day, and probably the next day too and then many after that. So I put my keys and the milk on the doormat and went back to look again at the hedge and the lawn, and something clicked in my head. I needed to walk in a park. It occurred to me to make a call, ring in sick, but I've never been sick a day in my life, and besides it just didn't feel important. What felt important was to get to a park, and so I did, but it was not enough so I used the cash in my pockets to take a train out of London and I got off when I saw nothing but trees and fields.'

'And here you still are,' Neil says.

'Well, sort of, but not quite. You see I was cruel. Caroline had no idea where I was or what had happened to me. She woke up to a half-made cup of coffee and my keys and the milk on the mat. She thought I'd been abducted. Soon a nationwide hunt was set up.'

'Hey, I think I remember seeing that on the news!' Neil can vaguely recall the picture of a very strait-laced man with dark, smoothed-back hair and a crisp white shirt. That was way back, before he went to college, before his A levels even. The news said he had been a big cheese at a major bank. It was big news at the time, and it was expected that a ransom note would appear, but none did.

'It was very cruel.' Quentin shakes his head. 'They found me in Cornwall. Caroline thought I must have gone mad and she had me sectioned. I ran away but, unlike the first time, I left a note. They found me again, and this time Caroline had the sense to talk to me, and I came up with a deal. She got the house, the cars, the bank accounts to play with and I got a thick winter overcoat. She agreed quite easily – I remember because, despite being the one who walked away, I was quite hurt at how easily she gave me up. Anyway, she said she would not make a fuss if I agreed to one condition. I have to go home once a year for Laurence and Benedict's birthdays, the twenty-fourth and twenty-fifth of June. She said this was my duty to the boys.'

'Do you go?' Neil asks.

'Every year, and every year they try to talk me into returning, and every year James just happens to be there. He's an old friend of mine who's a doctor, and every year there's a new tweed coat, a new pair of walking boots, a bundle of socks and a thick jumper and a haircut from Caroline's hairdresser.'

'Do you ever think of returning – you know, to live, for good?'

'I might, one day, just for the winters.'

'Does she miss you?'

'I think perhaps during the first year she did, but now she's learnt how much more fun life is when she's not running around to someone else's schedule. She likes to holiday, and she spends a lot of the year abroad, something we never did together.'

'So where does all that fit into your theory that our lives are the worst we will tolerate?'

'Perfectly,' Quentin says, and it seems that the subject is closed.

They walk on, following the curve of the canal, making good progress.

'Do you really want to walk with all those people? You strike me as a solitary sort of chap.' Quentin stoops to pick up a cigarette end, examines it briefly and then flings it into the bushes.

'Well, I would rather not, but it's sort of taken on a life of its own. They are calling it an art piece now.'

'I do miss the Chagall.'

Neil wonders if he has misheard.

'And the Dufy.'

'Are you saying you have a Chagall and a Dufy?'

'Um.' Quentin's eyes have misted over and he is gazing away at the horizon.

Gradually, their footsteps fall into matching rhythms – not like soldiers marching, just friends in tune. Tall trees line the towpath now, the edge of dense wood that stretches nearly to the locks that are just visible in the distance.

'You and I are not so different, it seems.' Quentin breaks the silence. 'Maybe your trip to London will become a way of life and I'll be seeing more of you … I'll just pop in here for a piddle.' And he steps off the towpath and into the trees.

Neil walks a few steps further and then stops to wait for Quentin. 'I'm not sure I could live this way permanently,' he remarks, but it doesn't feel a hundred per cent true. 'But then again, how do you know when this way of life suits you, eh?'

He waits for an answer.

'Quentin, I said how do you know?'

But there is no answer, and a surge of adrenaline courses through his legs.

'Quentin?' He runs back to the spot where the old man stepped off the path. 'Quentin?' he calls into the woods, his voice echoing off the trees.

A bird shrieks and twigs fall as it flaps its way to open sky. He knows Quentin has gone, and he also knows why.

Returning to the path, he eyes the locks in the distance. How many people will be there with his raft, making it into some kind of circus attraction? He is almost tempted to follow Quentin's footsteps into the wood and become lost himself.

'Except that would mean no Kim, and that is more than I can tolerate.'

He takes out his phone to take a picture of the spot. He wishes he had videoed Quentin for Kim; she would have loved him. He checks the phone's battery and tuts; it seems he has been draining it by recording a video of the inside of his pocket. He presses what he thinks is 'delete' but the device starts to play back the recording of the dark interior. Just as he is about to press again to delete it, he hears Quentin's voice, miniaturised and captured on the phone. He has recorded their conversation – muffled, but audible enough. He saves it under the name 'Quentin'.

Chapter 24

As Neil approaches the locks, of which there are in fact four and not sixteen, he does indeed sense something resembling the atmosphere of a circus. The people seem to have increased in numbers considerably, although this might just be because they are condensed into a small space and not strung out along the towpath as they were when the raft was on the move.

It is a colourful sight; some of the children hold balloons, and others are wearing paper hats, the sort that Neil has only seen in Christmas crackers.

Bushy-Mush comes barrelling towards him, tongue hanging out, a smile on his little face; he is enlivened and excited by all the people. Neil pats the little dog, and Bushy-Mush does his best to jump into his arms, but his short legs won't leap that high so Neil squats to pick him up and receives an enthusiastic lick on his face before the animal squirms free and runs back to the crowd.

If it wasn't for Fuzzy-Pants needing food, he would slink away again right now.

'Ah, Quentin, there's a lot to be said for your lifestyle,' he mutters.

There are two television vans and a radio van by the locks. People stand on the bank and stare at the raft, taking photos of Kim's piano.

A group of three are standing close to the raft and seem to be engaged in a serious discussion. As he draws closer he can hear them talking in hushed tones.

'Yes, but if no one has checked how do we know he is in there?' one says.

'Has anyone checked?' another replies.

'We can't just go in, it's his home – has anyone knocked?'

Another group of people have sat down in a circle in a field adjacent to the canal, and one of them is playing a guitar. An ice cream van is parked beside them and a hotdog wagon is next to that. The car park by the lock-keeper's cottage is full of assorted vehicles, and people are wandering back and forth, dogs winding between legs, couples holding hands. An artist has set up to draw sketches – caricatures, in front of simplified line drawings of the raft.

A child wanders across his path, munching

candyfloss. The television and radio reporters are interviewing people at random, it seems. Maybe he could ask someone to go into the raft and feed Fuzzy-Pants and he can just hang back, merge with the crowd.

A man in a boiler suit pushes through the crowd. 'So, where is this Neil person?'

'On board, asleep,' someone says.

'He's never asleep with all this racket,' the man in the boiler suit replies.

'Who wants to know, anyway?' a defensive voice asks.

'I live there.' The man in the boiler suit points to the cottage by the road that leads up to the locks. 'I'm the lock-keeper. This is a public right of way and you lot are blocking it.'

'We're just waiting for Neil to wake up to take us through the locks.'

'Well, give the man a nudge. Look over there – you see that, that's a canal boat coming the other way. If you don't make a move you'll have to wait for that to come through.'

He steps close to the raft. 'Neil, Neil?' he calls, and a hush falls over the crowd. The only response from the raft is a pitiful mewing. 'Neil, are you there?' The man repeats, and there is another mew and Neil, for the sake of Fuzzy-Pants, cannot hold himself back.

'No, I'm here,' he says. Now the crowd falls silent and they all turn to stare at him. He pulls the front of his hat down to cover his eyes, a wall against the stares, as he steps onto the raft and goes in to feed the kitten, closing the door behind him.

One of the group that was whispering says, 'How do we know it's him?' But the others hush her.

Neil is glad he is inside but he peeks through the gap on the hinge side of the door to see how the crowd are reacting to his presence. They show some interest, but not as much as he had expected, and he feels almost redundant, secondary in importance to the raft itself.

Several voices outside begin to call his name. The lock-keeper is most vocal, followed by the press. He wishes Jasper and Jez were there to entertain the crowd, or even Sleet, who would revel in the attention. He takes his time feeding the little kitten, who purrs loudly. There is a smell of cat pee and the boards in the corner are stained dark. 'Poor little thing.'

Neil strokes her as she eats, and when the food is gone she tolerates his petting a little longer and then curls up to sleep. His name is still being called from outside, and reluctantly he opens the door again, to be met with a barrage of questions and a blinding series of flashes.

'Neil, how is your journey going?'

'Neil, can we get this raft through and moving on please?'

'Neil, what does Kimberly think of your journey, will she be joining you?'

'I posted on your Facebook page.'

'Neil, will you be selling the raft when you get to London?'

'Neil, will you sign my autograph book?'

'Good work, Neil, not before time.'

'Nice one, mate.'

'Is this your dog, Neil?'

'Could we have an interview, please, Neil?'

The people on the bank, and the members of the press, speak to him in a familiar tone, as if he is well known to them, and Neil wonders if this is how celebrities feel. How often has he felt he knows an actor or actress just because he has seen them in a few films, read an article or two about them? He even once said to Kim after watching a film that he thought he and the star would make great friends if they hung out together, but then Kim told him one or two things about the actor that really put him off. Is it that same illusion that he can hear expressed in the people's voices now, that of familiarity with someone they believe they know but really don't? Have they just filled in any bits they don't know about him and think they have a full picture in their minds?

'Neil, what do you think of the sculpture Sleet has made of the raft on the waste ground beside your old home?'

This one makes him laugh, and as he laughs the whole performance seems hilarious. This crowd of people following along behind him is the funniest thing, and the media interest in him and the raft is bordering on the ridiculous. Like Ian said, it is all just a moment in time, and tomorrow or the next day he will be unimportant and forgotten. The tension in his neck relaxes, his frown drops away and he smiles.

'I say good for Sleet for seizing the moment.' He laughs.

'You think he is taking advantage?'

'No.' Neil ponders a second. 'I think he is doing what he believes in.'

'Neil, can we do an interview for the BBC. Not here – perhaps a quieter corner?'

'ITV, Neil, *News at Seven*, a word if we might.'

'What does Kimberly think of what you are doing?' A grey, fluffy-topped microphone is shoved into his face and his smile drops.

'I don't know what she thinks, we haven't spoken.' And with this, he goes to open the lock gate.

This is the question that has been at the back of his mind for a while. When he started, he was doing something rather than nothing and that took his mind completely off the reality of him and Kim. Now that he and the raft have been in the news, in the papers, she is bound to have seen it, so how does she feel? He should call Sleet, find out if he has been in touch with her. If he hasn't, maybe he can contact her. It is so easy to get caught in the moment and not think about consequences. He sighs. Isn't that exactly what the problem was in the first place – him not thinking ahead, always caught in the moment?

He looks at the television van. It seems odd that Kim's new employer, Channel Doc, is not there. That would have been a good move for Kim, to use her insider information, a personal viewpoint. Surely she would not hold back because she is still angry with him? No, that makes no sense at all. In fact why has Channel Doc not used her in that way, pushed her into the limelight, forced her to take centre stage? What has stopped her? Is she is all right? The more he thinks about it, the less it fits.

People are trying to help with the lock gates. Five of them are pushing on the water gate, so Neil walks away, superfluous. He unhitches the tow rope ready to pull the raft through. The lock-keeper is hovering.

'Hey, mate.' Neil calls him closer and talks quietly in his ear. 'Can you take the raft through the locks to speed things up? There's something I need to do.'

The lock-keeper starts to object but when a microphone is pushed in their faces he sees Neil's point and takes the tow rope.

'Neil!'– 'Neil!' Now he is free, the press hound him.

'Guys.' He holds his hands up, palms towards them. 'There comes a time when a man needs to stand behind a bush to obey the call of nature, so give me a little space, okay?' The male reporters immediately back off, the women taking just a microsecond longer as Neil slips away from the crowd and goes behind the cottage. Pulling out his phone, he recalls Kim's number and immediately feels sick. It is so much easier just to keep walking, and as long as he is moving and she is at the end of his journey he does not have to deal with the reality of whether she will actually want him back or not. As long as he keeps walking, he feels like he has the control. But now, standing behind the lock-keeper's cottage, pressing the numbers on his phone, the power is clearly Kim's. Please let her have seen the raft on telly and let her think it is cool. Please.

The phone rings. He mops his forehead with his sleeves, the faint smell of lavender lingering. It continues to ring. Maybe she is at work and cannot answer her phone – in a meeting, talking to the boss, keeping her connection with Neil a secret. If she is keeping her connection with him secret, that can only mean she does not want him, that she is embarrassed to know him. But maybe not – she was never openly affectionate to him when Sleet was around. She is quite a private person in that way. Maybe she is keeping her private life just that – private.

There is no answer and nor does it click to voicemail. Does that mean anything? He presses the record button on his phone to video and turns it towards himself.

'Kim, I hope you are okay … I hope I haven't embarrassed you with this venture. I hope Channel Doc doesn't pressure you to do anything you don't want to do.'

He clicks it off. He feels a little better even though of course it will make no difference to Kim, right now. Can he remember Sleet's number? He tries what he thinks it might be but a woman answers in a Liverpudlian accent.

'No Sleet here, mate, sorry,' and the phone goes dead again. He could call Ian. And say what? 'Find Kim' are the words that rush to his mind, but he does not want a journalist landing on her doorstep. He could text Ian and ask him to tell Sleet to call – that might work. His thumbs go to work, composing the message:

Ian, woke late, raft gone without me, caught it up. Huge circus of people following now. Can you give Sleet this number, tell him to call or text. At Sixteen Locks which is actually only Four Locks, if you have an idea where that is.

After running a hand through his hair, he replaces his hat firmly on his head and, bracing himself, he turns to meet the band of people again. The thought of Sleet calling him gives a bounce to his step. He can also hear Kim in his head. If she were here she would be encouraging him to grab this opportunity, to make the most of what is happening. He can almost feel how she would be behind him, steering him towards the camera. She might even approve of this creation Sleet has supposedly built on the waste ground by their old flat.

'Building a sculpture of the raft – nice one, Sleet,' he chuckles as the reporters approach him again.

For the first interview, he imagines he is Sleet and tries to think how his friend would answer. By the time the raft is halfway through the locks and he has done no fewer than five interviews, two on camera, he is feeling in the swing of the whole thing. A photographer asks him to pose with Bushy-Mush in his arms.

'Thanks,' he says, after he has his shot. 'We're off to London now to talk to Kim. Can you give us her contact number or address or something please?' The pressman waits expectantly, his pencil poised over a notebook.

'No can do,' Neil says. 'She has a right to her privacy.'

'Yes, but she is part of this whole thing.' The photographer seems astonished.

'If you wrote a love poem, would you print your beloved's name and address alongside it?' Neil says. Quentin would quite like that reply.

'Ah well, sorry to say, she will be tracked down anyway. Besides, we already have girls ringing up saying they are Kim. Better to get the right girl, I'd say.'

He strides off without waiting for a reply. Neil is rooted to the spot. A wave of panic shoots adrenaline across his chest and down his limbs. The press are hunting Kim, and girls he has never even met are claiming the piano is for them.

'What the heck have I done!' He looks around at all the people that surround him – the press, and the crowd behind. Have any of the girls in the crowd here claimed to be Kim? He takes a step back. Him in the spotlight is one thing, but the press hounding Kim, people pretending to be Kim – it feels terrifying, as if his life is spinning out of his control. Kim will be furious … Or perhaps not. Perhaps she will be amused.

The lock-keeper has the raft through three of the gates now and is opening the fourth. The circle around the guitar player has grown, and the field they have occupied has taken on the appearance of a festival, with blankets laid out on the grass, picnic baskets, ice creams and hotdogs, and lovers embracing. There is only a small group actually around the raft, and those who were helping with the lock gates seem to have lost interest. A boy of about nine or ten hovers with a notebook and pencil, looking nervous.

'Do you want an autograph?' Neil says, to be helpful.

'No.'

Neil raises his eyebrows at this.

'Can I have an interview for the year five magazine?' the boy says and Neil smiles. It's definitely a weird day – one of the weirdest!

'Sure. Do you have questions?' He feels he has answered everything he could about the Pianoraft today in one interview or another. He is getting really good at sounding like a real artist.

'Yes, what will you do if the raft sinks?' the boy barks.

'Great question.' Neil laughs. It feels refreshing to have a new thought about the raft. 'Do you mean if the piano went down too, or would that still float?'

'The whole lot, gone.' The boy sounds so serious.

'Okay.' Neil pretends to scowl, to look serious too. As he mulls over his reply he realises that, actually, it is a very good question. Apart from seeing Kim, begging her to take him back, he has not given a thought to what he is actually going to do with his life in London if she accepts him back into her life. But maybe, on the back of all the press over the Pianoraft, he can try to find a gallery that will take his work.

'I would walk the rest of the way to London, find Kim, marry her and paint pictures for the rest of my life.' He plays the game, creates the happy-ever-after for the boy, and he quite likes the sound of his own fantasy.

'What sort of pictures will you paint?'

The questions in this interview are much harder than the BBC's or ITV's.

'Pretty ones.' He knows he is being patronising but what else can he say to a ten-year-old?

'Do you think the world wants pretty pictures any more?' the boy counters, not fazed in the least. 'Grown-ups seem to like war more.'

'You're a tough interviewer,' Neil says, hoping to make the boy smile, but the child's face remains straight. The question saddens him and he has no idea how to answer.

He is saved by a cheer from the crowd as the raft is pulled out of the bottom lock.

'Sorry, little man, I have to go,' he says, and he pats the boy on the shoulder and starts to walk away.

'Hey, mister,' the boy calls after him. 'Nice hat.' The boy grins a very wide smile and then runs off to a woman – his mother, presumably – waiting by a car. She smiles and waves at Neil.

Chapter 25

Taking up the tow rope, Neil sets off, wondering if he can sneak away, maybe with just one or two stragglers. But as he begins to get into a rhythm, a general hum of noise and movement behind him tells him that the crowds are decamping and that the number of people on the footpath has grown rather than shrunk. He is quickly surrounded by enthusiastic supporters. A woman next to him, in a tie-dyed shirt, chats about this and that for a while, and then lowers her voice to explain that she separated from her partner recently. It seems there was some petty squabble and the relationship broke down. She laughs, playing down the significance of what she is saying.

'I'd have been satisfied with some flowers,' she says, 'and we'd have made up. It's not as if I was asking him to tow a piano the length of the country!'

Neil picks up on her sadness and tries to make the right noises. She is very thin and her hair is entirely white, and if anyone were to judge on looks alone, she would be cast in the role of agony aunt and he would be deemed to be the one with the problem. If it was not for the seriousness of her voice, he would probably smirk at this miscasting, but as it is, having her talk to him in such personal detail and with such seriousness is giving him an unfamiliar sensation. For a start, it makes him feel very adult, a characteristic Kim often said he lacked, but he is also feeling – how would he describe it? … It is the same feeling as the one time he got to hold Sleet's sister's baby. It felt as if he was being entrusted with something so very special, to which any indelicate handling could do so much damage. He had counted her toes and fingers and taken in the smell of the fluffy down on her head, and he had felt such a sense of honour to be experiencing the closeness of this new life. Yes, that is what he feels now – honoured that this thin lady with the white hair is sharing her emotional life with him.

'Kim will be waiting for you in London, mark my words,' she says sagely. 'She already knows how lucky she is to have a man do this for her.' She indicates the pantomime that surrounds the raft. Neil is not so sure.

Over the course of the day, various people talk to him – some jovially, about art and adventure, whilst many confide intimate details of their relationships to him, and the feeling of being asked to hold something as precious as a newborn comes to him again and again.

One woman, about Kim's age, says, 'She must be loving this, watching the news, seeing your progress towards her, delivering this piece of art – so romantic.'

He wants to believe her but can't help wondering why Kim is keeping her distance and staying so silent.

The crowd all eat lunch on the hoof. Some of the families with small children stop to eat but then catch up a few minutes later, all marching at a brisk pace.

One of the fathers chants, 'We had a good home but we left, right, left, right,' the children repeating it after him, their arms swinging, eyes shining, as they troop one behind the other, playing at soldiers.

Neil is constantly being handed sandwiches, slices of nut roast, boiled eggs, packets of nuts or crisps. It makes him smirk, to think that just a day or two ago he was wondering how he was going to find enough to eat on the journey. By late afternoon, he has eaten so much he feels the need for a lie down, so with Fuzzy-Pants as his excuse he climbs on board. Inside the cabin, the noise of the people is slightly muffled. The dark patch of wet on the floorboards in the corner has grown and the place really stinks of cat pee now. He must make a point of either taking her out or providing some cat litter or something. He delights in feeding her bits of hard-boiled egg.

'Ah my little fuzzy friend, it's a bit of a mad life!' They are both startled by an electronic buzz, and it takes him a second or two to recognise that it is his phone. He takes it out cautiously and looks at the number, recognising it immediately as Sleet's.

'Of course!' he exclaims. 'It was six-seven at the end, not seven-six! ... Hey, Sleet!'

'Hey, big man.' They both laugh. 'So it seems my plan worked, then,' Sleet says.

'And what plan was that then?' Neil waits for the punchline.

'Oh, you know, the standard plan ... Get you drunk, throw you on a raft, push you off to London and wait for you to get famous. That old plan.'

'Ah yes, that one. Well, if this is all your doing can you tone it down a bit?'

'I liked your interview for ITV on the lunchtime news, very slick, you almost sounded like me.'

'You taught me everything I know,' Neil banters.

'So, you'll be pleased to hear that your student loan is now paid off.'

'You're kidding me.' Neil's eyes widen at this news. 'The lot, all of it?'

'Yup, all of it, so now I'm starting a fund to put on an exhibition in London. We'll rent a gallery and put on a big splash. When do you think you'll hit London?'

'Well, it's hard to know, really. I mean, I'm not sure where I am or how far I'm travelling each day,' Neil says vaguely.

'Well, you must have some idea of where you are – what was the last town or village you passed through?'

'There was a Sixteen Locks, which was actually Four Locks, a while back, but that was hours ago. I really have no idea how far we've come.'

'Can't you find out? Have you no one there who is map-reading, some middle-aged walker in a kagool?' Sleet's words are clipped.

'They are nice people, Sleet. Why are you being so derisive?'

'I'm not being derisive, I'm just being practical.'

'So when did you become all serious and official?' Neil tries to inject some laughter into his voice but it falls flat. 'Besides, can't you trace the progress online? Find Sixteen Locks, then I can describe the landscape here or something and you can work it out that way.'

'Okay, hang on, I'm just looking at a map now. Oh, okay, so you're *there* … and yesterday the *Daily Press* said you were *there*. Oh right. So, if you keep going at this speed …'

Sleet's voice tails off, and all Neil can hear is mumbling. Then he comes back on the line again, confident, businesslike.

'Right, so I'm going to hire a gallery for the twenty-fourth. I reckon that would be perfect timing.'

'What if you don't get enough donations?' Neil hates these schemes of Sleet's when all the loose ends are not totally wrapped up.

'Then I'll blag the gallery into doing it for less. Trust me, they'll want the exposure. The TV lot are sure to come.'

'Er, Sleet, mate.'

'What, what's up?' Sleet's voice is buoyant.

'Have you heard from Kim?'

'Ah.' Sleet goes quiet and an icy sensation creeps over Neil's forearms. He pulls his jumper sleeves down.

'What is it?'

'Well, I don't want you to panic, but I can't find her.' Sleet sounds unsure.

'What?'

'She's safe, we know that, but no one knows where she is. Well, not exactly.'

'Have you been round to her parents'?' Neil can taste bile in his mouth.

'That's how I know she's safe. She called them, in fact she's called them a few times. Apparently, she said she's fine but she hasn't given them an address, at least that's what they are saying.'

'Did you get her number?'

'Apparently the number was withheld.'

The icy film has crept up his back.

'Are they worried?' Neil tries to gauge the seriousness of the situation. Kim's parents could just be keeping him away, seeing this as a new start for Kim. They liked him to begin with but were not impressed that he was still on the dole after the first year, and now, on the rare occasions that they do speak, they are polite but cold.

'Not in the least. They say she sounds chirpy, that she's busy and that she'll give them numbers and addresses when she's settled. I mean, I get it, she's only been in London a few days, not weeks. Give the girl a chance, and all that.'

Neil is grateful for Sleet's optimism, but he doesn't entirely believe it.

'Time must be seeming so different to her,' he says. 'I feel like I've been doing this journey all my life now, but I bet for her, with her new job, the days have just flown. How do you think she is going to react to the TV interviews, Sleet?'

'You're the artist-hero, mate – how could she not love you!' His tone becomes alive again.

'So why has she not been in touch?'

'Is this your old phone?'

'No, one I was given.'

'Where's your old phone?'

'It went dead the day we left.'

'Then how can she call you?'

'She could have called you?'

'Be realistic, it would take a national disaster for her to stoop to calling me. I was never her favourite person.'

'Well, can you find her, please, mate – talk to her, give her this number? The press say they are going to track her down. They say other girls are calling, pretending to be her. It's all a bit mad. I just want to know that she's not angry with me for all this, you know?'

'She won't be angry, I know that for sure. Isn't this the sort of thing she was always pressing you to do, wanting you to make some big jump into the art world? Do something with your life – be someone?'

'Yeah, I suppose.'

'Yeah for sure! Come on, Neil, you know she was frustrated with you. That's why she took off alone. She'll be in touch, mark my words. Her new job will be full on right now, so let's give her some time.'

'Well, that also concerned me. If she is at Channel Doc, why hasn't she used her connection with me to give herself a boost up the ladder – you know, get them to let her interview me? That would be the scoop that everyone else seems to be looking for.'

'Dunno, mate – ah, but did I tell you, I made a sculpture of the raft from all the rubbish dumped by the side of your old flat, and guess what! Greater Lotherton Council have bought it to put out the front of the library!'

'No way!'

'Way!'

There's a beep.

'Ah, that's my battery again. They should design these things with solar panels permanently attached so you never have to recharge them,' Neil moans.

'You sound like my dad.'

'Sod off. Look, I'm going to put this thing on charge. Please, please, get this number to Kim, all right? Somehow.'

'I'll do my best, and I'll email her too. Oh, and I'll tell her that you'll be in London, let's say Hackney Wick, on the twenty-fourth, okay? So don't be late – ha ha.'

The line goes dead.

Even with the chatter of people outside, the raft suddenly seems lonely. Neil strokes Fuzzy-Pants and lies down next to her so his nose buries into her soft fur. Why the hell did he not just buy the ticket to London at the train station with Kim? It would have been so much easier! The noise outside, the constant people all around – it's irritating.

He closes his eyes; he will sleep as long as he can. Maybe he will feel better when he wakes up.

He must have been tired, as he sleeps through the evening and wakes up very early the next day. Scooping up Fuzzy-Pants, he takes her outside to pee. Tents are strung along the towpath, ghostly shapes in the half-light, each one zipped up tight. The little cat jumps about excitedly, and Bushy-Mush turns up from nowhere and seems just as happy to see Fuzzy-Pants on the towpath as Fuzzy is to be outside. When they stop leaping about and start sniffing each other, taking their time, Neil takes the opportunity to grab them both and put them in the cabin, closing the door firmly.

Then, making as little noise as possible, he unties the mooring line, and with a tug the raft starts to move. The piano judders and he looks at it in alarm. The tarpaulin is not covering the instrument, and he notices that all the polish has gone off the top. He must cover it over again, do his best to protect it, but right now it feels more urgent to make his escape.

He walks steadily, towing the raft and checking behind him every few steps. No one follows. The feeling of being alone allows him to breathe more freely. The countryside on either side of the canal is still and shrouded in low-lying mist. The world is perfect and it only gets better as the sun breaks through the huge white fluffy clouds to cast shafts of light onto the hills.

Once he is a safe distance from the camp, he decides to let Bushy-Mush out, only to find he is curled up asleep with his feline friend. Neil returns to pulling and his thoughts drift to Kim. Is she awake yet? What time does her day start? What is the flat like? The postcard Sleet stole suggested a window that lets in masses of light – that's where she wants to put the piano. Maybe he could grow tomatoes in growbags by the other windows, fill the place with plants, bring the outdoors in. He can imagine Kim stretching on clean white linen, the sun pouring over her from the oversized windows, and him in the kitchenette making coffee, like Quentin did every morning for his wife. But if he ever feels like walking out, he will talk to Kim first, get her to come with him. In fact, they should have some of those adventures they were always talking about. Maybe by working in London and saving what they can, he will be able to afford to take her abroad, to India, Cambodia, Cuba – all the places they have dreamed of, that have so far been beyond their grasp. It might inspire his work; the colours are sure to influence him.

His dreams fill his mind and bring energy to his feet, and pretty soon he has forgotten the group of hangers-on. Consequently, it's a shock when he stops for a breather and finds a ragged group of people following in his footsteps, and his first emotion is resentment.

'Morning,' a woman with a dog on a lead says, breathing heavily as she catches up with him. 'Sorry, we were late getting up. Did you sleep well?'

Others join them, smiling, jolly.

'Morning.' Neil cannot find a smile. He was enjoying being with Kim in their make-believe flat. He was about to cook her pancakes before she went off to her very important job with Channel Doc.

'Would you like me to take that?' The woman with the dog puts her hand out for the rope. He gives it to her, and the group chatter amongst themselves: sleepy, half-awake sounds. Walking ahead on his own, Neil finds he cannot bring the daydream back, or at least not so that it feels real.

After half an hour, a small canal boat catches them up and offers a tow, and it's a relief to Neil that the general consensus is that he should accept, even though it will mean them walking a bit faster or being left behind.

When he hesitates, someone says, 'Kim is waiting.'

So the rope is passed over, and the canal boat captain smiles and introduces himself as Dan, or Dom, or maybe even Ben. Neil shakes hands with him to show his appreciation and then opts to travel in the raft, preferring his own space. He spends the afternoon sketching the inside of the raft and the animals and then the passing countryside. He does one or two images from memory, of the banks of reporters and the crowds of people, which turn out rather dark. Using a rubber, he cuts back into the marks he has made to lighten them up, but what he is left with is smoky and slightly dreamy. He is so engrossed that when the canal boat man calls to say they have arrived it feels like a jolt and he wonders where they are.

Predictably, it turns out to be another towpath pub – this time, The Carping Crusader. The landlord comes out and slips something into the hand of the boatman, who gives Neil a cheery wave, jumps back aboard and turns round, heading back the way he came. In the distance, Neil can see the jumble of people who were following him still coming down the towpath. They are not so far behind.

At The Carping Crusader there are local television and radio vans, and the two reporters greet him warmly. Both want an interview. Neil does his best not to be short with them but something has shifted inside him. He wants to be alone now, or rather he wants to be done with this journey and be with Kim. The landlord offers Neil his dinner on the house, and he also invites the television and radio crews inside; the pub fills with their equipment, lights are brought in, and the small space becomes claustrophobic. It feels like the camera is only inches from his face as he eats.

People loiter around, not knowing quite what to do. One asks if she can go out and play the piano, and soon a very accomplished version of 'My Funny Valentine' comes drifting in through the pub windows. The radio man is quick to join her and capture the performance, and the television crew are not far behind. It sends shivers down Neil's spine, especially when she gets to the lyric 'You make me smile with my heart, your looks are laughable, unphotographable, yet you're my favourite work of art.'

'So, what's this raft all about then?' The landlord interrupts his reminiscing. 'I saw it on the television but the sound was down, always is in here.' He points to the small, wall-mounted television at the end of the bar.

'It's a piece of art,' Neil replies without hesitation.

'Oh yeah? Art, eh? Well, that will always bring all the fun of the fair. You want a drink?'

'Thanks,' Neil replies automatically. 'Actually, can you make that an orange juice?' Kim would be impressed.

The song comes to an end and the camera crew returns indoors and closes in on him as he drinks the orange juice. The group of people that were following arrive and they all try to get into the pub, and the landlord's wife appears behind the bar to help serve them all.

The woman with the camera crew squeezes in beside Neil.

'Neil, do you have anything to say to the people to whom you have brought such hope and joy with your demonstration and art?'

Neil notes that she has worded her question carefully to cover all that the raft might be. He clenches his fists; he just wants to eat his dinner and have a glass of orange juice in peace. But then he has an idea.

'Yes, I have a message. It's not for the people.' He looks straight into the camera. 'It's for Kim. Kim, I should have bought a ticket and gone with you to London. It was dumb not to. A lot has changed since you left.' He pauses for thought. 'Mostly inside of me. I have so much to tell you, to share with you. I'll be in London soon. Check your emails.' He turns to the reporter. 'That's it.'

And he downs the orange juice, thanks the landlord and leaves too quickly for the television and radio crews to follow with all their paraphernalia.

Chapter 26

As Neil leaves, it's as if a bell has been rung and time called. Drinks are left half drunk, and a stream of people follow him out of the doors and down the slope to the water's edge.

'Aren't we staying the night here?' a voice in the crowd asks. Neil doesn't want to answer. Anger boils in the pit of his stomach. Where did that feeling come from? Was it the microphone in his face whilst he ate? No, he is angry with himself, with the mess he has made of things with Kim. How easy it has been to con himself that she will just be there waiting for him in London. That he will be forgiven and they will just carry on living together as they have done for the last two years, as if nothing had happened. But now he is begging over the television for her to get in touch because she can't be found. He can no longer continue with the illusion that as long as he keeps walking all is well. He cannot bear to think about what it will mean if she is not there when he reaches London.

'I need to walk,' Neil replies, and those who had started to pitch their tents hurriedly begin to dismantle them, and others buckle up their rucksacks. A ripple of excitement at the possibility of a starlit walk charges the crowd. Bushy-Mush is as excited as anyone and he runs back and forth through the throng of people. The little dog has become very adept at leaping from the bank onto the raft and landing in a skid that ends with him shouldering the door of the cabin. He then jumps back, his paws scrabbling on the muddy bank, and repeats the process.

As Neil walks, he tries to block out his thoughts, concentrating on each step, expending his angry energy.

'You want me to take the rope a while?' It's Tristan, spokesman for the philosophy group. Neil thought the students had peeled off a while back.

'No, you're all right,' he says. He just wants to walk. The moon rises in the sky, lighting the way, and owls hoot as they head deeper into the countryside. A part of him knows that it is unfair to keep the people walking into the night but until his feelings subside he is urged on. Anyway, they can choose for themselves what they want to do, can't they?

'Sure you don't need someone to take over from you?' Tristan says a little later, yawning. Neil gives in this time – not to having the rope taken from him, but to stopping for the night. He senses a collective sigh of relief from the others as he ties up the raft to a tree. Head torches come on and tents are erected. He quite likes seeing this – the tents springing into shape as soon as they are unzipped. The chatter quietens, and the zips of sleeping bags and tents can be heard in between the owl calls.

Bushy-Mush has curled up in the centre of the mattress but Fuzzy-Pants is awake, fighting with one of Neil's jumpers, her front paws and teeth maintaining a tight hold as her back legs kick away.

'Come on, Fuzzy, sleep time now.' But she thinks it is a game as he tries to take away his jumper. In the end, he lets her have it and uses a T-shirt over his shoe as a pillow. The green cushion that Bill gave him has long since been lost. He suspects Bushy-Mush took it for a walk and it never came back.

He lies on his back and flicks on the phone. 'I don't think I've shown you the inside of the raft before,' he tells the absent Kim. 'Look, there is Bushy-Mush, and this cheeky little girl is Fuzzy-Pants, on account of her long hair and ridiculous markings. Can you see, she looks like she is wearing short white trousers. I sleep here. As you can see, there's not much room, but your chair is there.'

He is not sure what else to say so he looks at his reflection in the camera. If he says anything about how he is feeling right now he is going to come undone, so he switches the phone off, tucks it inside his shoe and closes his eyes.

The morning brings a chill and it is the cold that gets him up. He hasn't lit the pot-bellied stove yet, but now seems like the perfect time to try it. The domed tents in the field next to the towpath give the impression that giant moles have been busy in the night. Nothing stirs, all is quiet and Neil relishes the stillness as he gathers bits of wood, broken branches and twigs from the hedgerows. By the side of the field is a coppice, and here he finds a pile of logs, which he carries back to the raft. It occurs to him that he doesn't have a light, and he thinks of Quentin.

'Now, how will I ever track you down to see you again?' he asks his missing friend with a touch of sadness in his heart. He begins a tiptoed tour of the tents. Outside some of them sit Primus stoves, and one, thank goodness, has a lighter balanced on top. He makes a note of which tent it is and then returns to the raft and sets a blaze going. The stove draws well, and soon the wood is roaring, flames licking up the chimney, and the cabin warms up in no time. He will need more wood if he is to keep it going, though, and so he returns to the coppice for another few armfuls, dropping the lighter off on the way back. He returns to find Fuzzy-Pants stretched out in front of the fire and the place pleasantly warm.

He sits on the edge of his mattress and warms his toes, and all the thoughts of the evening before return to him and, despite the relative comfort now that he is warm, his head sinks to his chest, his shoulders slump, and there seems little point in doing anything but sitting there.

From the window on the side of the cabin facing the water, he can see the coots swimming around absently, and behind him, through the solid wall, he can hear the tent-dwellers waking up. They laugh and chat and the noise increases, and soon he can smell bacon cooking. Bushy-Mush whines to be let out. Neil kicks the door with his foot and his furry friend makes his escape. Fuzzy-Pants continues to bask in the heat.

'You know what, Fuzzy,' he begins, 'if she's not there in London waiting, what's the point in going on?', and he wonders what the people outside would do if he just walked away. Maybe they would continue the journey without him. He could do that – just walk away, forget the whole thing. That would be facing the truth – real life, as some might call it. But what then? Work for Sleet's dad again?

'Oh my God, can you imagine how annoyed Sleet would be if I jacked this all in?' he says to the cat, but there is no joy in his voice. 'And the alternative? Keep towing just to focus on something other than this hole in my chest that Kim left behind her?'

Fuzzy-Pants rolls onto her back, exposing her tummy to the heat.

'That doesn't seem like a very good reason.' He slips out his phone and presses record. 'Kim, you might never get this recording. In fact, you probably won't, but just so I can have some closure, as they call it, I want to say something. This whole thing from the beginning was a ridiculous and pointless exercise. I was just sticking my head in the sand to avoid the realities of life, as usual, just as I did in the days before you left for London. No sense of reality. No wonder you had just had enough and walked away. I think I would have, too. Well, over the last twelve hours, being surrounded by this ridiculous circus that some have named "the romantic quest of the century" and others have labelled "extreme performance art" and yet others "a load of woodpulp", I have hit reality face on and I see what I am doing for what it really is. It's just more prevarication, a prime example of shying away from getting on with life. Had you been here, you would have told me that from the start. I know you've seen straight through me. I mean, let's face it, I've been all over the news and there is no way you could have missed this embarrassing episode – my fifteen minutes of fame. Honestly, I think Andy Warhol will be turning in his grave! But you, having seen it, have not contacted me, and nor have you appeared on Channel Doc making a name for yourself. No, you've made your opinion clear by staying silent. I get it. I hear you, and believe it or not I understand. I just wish I could see you again just to say … Actually, I have no idea what I would say. Maybe just ask to see your face one more time, just to really accept I have well and truly blown it and to say – yes, to say that I really do wish you a good life.'

He clicks the phone off, lies next to Fuzzy-Pants and hides his wet cheeks in her warm fur.

Hours later, he blinks and yawns; the heat of the stove and the early hour must have sent him to sleep again. He takes a moment to orientate himself.

Fuzzy-Pants is relieving herself in the corner of the cabin, and the smell begins to permeate the air. As he rouses himself, he realises the raft is moving and, looking out of the window to the water, he sees the opposite bank slipping past. The choice of whether the raft should go on or not has been taken from him.

'I wonder how many other people on this journey are also avoiding reality,' he muses. 'Goddamn, Fuzzy, that stinks.'

The smell forces him outside. He really must get her some cat litter, or make a little bridge that she can use to cross to the bank when they are stationary. Anything but allow her to keep doing what she is doing.

'Morning, Neil.' Tristan is pulling the rope again. His skinny arms and legs show every taut muscle that is called into play to pull the weight along. What is *he* avoiding, for example? A midterm paper, perhaps, or choosing a subject for his final year; or maybe he just doesn't like his course at all and this is a way of avoiding that reality.

'You said you were second year, right?' Neil asks.

'Yup, but I feel like I'm just treading water,' Tristan says.

Ah, so that's it; he isn't happy with his course.

'I just want this year to pass so I can get stuck into my thesis.'

So, he does like his subject, but maybe he is having difficulty finding a topic for his thesis? Maybe he's avoiding that?

'Are you struggling for a topic?'

'I've narrowed it down to a choice of two avenues of investigation.' Tristan sounds enthused. 'Either "Can we help others without helping ourselves?", in which I want to investigate the perceived altruism of giving without receiving – materially, at least – or I quite fancy "The inescapability of mental externalism". Fascinating, don't you think?'

The question catches Neil off guard. 'Ah, so you're here pulling a raft to avoid thinking about which you want to do?' he says, with a knowing smile and a wink that is meant to convey his understanding of the whole position.

'Good Lord, no! I'm here firstly because I believe wholeheartedly that we need to make a stand against the growing war machine that has become just another part of modern-day life, but also so I can think about the inescapability of mental externalism while gauging whether I am helping myself through giving without materially receiving. It's win, win and win!'

'You want me to pull for a bit?' Neil says, wishing now that he at least hadn't winked. Despite being a teenage boy, Tristan is so much older than he is, in some ways.

'Actually, if you have no objection, Paul and Julia asked if they could pull for a while.'

Paul and Julia, who have been following close behind, now step forward, eager. To Neil it seems like they will snap if they pull too hard; they cannot even be out of school.

'Sure,' he says, and he stops walking so Bushy-Mush can catch up. The little dog loiters, savouring a wealth of interesting smells, and it is a while before he joins Neil, by which time they are far enough behind the group not to be overheard.

'It seems it's just me, then, avoiding the world,' Neil says. A chaffinch replies with a tuneful warble.

In the days that follow, Neil finds that walking some way behind the raft and the crowd, which seems to grow ever bigger, suits him best. The chill of that morning when he lit the little pot-bellied stove does not return – both days and nights seem to be getting warmer. Most days, he walks with just a T-shirt and jeans on. He fixes up a cat litter tray of sorts, using a sandwich box and soil for litter, and if he cleans it morning and night the cabin is mostly odour free. He tries building a little bridge to the shore but Fuzzy-Pants is too timid to cross over the water, even when

Bushy-Mush delights in showing her how, again and again.

His days and nights take on their own rhythm. He seems to wake at the same hour, walk for four hours or so, rest for a while, walk another four hours and then bed down when it goes dark. His leg muscles grow stronger and he doesn't ache like he did in the early days, although he is aware that he seldom pulls the raft any more: everyone else is doing that. The crowd sometimes grows quite big, and the time for which each person pulls is very short. At other times there are fewer people, but he is never alone. At each new town they are welcomed by a local television crew or radio station, usually waiting by the first pub. He patiently answers all their questions and he keeps in touch with Ian as agreed, but it is the conversations with Sleet that concern him.

'Look, mate, I've tried everything to find Kim but her parents are not being very forthcoming,' Sleet says during one phone call.

'Not really surprising, I guess. They never liked me much, you even less,' Neil replies.

'Don't get all down about it, she'll turn up. She's probably watching this whole thing and waiting to surprise you in London.'

But neither of them believe it; that would not be Kim's way.

'Can't you press her parents? Hey, have you tried her at Channel Doc?' Neil brightens at this thought.

'Of course I have, but the girl on reception kept harping on about confidentiality agreements. I couldn't say too much as I figured you wouldn't want me to say it was the guy from the raft – I presume there's a reason why she has not owned up to knowing us.'

'Yeah, well, you did right there.' But there is something in the way Sleet is talking that makes Neil wonder how hard he is actually trying.

Between interviews and calls and texts and the constant demands from the crowd of people, Neil finds that he likes walking all day. He appreciates the time it gives him to study nature, to watch the smaller things in life: the way the birds land on the thin branches and then bounce, their heads staying still; the way a dog that belongs to one of the people walking with him runs with its back legs slightly to one side. He watches the movement of the canal water against the banks, in the raft's wake. The chatter of the people blends into the background and he listens to the drum of his feet – step, step, step. All day long – step step step. On gravel, it is crunch, crunch, crunch, and on mud, squish, squish, squish. On tarmac the sound is harder, and through grass there is a soft swishing to it. With these sounds he tries to block out the future and thoughts of what he might do when this is all over. Maybe he will find Quentin ... But this thought is too sobering and he pushes it firmly away and looks for something else to focus on.

He starts to time his breath by his footsteps, and his breathing deepens, and he notices this brings his heart rate down. His thinking slows too, and after some time has passed, he no longer thinks at all; he just exists.

The days follow nights follow days. He loses track of where he is in the world. The press and television and followers are still there, only he no longer feels part of what is going on; he has become a bystander of his own creation. The only thing that lifts him from this solitary place is the news that no one can find Kim; there are rumours she has gone abroad, some say America, others say India. The media are making the most of this hunt for the missing girlfriend. Sleet is silent on the matter – no texts, no calls. Ian is in the dark as much as anyone else. Members of the crowd buy newspapers in the villages they pass through, and they read them aloud to eager ears.

'Hey, listen to this one! "Several girls have come forward recently, claiming to be Kim, but now we can reveal that Kim is in fact a man. He lives in

South Kensington and lectures at the Royal Academy of Arts."'

The reader turns to call to Neil, who is walking behind as usual. 'Is that true, Neil?'

'No,' he replies; the company laughs and he manages a smile. What was it Quentin said about being alone in a crowd? But he also said it is all in the head. What was the trick of the head? Oh yes – Quentin said to look outward.

'Listen to this one. "Is she real, or is Kim a metaphor?"' Again the reader turns to Neil.

'Metaphor for what?' Neil asks, trying his best to sound interested, to look outward.

'She is real, right?' someone else asks. It is the man with the dog whose back legs run off-centre.

'She's real,' Neil replies, and they walk on.

After a few days, Sleet calls.

'Hey, buddy boy, guess what!'

'You've found her?' The question springs to Neil's lips.

'Ah, no, but, erm, well, listen to this! They want you for a spot on *Art News Weekly* tonight. In fact, they want you so much they are willing to send a car to pick you up, take you to London, record the programme and then they'll run you back to the raft afterwards. What do you say?'

Sleet sounds so excited it seems a shame to let him down, but right now Neil is happy. No, not happy. Perhaps content. No, it's not that either. He is comfortable where he is; he doesn't need a fast track to London.

'Er, wow, well, what can I say? I do get the notion you are working very hard at all this, but you know that I started out on this raft to find Kim, just to get back together with her–'

'Yes, and that's what you'll do,' Sleet interrupts.

'Listen, Michael' – that gets his attention; he hasn't called Sleet by his given name since they were about five – 'to be honest, I think this whole thing has got out of hand and, well, to be honest – there is no soft way to put this, but – the long and the tall of it is that I am done with it.'

There, he has said it. Maybe Sleet can come down and tow the raft himself, be the person the people follow.

'Have you gone potty? So we don't know where Kim is, but look what you've created. This is art! Come on, Neil, what else are you doing with your life?'

And that's it. There is the truth, the plain and simple reality. What else is he doing with his life?

What else is he planning to do? What would he do if he stopped pulling the piano?

'Neil, here's what you do, right.' Sleet's tone of voice sounds just like Neil's dad. 'Pull the raft, have a London show, get famous, make some money and draw sketches for the rest of your life. You lucky bugger.'

Sleet adds the last sentence on with a teasing tone but Neil can hear a touch of jealousy behind his words.

'Besides, if you stop pulling the damned raft I get to spend the rest of my life being a sad clown instead of your agent and manager and that would be on your conscience.'

This makes Neil chuckle.

'Can't you come and pull with me for a bit?' he says.

'I'm in London tomorrow arranging your show, but we can meet up tonight if you do the *Arts News Weekly* thing.'

'I really don't fancy that.'

'Well, if you don't do it they're going to ask me. Your choice,' Sleet quips.

Neil feels the laughter poke at the inside of his ribs. It swells through his throat and explodes, louder than he anticipated, into a real guffaw. It feels like such a relief.

When it subsides he says, 'You do it, Sleet, you deserve some limelight, and besides, you'll be really good at it, talking all arty with those boffins they have on.'

'You sure?' Sleet asks. 'It's a paid gig. If I do it I get the dosh.'

Neil snorts. 'You know what, I think I almost miss you.'

'Course you do,' Sleet answers without hesitation. 'Right, so I'll do that tonight and I'll see you tomorrow.'

'Oh, so you'll come and help pull?'

'No, mate, it's the twenty-third. Tomorrow is the twenty-fourth – you'll be pulling into London. Judging by where they are saying you are right now, you'll probably be able to see the orange glow of the big city tonight, and I reckon you'll be there by lunchtime tomorrow.'

'Tomorrow – you're kidding me?'

'No, no kidding. There's a good pub at Hackney Wick.'

'Tomorrow, it's over?'

'Yes. We can have a quiet lunch there before going on to the gallery.'

A churning that starts in Neil's belly shivers up through his chest. He is not sure if he is going to laugh again or, this time, cry. He has done it! He has pulled a piano on a raft to London. Did he ever doubt he would? Yes, every single day.

'I've done it! London!' he cries.

'Of course you have, and like I just said, we can have a quiet lunch at the pub at Hackney Wick before going on to the gallery.'

Neil is laughing as he speaks.

'Sleet, haven't you seen how many people are pulling this thing? The idea of a quiet lunch is a joke.' He is enjoying the conversation now, excited by the idea that tomorrow it is over, tomorrow he can go and search for Kimberly himself. He's done.

'Well, maybe we'll go straight to the gallery. The opening is at nine, and we might have to go and buy something for you to wear first.'

'Can you hear yourself, Sleet? Go and buy me something to wear – you sound like my mother.'

'Just thinking about your future,' his friend says seriously.

'Now you sound like my dad.'

'Well, while you've been wandering along, pulling a blinking piano, I've had some short, sharp training in marketing, and you know what, I think I'm pretty good at it.'

'Sleet, my friend, I think you were born for it.'

'Thanks! Now we have the gallery and the wine and all that nonsense at nine, but it would be great to create a good atmosphere before you enter.'

It sounds Sleet is a world away, in a parallel universe. The way he is speaking is so alien Neil cannot believe that tomorrow he will be heading into that universe.

'Can you think of anything?' Sleet asks.

'Sorry, think of what?' He has not been listening.

'Something to create a buzz on the street before people go into the gallery. I don't know, something to attract the eye, to gets people's attention.'

It comes to Neil with no effort at all, and it feels so delightfully complete that it takes all the tension out of re-entering the real world.

'Sleet,' he says, 'find Jasper and Jez, a pair of jugglers, last seen performing in Ruttingham. They are great people, and they'll create an amazing buzz. Also, they were part of the raft's journey so they would be perfect.'

'Ah, that's my man,' Sleet exclaims. 'Together, you and I, we will conquer the world.'

Neil can hear him grinning as he talks, but before he is ready the phone purrs and Sleet is gone.

Chapter 27

The glow from the big city is not just slightly visible, as Sleet predicted – it outshines the stars so much that Neil can see nothing of the night sky. After absorbing all Sleet said, he is quite excited by what lies ahead, but deep in the pit of his stomach there is a dull ache due to the lack of contact from Kim.

Despite his excitement, he sleeps well, but he is woken early by Fuzzy-Pants scratching away at the soil in her sandwich box litter tray, and then an aroma permeates the cabin and Neil kicks the door open. Bushy-Mush runs out and the sun streams in. The day is glorious. Small white clouds hang in the sky, far off at the horizon, and the sun is warming the air, promising the heat of the summer to come.

A text from Ian arrives, saying he believes that Kimberly is no longer in London, that she has gone abroad, but it sounds like he has heard old news. No one, it seems, is really sure if Kim has gone to ground or moved away. Sleet has been useless in this matter, too, but then what would be his motivation? He and Kim never really got on, anyway, and Sleet was always much happier when it was just the two of them down the pub. But Neil doesn't really believe this of Sleet – that he would intentionally stop him from getting in touch with Kim.

This morning, the circus are slow to emerge from their tents.

Tristan yawns as he packs his tent; there is little energy in his movements.

'You all right?' Neil asks.

'Yeah.'

'You seem a bit – well, I don't know.'

'I'm fine, it's just adjusting, isn't it? One minute walking in the countryside, and then, later today, we'll be in the heart of London and standing up against the very people who propagate war.'

It takes a few moments for Neil to see the day from Tristan's point of view. Looking inward to his own world, Neil had seen no point if Kim was not there, but on the other hand, maybe she, maybe the two of them, maybe their whole relationship, was just a path, a vehicle to reach this point when Tristan will face the 'people who propagate war', as he puts it, and when Sleet will find his niche as an art agent and manager, and he, Neil, will become a credible artist. Is this 'looking outward', as Quentin suggested? Is this what he meant?

As they draw near to London, more people join them. Some come just to gawp, and others seem to derive their own meanings from the journey. Neil hears many different opinions and points of view. The

345

majority encourage him to keep going and suggest that he produce more artworks. The philosophy students come to him one by one and thank him for the journey. Many of the others who have been with him for a good part of the way make a point of saying a word or two – not much, nothing profound, just to make contact, but Neil is deeply touched by this. It seems that everyone who walked with him, for a long stretch or just for the last day, has their own idea about him, about the project, the raft and the piano. Neil avoids expressing an opinion. Instead, he lets people talk and he delights in all they have to say, not because what they are saying has any direct connection to him but because they feel close enough and trust him enough to open up to him. It feels like an honour, a privilege, and the world takes on new colours.

The canal widens, and beyond the trees that edge the waterway are skyscrapers. On his phone he films all he sees and then turns the camera on himself.

'Oh my God, this is amazing, I wish you could experience this!'

But he is aware that what he is experiencing is mostly his own awakenings, an awareness of the feat he has accomplished, of the fact that he has fulfilled his intention. And it is not only he who is amazed by what he has done: it seems that the world around him is amazed and excited by his journey too. He clicks off his phone and continues with all his senses on alert.

The pace seems to pick up as the canal winds into the city. There are more people walking and running on the towpath now, and canal boats are moored all along either bank. Many of these are piled high with bicycles, firewood and potted plants. The people calling these places home come out, and with boathooks they assist him on his journey, pushing him from one boat to the next, the crowd following on the banks.

The closer they get to the centre of London, the larger the crowd becomes. Some bring children, others carry placards, and a few have musical instruments. A jazz pianist jumps aboard, and someone comes forward to accompany him on the trumpet. The people living on the boats moored to the canal edge come out to join the party, and the group grows and grows. A saxophonist appears from nowhere and joins the piano and trumpet player. They play 'Take Five' with style and confidence. It's one of Kim's favourites.

Camera teams hang over the bridges they pass underneath, and people lean from office windows to shout hello and click their camera phones. Bushy-Mush is frantic with the energy of the event.

Neil wonders how many of the onlookers are expecting Kim to run through the crowd to him, for him to swing her off her feet, whilst the media incessantly clicks its cameras and captures the moment. But he knows that this is not how it will be. She helped him get here, helped him to reach this point, and now it is his job to use every avenue that is open to him to establish himself as an artist.

'Thank you, Kim,' he whispers, and he reads a sign on the wall on the other side of the water that announces that he has reached Hackney Wick. He has arrived – and up ahead, if he is not mistaken, is Sleet in a suit, with a camera crew. In a suit! He laughs out loud and takes out his phone to record this momentous occurrence. He films Sleet and Sleet's camera team films him. He draws closer and closer until Sleet's feet can no longer stay still and he runs to his friend.

'By 'eck, but it's reet grand ta see thee' – as he pulls away, Sleet tries to cover his embarrassment by exaggerating the Yorkshire accent they both find so comical. The piano, trumpet and saxophone are going full swing and they have to shout to be heard above the din. In no time, more camera crews have arrived, as have hamburger stands, tea and coffee stalls and the inevitable police in their high-vis jackets.

The press mostly leave him alone – it seems they are here to cover the event, but are behind safety barriers, and Neil is relatively safe from their attentions. It feels like a public celebration and Neil is caught up in the wonder of it all, looking around himself at the spectacle of the gathering.

But for Sleet, all necessary 'hellos' have already been said, and he is not in the least distracted by the commotion. He speaks to the police, who clear a space by the side of the canal, and a flat-backed truck and a crane are manoeuvred to the canal side. Neil is amused to witness Sleet cooperating with the police, rather than being cautioned for drunkenness or disturbing the peace, which has happened more than once in Greater Lotherton, and he records this on his phone too. The pianist is ushered off and two men with chains jump aboard the raft.

'What are they doing?' Neil feels a sense of violation.

'We need the raft in the exhibition,' Sleet says and he waves the crane driver closer.

'Hang on,' Neil exclaims, 'that's my home.'

'That's the art,' Sleet replies and continues gesticulating.

'For Christ's sake, wait!' Neil shouts and he rushes to the raft, pushing past one of the men, who is wrestling with one of the huge metal hooks that hang from the crane.

'Where's he going?' one of the men shouts to the other.

'Hey, we can't move it with you in it!' the other says as Neil pulls open the door to the cabin.

Inside, Fuzzy-Pants is fast asleep on his best jumper. Scooping her up, he stuffs her down the neck of his T-shirt and grabs his jumper and his cowboy hat, then fixes the latter firmly on his head.

'Oi!' The door opens; it is one of the men. 'Did you hear me? This is a work of art, you can't be in here.'

Neil doesn't know how to respond to this. It is all too sudden to know what he is feeling.

Sleet is now signing a sheet of paper on the truck driver's clipboard.

'Do I get my home back?' Neil asks.

'You get better than that,' Sleet says, and he throws his arm over his friend's shoulder.

'Where are we going?'

'You'll see.' Sleet is all smiles.

The party by the canal continues as they walk away. There is a cheer when the raft is lifted out of the water. The blue barrels underneath hang off the wooden structure, looking very poorly attached. Neil wonders how much longer the whole thing would have lasted. The building of the first part of the raft, behind his and Kimberly's flat, seems a lifetime ago, but he can still remember the sound of her laughter as he towed her up and down a short stretch of the water, and her arms around his neck the first time she jumped on board and the whole thing rocked.

'This way.' Sleet leads him between two substantial buildings that were once mills and factories but are now trendy eating places and artists' studios. Ten years ago, no one wanted these properties, but today they are full of elite arty types who are the only ones who can afford them. Sleet seems to know where he is going, and he turns into the cobbled yard of one of these Victorian buildings. Across the yard are a pair of wide double doors, and set within one of these is a smaller door, for which Sleet has the key. Inside, a large industrial lift takes them up. Sleet pulls a hip flask out of his suit pocket and offers it to Neil, who shakes his head and laughs.

'Ha! Some things never change,' Neil says.

Sleet takes a swig, grinning. Neil watches the neatly whitewashed stone walls pass as the lift climbs up and up, and then with a clang it comes to a halt. Sleet slides the concertina grill back and they step out into a narrow corridor with a metal door at the end. Key in hand, Sleet opens this to reveal a space of the kind Neil has only seen in the interior design magazines Kim used to buy. It is completely open plan and totally white. The floors, the walls, the sofa – even the canvases on the walls are mostly white. The furniture is dwarfed by the size of the room, and the rafters above their heads have also been painted white. But what makes the space so amazing are the windows all down one side, which provide a panoramic view of the surroundings and the canal for some distance either way.

'It's on its way!' Sleet says, and he points.

The raft is being carefully positioned on the back of the lorry, and as the ropes from the crane are detached they can hear the distant cheer of the people. Neil hopes that they have tied the piano on firmly, and he worries that the rocking chair might have fallen over inside and smashed one of the windows.

'Where's it going?' he asks. Everything is suddenly moving so quickly, and changing so fast, that he feels detached from the raft and from the whole journey, as if the process that he started has now taken on a life of its own and left him behind.

'To the gallery.' Sleet stops staring and sounds all businesslike again. 'Right! Through there is the bedroom. I thought it would be quicker if I just got you some clothes, so there are some things on the bed that should fit. Choose what you like. We have this place for the first two weeks of the exhibition, and by then I reckon we should know how things are going and we'll know what we can afford for your studio.'

'Where – here, in London?' Neil looks through to the bedroom, where trousers and shirts are laid out on a big brass bed. He cannot remember the last time he wore a button-up shirt – his granny's funeral, probably.

'Well, yeah. If we want you to be taken seriously as an artist then London is the place. I mean, we don't have to be here all the time, but you need a base, and a studio, somewhere to invite people to see your work. There's a good chance, I've been told, that there will be one or two bigwigs who will be asking to sit for a portrait, collectors of emerging artists' work, those sorts of people, so you can't have them jumping on the train and using up their day to go to a poky place in Greater Lotherton, can you?' He seems to find this funny.

Neil wants to talk about Kim, to involve her, somehow, even though she is not here. She would love this place. He looks around the all-white room and then out of the window across London.

'Who's paying for all this?'

'Ha! I told you I was good at this stuff. The gallery are paying. There were a few who wanted to take you on, so I just played them off against each other. In the end it doesn't really matter which one took you because, as you can see' – he nods to the crowds, still gathered by the canal even though the raft has now gone – 'the people are going to come to you.'

'Where's the fridge?' There is a row of flat white doors along one wall in the kitchen area, but none of them have handles.

'Ah yes, a beer!' Sleet presses the front of one of the cupboards and it springs open.

'No, milk.' Neil grabs the carton from the fridge door.

'Milk?' Sleet pulls a face. 'It sounds like you've lost your way in your travels.' He frowns.

Neil presses open one cupboard after another until he finds a bowl.

'It's for Fuzzy-Pants.'

He scoops his little furry friend out from inside his T-shirt, and then he remembers the dog.

'Oh, crapola!' he exclaims.' Where the heck is Bushy-Mush?' Neil puts the kitten on the floor by the bowl of milk and heads for the door.

'Don't panic,' Sleet says. 'Look, he's there.' And sure enough, the little dog is below them in the courtyard yapping his head off. It's the first time Neil has heard him make such a fuss since Cyril picked him up at Bill's yard.

'I've got to go get him.'

Neil is out of the door, taking the stairs two at a time. Bushy-Mush's tail wags madly at the sight of Neil, and for once the dog doesn't struggle to get out of his arms as he carries him back up to the enormous apartment.

'Well, my little chum,' Neil says to the dog, 'wait till you see this place we are staying. No food spillages on the floor here, and you'd better tell Fuzzy-Pants there is definitely no peeing in the corner.'

'Right,' says Sleet. 'I have to go and organise the opening this evening.' He pats his pockets, muttering, 'Keys, wallet ... See which clothes suit you and get rid of the ridiculous hat. You look like Yul Brynner in that old film *Westworld*.'

It was a film they borrowed from the video shop once, when they were still at school, and for weeks they walked like robots, drew imaginary guns on each other and exchanged creepy stares across boring classrooms.

'I thought I was more like James Dean,' Neil says.

'You wish. Right, make yourself at home, crack a beer, I'll be back in a bit. Oh, and by the way, before I forget, Phee says to say congratulations, and she'll try to make it down, but can't promise anything.'

'Phee?' Neil replies. 'Are you still in touch then?'

'Yeah, well ...' Sleet looks at his boots and shuffles slightly.

'You sly dog!'

Sleet colours slightly at this, grins, and turns to leave.

Once the door clangs shut and the whir of the lift stops, Neil watches Sleet march across the yard and around the corner until he is out of sight.

'Well, guys, what do you make of all this?' Neil asks his animal friends.

Bushy-Mush is drinking Fuzzy-Pants' milk and Fuzzy-Pants is trying out her claws on the arm of the sofa.

'No.' Neil flies over to her and holds her little feet. 'That, my little friend, is a definite "no" in this place. The sofa alone would cost a year's rent.' Neil keeps hold of the cat and finds the bathroom. The towels are fat and fluffy, but at least he might be able to afford to replace one of them if the little kitten ruins it with her claws. He puts it on the sofa and sits Fuzzy on top. Against one wall, at odds with the white theme, is a very large flat-screen TV, and Neil clicks it on out of curiosity. Maybe some of the footage of him will be showing on one channel or other. Maybe the noise of the television will counteract the ringing silence now that he is without the circus of the crowd that accompanied him.

The TV lights up, showing Neil's face larger than real life, him and the raft, Bushy-Mush racing along the towpath. He laughs and grimaces at the same time. He hadn't realised how gangly he looks. The camera scans to the crowd and he laughs again as each familiar face is focused on. It cuts back to a woman in a studio announcing the next item of news, so he clicks to the next channel. There he is again.

'Oh my God, Bushy, look at us.' He clicks and there he is again. 'We're on every channel, Bush!'

He sits wide-eyed, not quite believing what he is seeing. The film cuts to the front of a gallery, and a man in a suit talks to another man in a suit about the opening this evening, and there, in the background, he can see Jasper and Jez practising their routine.

'Guys!' Neil speaks to the screen. 'Look Bushy-Mush, it's your friend Jez.' The dog wags its tail and looks at Neil's finger. The sight of his friends brings a bubble of happiness to Neil's chest, and he flops on the sofa next to the cat and puts his feet up on the coffee table, forgetting where he is.

The programme switches to something else so Neil channel-hops for a while and then goes to investigate the bedroom.

'Oh yes, clothes. What the heck has he bought me?'

He looks at the shirts and catches himself in the mirror, which takes up practically a whole wall. He has on a pair of black Levi's jeans that he got from a charity shop. They are Originals from way back, the material all stiff, the edges of the pockets frayed. His black jumper no longer smells of lavender and the hole that the hotel people kindly stitched under the arm has come undone again – or was it the other arm? Anyway, at least on the whole he looks cleanish, but still, a shower wouldn't hurt.

After half an hour spent relishing the hot water and then having a shave, he looks over the new clothes again before climbing back into what he arrived in. The door opens just as he scrapes his wet hair back against his head and clamps his hat on top.

'You not ready?' Sleet says.

'Yeah, I am.' Sleet has three white plastic bags with him and the smell of spices fills the air.

'No, I mean the clothes.' Sleet goes to the kitchen, finds some forks and, after depositing the plastic bags on the counter, pulls out one takeaway tray after another. Neil doesn't answer; he takes a fork and gets stuck into the curry straight out of the containers.

'Aw, I'd forgotten how good they can taste,' Neil moans.

'Life on the road, eh?' Sleet quips and takes a beer from the fridge. Neil is about to accept one but declines instead.

'Grab me that lemonade,' he says, and Sleet gives him a withering look but obeys.

After their curry, Sleet has one more try at getting Neil to change into the new shirt.

'I'm happy in what I have on,' Neil says. Sleet shrugs.

'Ah well, I suppose you look like an artist, anyway.' And, sniggering, he leads the way out of the flat.

Chapter 28

Jasper's hug is vice-like.

'Thanks for the gig,' Jez says. Bushy-Mush jumps up, demanding attention.

'Thanks for coming! God, it's good to see you guys! And now you've met Sleet!'

Neil feels a little breathless; his heart is pounding with the excitement of seeing his friends again. It feels like a confirmation that they are a permanent feature in his life, and this feels reassuring, stabilising. But no sooner is he comforted by this thought than it occurs to him that he is once again at a London gallery that has all his work on the walls. Unbidden, his mind races with memories of his last exhibition, flashes of collapsing fascia boards, torn canvases. And Kim – there is no Kim. A little stabbing pain twists in his heart. He cannot process everything at once.

'I have indeed, a man after my own heart.' Jasper gives Sleet a sideways look through narrowed eyes. They seem to be sharing a private joke.

'He's managing us now,' Jez explains. 'We have a gig every night this week in London, thanks to him. There's here, another opening night tomorrow and then here again for some midweek affair and then … I forget. Anyway, it looks like we'll be around.'

'Just call me Mr Golden Boy Manager.' Sleet lifts his nose in the air.

'Hellfire, Sleet, I leave you alone for a few days and you take over the world.' Neil knocks Sleet's arm with his elbow.

'Could say the same about you!'

'Right, we need to practise that last bit again, Jasper. We'll catch up later, right?' Jez says.

'Course,' Sleet calls over his shoulder. He is already leading Neil inside, where the contents of his portfolio are displayed on the walls. Some of his work has been mounted and framed, and sketches have been taped to the wall in an area that simulates his working space; in front of these is a table with pencils and watercolours, and a paint-splashed chair, as if he has been working there and will be returning. In the centre of the room is the raft, grounded, resting on its blue barrels. The piano is by the wall, in a space of its own, spotlighted like an old master. With the careful lighting and the white walls, the place has a calm, serene atmosphere. But not, Neil notes, anything like the peaceful calm on the canals.

'I wanted them to sink the floor so people would get the impression of the raft being in water, everything at eye level, but they said it was out of the question, so they are erecting a viewing platform.

People will walk up about here, along past the raft and then down here, where the piano will face them.' Sleet waves his arms about to demonstrate.

'What's this? Is it the catalogue entry number? I didn't realise I had so much work.' Neil looks at a little plaque next to the raft, and another by the piano.

'No, that's the price, you dumdot,' Sleet scoffs.

Neil's first reaction is to laugh, then his hand covers his mouth and his eyes widen, 'You can't charge that, that's just ridiculous! It's a bunch of dumped barrels and some discarded wood!' He speaks through his fingers.

'Shh, keep your voice down. Of course it's ridiculous.' Sleet moves closer to him, his eyes dancing. 'But it makes all your sketches look like a bargain so there's psychology in the markup.' Sleet taps his temple. 'Besides, I don't expect we will sell the raft. Who the heck would want it, and where would they put it?'

'But what if no one buys anything – will we owe the gallery?' Neil is suddenly struggling to breathe.

'Not a bean, my friend. Oh look, here's the viewing platform.'

Six men manoeuvre scaffolding poles and sturdy wooden planks in through the door and up to the raft. In minutes, they have erected a very sturdy set of steps with a platform, and another set of steps down the far end, facing the piano.

'What do you think?' Sleet asks. 'I think it looks good.'

'Can people go in the raft?' Neil asks.

'No, it's art! Why?'

'Well, I've got a sketchbook up there, and I didn't really want it to go missing. Stuff I drew on the journey.'

'Oh my God, that's brilliant, let's see!' Sleet looks like he will burst.

The raft feels strangely solid as Neil steps onto the deck. Inside, the cabin seems cold and empty; his feet echo on the wooden floorboards and it smells of cat pee and unwashed clothes. It's no longer an inviting space and he is quick to get out. At the bottom of the steps he almost collides with the piano.

'Watch it, that piano is priceless art, that is!'

Sleet takes the sketchbook. 'Crikey, you've really improved. I love this one, and that one of the coots. Wow, and I really love these dark ones. These are great.'

He looks around the walls but they are full of Neil's college work – there is no space for more.

'Hey, I know,' he says. 'We'll have an auction. Brilliant idea.' Sleet's whole being seems to be buzzing ever so slightly. 'We'll auction the first for a charity of the buyer's choice, so that should bring a high price, and then the ones we auction after that, to raise money for your studio, will seem like a bargain.'

'You know, I don't think I recognise you – when did you become Mr Tycoon?' Neil says.

'I'm just having fun.' Sleet replies, his face shining, giving him the appearance of being a boy still. The whole 'sad clown' act has gone.

'I'm pleased for you,' Neil says.

'For us,' Sleet replies.

People begin to show up earlier than expected, and Jasper and Jez are quick to start performing, involving the first guests in their act as they usher them indoors. The room fills with smiling people and Neil's butterflies evaporate as he quickly realises that no one seems to recognise him. He can wander round the gallery, listening without having to join in.

'Ah, you see, life is a journey,' a grey-haired man is explaining to a slender woman with long gold earrings.

'Once, knights on horseback would fight duels for the ones they loved, but I think I would rather have a piano delivered, or maybe a puppy,' a blonde woman in a yellow dress says to her friend.

'It's difficult to produce original art these days,' a woman with a halo of grey curls informs a young man in a smart suit. 'Everything has been done, and more and more young artists are pushed to make statements rather than create something beautiful.' She sneers at the delaminating piano.

Neil finds the whole thing amusing until Sleet bangs a little gong and the room goes silent.

'As if tonight was not exciting enough, we have an unprogrammed event,' he announces, beckoning Neil over to him.

Neil wonders if he can just duck behind an easel, but all eyes have turned on him and the murmurs of the assembled people fill the room. He lifts his hand to give a little wave but it feels stupid, so he touches the front of his cowboy hat instead, as if he is in an old western.

'During the journey,' Sleet goes on, 'Neil here captured all he saw in some unique and very personal sketches.' Heads turn to look at the walls. 'No, they are not on the walls, they are here. Some of his best works, to my mind.'

Sleet holds up the sketchbook. Another murmur passes around the room. Sleet explains how the auction will work, and no one speaks or moves. A youth in an apron, carrying a tray of champagne glasses, slinks through the crowd on silent feet.

'So let's begin.' There's a slight tremble to Sleet's voice and Neil can tell he isn't getting the reaction he was expecting.

'So, lot one, *Coots and Boots*. Where will you start me?'

There is silence. Neil backs a little towards the wall.

'Open to offers, as ridiculous as you like.'

Now Neil knows Sleet is feeling uncomfortable. He is letting the crowd decide the price whereas, surely, he should give them a starting point.

There is still no response; the room is silent. Neil almost wishes his pictures would fall off the wall like at his last exhibition – anything to break the long silence. People begin to fidget; high heels clack on the polished floor as a thin woman with an angular haircut shifts her weight. A man in a sharp suit coughs as quietly as he can into his hand but to Neil it sounds deafening. This whole thing is a ridiculous notion and Sleet has outdone himself in the realms of messing things up. No wonder all he has ever done is work for his dad and drink to excess.

'If ridiculous counts, I'll give you a fiver,' Jasper shouts through the door from the street. He is wearing a beret and, as all eyes turn on him, he puts a paintbrush above his top lip which he curls to his nose to keep it there. A ripple of laughter runs through the crowd and the tension dissipates. A group of people arrive and everyone has to shift to make room for them.

'So, a fiver I have.' The relief in Sleet's voice is obvious. 'Do I hear ten? Ten I have, do I hear twenty? Twenty, thirty, forty, fifty.' Hands are going up all over the room now. 'Remember, every penny of this money will go to a charity of your choosing.'

More hands go up and Sleet is struggling to keep pace.

'Five hundred pounds,' a voice near the door growls.

Heads turn at this, and there is a gasp. There are too many people for Neil to see who has spoken but he thinks he recognises the voice.

'Five hundred pounds it is – any advance on five hundred pounds? No? Okay, going, going …' Sleet pauses for dramatic effect. 'Gone! To the man in the tweed coat.'

Tweed coat? Neil's stomach flutters. He pushes through the crowds and there, by the door, giving his details to the gallery owner, is Quentin. His hair is cut, his face is scrubbed, his fingers are manicured and he has on a new tweed coat. Next to him, a pleasant-looking, mature woman hovers, and next to her are two younger versions of Quentin who must be Laurence and Benedict. Before Quentin spots him, Neil takes out his phone and films Quentin and the room, and Sleet on the platform, now auctioning off the second sketch. Hands are being raised all over the room; they are keen to buy. Laurence and Benedict break away from Quentin to look around the room with the pleasant-faced woman. Quentin, who has finished with the gallery owner, looks up and steps back, away from the crowd, towards the door.

Neil pushes through the crowd of people, who are laughing at something Sleet has said.

'Quentin,' he calls, but the laughter drowns out his voice and by the time he reaches the door Quentin is out on the street.

'Quentin!' he calls again, and this time the old man turns. He looks just like Neil expects a city banker to look, only his eyes dance and there is something distant about the way they focus.

'Ah, Neil.' His greeting is warm.

'What are you doing here? I mean, good to see you, but isn't this off your beaten track?'

'It's the twenty-fourth, right?' Quentin says. 'I made a promise to my wife and the boys that I would see them every twenty-fourth and twenty-fifth of June. It was they who pressed me into coming to this. Usually we go to the opera or just for dinner. I warned them I would be leaving them to it before long.'

'You bought the picture?' Neil says. The surroundings are at odds with his memories of Quentin and his tongue feels tied.

'Course, how could I not? I love coots and I love boots.'

Neil looks at Quentin's feet. He has on a shiny pair of brown brogues.

'I'll put it next to the Dufy.' He smiles and takes another step back.

'Won't you stay?' Neil asks.

'You sound like my wife.' Quentin smiles.

'I'm scared I won't see you again.' Neil is surprised at the force of the emotions he is experiencing.

'Well, I think if life has brought us together twice already, there is a good chance it may do so again.' And he turns and walks away.

'Quentin?' Neil calls after him.

'What?' he replies, but he doesn't stop walking.

'Change your shoes and take some matches with you next time you go walkabout.' Neil smiles.

Quentin's shoulders judder and Neil knows the old man is laughing as he turns the corner; then he is gone.

The street feels very empty compared to the gallery, the air fresher and cooler, and as he looks up to the stars Neil spares a thought for Bill and Cyril,

Joyce and Trevor, Pat and Phee. He narrows his eyes, trying to recall names and faces, but there have been so many over such a short period of time, so many lovely people. For a perfect ending now, he needs Kim to walk round the corner, her arms wide. He waits a moment, hoping, but this is real life, not a Hollywood film, and no one comes.

By the time he goes back in, the auction is over and Jasper and Jez are working their magic on the crowd, creating a party atmosphere. Sleet is busy, talking to one person or another. The gallery owner flits about, putting up little red stickers beside his sketches on the walls. When Neil does catch Sleet's eye, Sleet winks and grins but then continues the conversation he was having. As the evening grows late, Jasper and Jez leave, promising to be back the day after tomorrow.

Sleet is still talking, and Neil's energy is completely drained and he considers slipping away by himself. Bushy-Mush is bound to want to pee by now. But as the gallery empties and he can see his art on the walls, and the raft in the middle, he gets the sense that this is both the closing of one part of his life and the opening of another.

'A studio in London,' he whispers, to see if he likes the sound of it. Maybe it could be like Kim's place, with a big window letting in the light. Maybe if she is still in London, he might, given time, find her, or she might visit him. They could meet as adults, rather than just carrying on from where they were. This would give them a chance to see each other with new eyes. Or, to be more accurate, give him a chance to impress her with how far he has come. It's worth a try.

The gallery is emptying quite rapidly now. A few more red stickers are placed and finally Sleet ushers the last few people out of the door. The place looks so much bigger now it is empty.

'Wow, what a marathon, I don't know how you do it,' Sleet says to the gallery owner, who is looking through the receipts by the till.

'A lot of coffee,' the woman replies. 'Come on, I'll take you across the road for a bite to eat. That Japanese place will still be open. Do you like sushi?'

'No idea.' Sleet grins. 'Let's find out – come on, Neil.'

Neil is still looking at some of his earlier works that are off in a small side room. He has improved since he produced them, but there are still elements of his early work that he would like to use again.

'Can I join you in ten minutes?' he says, picking up a pencil and the remains of his sketchbook. All his drawings have been pulled out and sold but there are some blank pages left at the back.

The owner hesitates but then hands over the keys. 'Lock up when you come,' she says, and she and Sleet wander across the road.

The door bangs behind them, echoing in the vast empty space. Neil studies the way he used his pencil in his earlier sketches, so much bolder, more certain, with real vitality. He moves on to the next and the next, tracing his life through his work. Halfway through his college years, it seems, he lost his way, artistically speaking, but then the sketches get much stronger towards the end – darker but more mature. On the next wall are sketches he only just remembers doing, although he can't have completed them that long ago: the first is of the canal at the end of the garden in Greater Lotherton, so these must be from after he left college.

His breath freezes at the next sketch, which is of Kim asleep in their bed, the lines of the creased sheets mixing with the lines of her hair, and her face smooth and unwrinkled by comparison. The sight of her is so sweet it's like a bath of chocolate. He stares at the picture, drinking her in. There is a red sticker beside the sketch, but he doesn't want to sell it; it is too personal. Can he change his mind, ask for it back? It isn't the only one, There are other pictures from when they lived in the flat. The sight of them is bringing all his emotions to the surface. His footsteps echo in the smaller room as he walks slowly along.

He takes another step, and the ring of his shoe against the smooth painted concrete floor is joined by a resonance that he recognises as the sound of the piano. A single note has been struck. Didn't he lock the door after Sleet and the gallery owner left? The single note is played again. Another follows it. How dare they! It is not their piano to play. It seems bad enough that his life has been carved up and sold in pieces, but for someone to now invade his own personal space, this last moment alone with his sketches of Kim, feels cruel.

'How dare you?' He flies out of the side room and into the main gallery.

'Why not? It's my piano,' are the simple words that meet his ears.

'Kim!' Neil's legs won't move; all the bones his body have turned to dough.

'Hello.' Her voice is small but there is a tinge of defiance in her face as she swivels around on the piano stool.

'Kim,' he repeats. She looks older than he remembered, but there is also a glow about her he does not recall. Can he just wrap his arms around her and smother her in kisses?

'This is all very …' She looks around the gallery but does not finish her sentence. He cannot tell if she approves or not.

It may not be acceptable to hug and kiss her, but he is not going to let this moment pass altogether.

'I missed you so much ... I missed you from the moment you walked out of the train station.'

'Yeah, right.' She sounds small and hurt. 'So why didn't you get in touch?'

'My phone was dead, your phone was dead, I tried!'

'But there are other ways.'

'Kim, I just pulled your goddamn piano from Greater Lotherton to London to show you how sorry I was ...'

She looks at her lap.

'I spoke to you through the television. Didn't you see that?' he asks.

There is an almost imperceptible nod of her head.

'Kim?' He is beginning to wonder why she is here. 'Why didn't you get in touch with me? If for no other reason than that it was a great opportunity for you. You could have used the fact that you were Kim of this crazy raft thing to climb a few rungs of the ladder with Channel Doc. It wouldn't have had to mean anything between us if you didn't want it to.'

She looks down again. This is not the fun-loving, feisty Kim he knows. Something has happened.

'Kim.' He drops to his knees in front of her and looks up into her face.

'Oh, Neil,' she sobs, and he cannot help himself – his arms are around her, her head to his chest, and he breathes in the smell of her hair.

'What's happened, why didn't you get in touch?' he says quietly.

'How could I, when you were changing the world and I was living a lie?' she sobs.

'What do you mean, living a lie?'

'Channel Doc – I got there, and they never hired me.'

'What? But I don't understand.'

'They have a rule, as it turns out,' she sniffs. 'They don't hire pregnant women. Well, they didn't say it was that, of course – they made some excuse, said I wasn't right after all...'

Neil is searching her face, trying to take in what she is saying.

'They don't hire …'

He draws air in suddenly through his mouth and looks deep into her eyes. 'You?' He looks hard. Now he recognises the glow. And the aged look – she hasn't been sleeping well. 'With …'

'Well, it isn't anyone else's,' she says, and he can see the tension in the muscles of her face, the fear in her eyes that he will not be pleased.

'I wasn't sure if I should come. I mean it's life-changing stuff, right? The kind of change not everyone wants. I mean, here you are, shaking the world up. I imagine the last thing you need are any encumbrances right now. Besides, if the media get wind of this, they will have a field day. But having decided to keep it, I thought you had a right to know.'

Her voice trembles and she does not make eye contact.

'Oh Kim!' he exclaims. He cannot control himself, he is on his feet, she is in his arms and he swings her around and round until she protests that she is going to be sick.

'Oh Kim, this is just wonderful!' He puts her back on the stool; she smiles and it reaches her eyes, but she seems tired.

'Are you very sad about the Channel Doc job?' he asks.

'Yeah, well, you know, life dreams,' she says, perhaps trying to dismiss all the hurt she must be feeling.

'Bad judgement on their part,' he says. 'Channel Doc have no idea what they missed by not employing you. But, it looks like, with Sleet's able help, we will get by.' He looks up at the wall full of work, all sold.

'It is all pretty amazing,' she says. 'What does it feel like, changing the world?' She has settled in under his arm. How many times before have they been in this exact same position? Hundreds, thousands. It is as if they have never been apart.

'I don't know about changing the world. I mean, I still don't know really what I want to do, the sort of art I would like to produce.'

As he says the words, he knows it is not true – already, thoughts are distilling, ideas based on the sketch of Kim in the bed, the folds of the sheets, the folds of her hair, the smoothness of her features. A touch of Klimt, but without the gold – or maybe not, maybe a modern take on icons. A triptych of her from different angles.

'But what I do know is that it has to be with you.' And Neil lowers his head, searches her eyes and finds all he is looking for there, and with tenderness their lips meet.

When they finally break for air, it is Kim who speaks first.

'So Fuzzy-Pants, eh? What kind of name is that to give a cat?'

'A name no better than Bushy-Mush – what sort of name is that to call a dog?'

'Ah, but he does have a bushy mush,' Kim defends.

'And Fuzzy does have a fuzzy pair of pants on. When you see her you'll realise she could be called nothing else.' He strokes Kim's hair from her face. 'We've a nice place to stay, unless you want to go back to yours with the big windows?'

'You mean my broom cupboard with a window that looks onto a brick wall,' Kim admits.

'So you lied in your postcard?' Neil chuckles.

'So you read other people's post?' Kim counters, and she dips her head forward so their foreheads touch.

'You want to marry me?' Neil asks, and he feels he should be surprised by his own words, but it is the most natural thing in the world to ask.

'Sure. Make it soon, though, because I might be a bit busy in eight months.' She runs her hand over her so-far-flat belly.

'Would you like a quiet, private affair or would you prefer the whole circus act of being the Famous Missing Kimberly?' Neil asks.

'What was it really like, that whole attention thing?' she asks, and this time she strokes his hair out of his eyes. She is staring at him and gives the impression she is not listening to a word he is saying because she is so lost in the sight of him. He has always liked it when she does that.

'It was pretty surreal, actually. There were times when I wished you could have been there. Quite a few times, actually. Oh wait!'

And he takes his arms from around her to fish his phone out of his pocket.

'Look,' he says, and he randomly selects one of the videos he made and plays it back.

'Oh my God, do you have more of this?' She has stopped staring at him now and takes possession of the phone.

'Yes, I pretty much recorded every day to pretend you were there, so I could talk to you,' Neil says, expecting a kiss and a thank you. Instead, Kim is glued to the phone, flipping to the next recording.

'You don't know what you have, do you!' she says, eyes shining.

Chapter 29

'Of course I like it,' Neil says, 'but I still say Benedict is not the best name for a girl.'

'Trust me, it will give her a better chance of not being judged until she meets people face to face when she is grown. It will also make her more memorable.'

'The world will have changed by the time she is grown, and anyway, let's face it, if she is anything like her mother she will be very memorable,' Neil replies.

'They keep saying the world has changed, that women have equal rights, but we still only earn a fraction of what men earn in the same roles in industry.' Kim is at her desk, working on her latest project.

'Except you, who earns more.' Neil is sketching Benedict, or Bennie, as he calls her, who is lying on her back on the rug, making gurgling sounds.

'I'm only as good as the last thing I produced. There are no guarantees that there will be any takers for the next one.'

'Ah, but your name is known and that's what counts.' Neil's sketchbook has had so many pages torn out for Kim to make notes on and pin to the corkboard that it is no longer stiff enough to use without support. He grabs a newspaper.

'No, not that one!' Kim says, and when he looks at it he realises it is the one with the advert across the front, announcing the TV premiere of Kimberly's documentary about the Pianoraft that she put together using the phone clips and news coverage. He puts the newspaper to one side and takes another.

'Did Sleet ring while I was out?' she asks.

'He says he has to stay in London a few more days to arrange my next exhibition. A big collector, not Saatchi & Saatchi, but someone else I've been talking to, wants me, or actually, I think he said us, as in you and me, to go the London gallery to present his new acquisition to the world. He's decided to put the piano back on the raft.'

'Good, that's where it belongs. Right, I think I'm done here, are you ready to go?'

'Do we really have to do this?' Neil puts down his drawing, slides to his hands and knees and crawls over to his daughter, making funny noises. Bushy-Mush thinks the game is for him and bounces off his two front paws.

'Not you, old man.' Neil strokes the dog and then picks up his daughter. 'Or you' – he uses his free hand to stroke Fuzzy-Pants, who has found a shelf above the radiator.

'Yes, we have to do it. Come on, we agreed – once a month.'

'But I hate Greater Lotherton,' Neil moans.

'You only hate Greater Lotherton because you've got used to Little Lotherton.' Kim pulls on her coat.

'There's more air here.' Neil knows he is whining.

'But there are no restaurants.' Kim takes Benedict's coat from the hook.

'Let's make it a quick lunch, then.'

'For goodness' sake, Neil, going for a meal with them is a good thing. It means my parents finally approve of you, for a start.'

'Yes, but if my dad goes on and on to the waiter about his famous artist son like he did last month I'm walking out.'

'There's no pleasing you, is there?' Kim opens the door and takes Benedict from Neil's arms and the car keys from the hook. 'It upset you when he didn't support you and now you complain when he brags! You were all in a mood when my parents didn't think you were worth much, and now you complain when they invite you to dinner. You brooding artists are always so full of angst.' She winks at him.

Neil closes the door behind them and looks up at the stars. The air is warm and it would be a beautiful night for a walk by the canal. Maybe he could just slip away, for an hour or two. The idea appeals so much he wouldn't mind if it turned into a day or two, actually.

'Neil.' Kim is in the car. 'Are you coming or am I going without you?'

He has a slight feeling of déjà vu, but this time the question is not a tricky one.

'No way, Mrs Neil Campbell-Blair, you're not pulling that one on me again.'

And he climbs in the passenger side and is rewarded with a kiss before they drive away.

If you enjoyed *The Piano Raft* please share it with a friend, and check out the other books in the Greek Village Collection!

I'm always delighted to receive email from readers, and I welcome new friends on Facebook.

https://www.facebook.com/authorsaraalexi

saraalexi@me.com

Happy reading,

Sara Alexi

Made in the USA
Middletown, DE
30 April 2017